***She and Crash would be alone
in the house tonight,***

Nell thought.

She turned away, afraid he would know what
she was thinking just from the look in her eyes.
Not that it mattered. He probably already knew
what she wanted. But he didn't want the same
thing.

Friends, she reminded herself. Crash wanted
them to be friends. Being friends was safe.

She moved out of his grasp, but not because she
didn't want him to touch her. On the contrary.
But she was afraid that if she stood so close to
him, it wouldn't be long before she sank back so
that she was leaning against him.

And friends didn't do that. Lovers did.

Dear Reader,

Happy holidaze! The holiday season always does pass in a bit of a daze, with all the shopping and wrapping and partying, the cooking and (of course!) the eating. So take some time for yourself with our six Intimate Moments novels, each one of them a wonderful Christmas treat.

Start by paying a visit to THE LONE STAR SOCIAL CLUB, Linda Turner's setting for *Christmas Lone-Star Style*. Remember, those Texans know how to do things in a *big* way! Then join Suzanne Brockmann for another TALL, DARK AND DANGEROUS title, *It Came Upon a Midnight Clear*. I wouldn't mind waking up and finding Crash Hawken under *my* Christmas tree! Historical writer Patricia Potter makes a slam-bang contemporary debut with *Home for Christmas*, our FAMILIES ARE FOREVER title. Wrongly convicted and without the memories that could save him, Ryan Murphy is a hero to treasure. Award winner Ruth Wind returns with *For Christmas, Forever.* Isn't this the season when mysterious strangers come bearing…romance tinged with danger? Debra Cowan's *One Silent Night* is our MEN IN BLUE title. I'd be happy to "unwrap" Sam Garrett on Christmas morning. Finally, welcome mainstream author Christine Michels to the line. *A Season of Miracles* carries the TRY TO REMEMBER flash, though you'll have no trouble at all remembering this warm holiday love story.

It's time to take the "daze" out of the holidays, so enjoy all six of these seasonal offerings. Of course, don't forget that next month marks a new year, so come back then for more of the best romance reading around—right here in Silhouette Intimate Moments.

Seasons Greetings,

Leslie J. Wainger
Executive Senior Editor

Please address questions and book requests to:
Silhouette Reader Service
U.S.: 3010 Walden Ave., P.O. Box 1325, Buffalo, NY 14269
Canadian: P.O. Box 609, Fort Erie, Ont. L2A 5X3

IT CAME UPON A MIDNIGHT CLEAR

SUZANNE BROCKMANN

Published by Silhouette Books

America's Publisher of Contemporary Romance

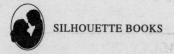 SILHOUETTE BOOKS

ISBN 0-373-07896-X

IT CAME UPON A MIDNIGHT CLEAR

Copyright © 1998 by Suzanne Brockmann

This edition published by arrangement with Harlequin Books S.A.

® and TM are trademarks of Harlequin Books S.A., used under license. Trademarks indicated with ® are registered in the United States Patent and Trademark Office, the Canadian Trade Marks Office and in other countries.

Printed in U.S.A.

SUZANNE BROCKMANN

wrote her first romance novel in 1992 and fell in love with the genre. She writes full-time, along with singing and arranging music for her professional a cappella singing group called Vocomotive, organizing a monthly benefit coffeehouse at her church, and managing the acting careers of her two young children, Melanie and Jason. She and her family are living happily ever after in a small town outside of Boston.

For Tom Magness
(1960–1979)
I never had the chance to tell you that
I'm glad I didn't miss the dance.

Prologue

Crash Hawken shaved in the men's room.

He'd been keeping vigil at the hospital in Washington, D.C., for two days running, and his heavy stubble, along with his long hair and the bandage on his arm, made him look even more dangerous than he usually did.

He'd left only to change the shirt he'd been wearing—the one that had been stained with Admiral Jake Robinson's blood—and to access a computer file that Jake had sent him electronically, mere hours before he had been gunned down in his own home.

Gunned down in his own home... Even though Crash had been there, even though he'd taken part in the firefight, even though he'd been wounded himself, it still seemed so unbelievable.

Crash had thought that last year's dismal holiday season had been about as bad as it could get.

He'd been wrong.

He was going to have to call Nell, tell her Jake had been

wounded. She'd want to know. She deserved to know. And
Crash could use a reason to hear her voice again. Maybe
even see her. With a rush of despair, he realized something
he'd been hiding from himself for months—he wanted to
see her. God, he wanted so badly to see Nell's smile.

The men's room door opened as Crash rinsed the dis-
posable razor he'd picked up in the hospital commissary.
He glanced into the mirror, and directly into Tom Foster's
scowling face.

What were the odds that the Federal Intelligence Commission commander had only come in to take a leak?

Slim to none.

Crash nodded at the man.

"What I don't understand," Foster said, as if the conversation they'd started two nights ago had never been interrupted, "is how you could be the last man standing in a
room with five-and-a-half dead men, and not know what
happened."

Crash put the plastic protective cap on over the razor's
blade. "I didn't see who fired the first shot," he said
evenly. "All I saw was Jake getting hit. After that, I know
exactly what happened." He turned to face Foster. "I took
out the shooters who were trying to finish Jake off."

Shooters. Not men. They'd lost their identities and become nothing more than targets when they'd opened fire
on Jake Robinson. And like targets in a shooting range,
Crash had efficiently and methodically taken them out.

"Who would want to assassinate the admiral?"

Crash shook his head and gave the same answer he'd
given Tom two days earlier. "I don't know."

It wasn't a lie. He *didn't* know. Not for sure. But he had
a file full of information that was going to help him find
the man who had orchestrated this assassination attempt.
Jake had fought both pain and rapidly fading consciousness

to make sure he had understood there was a connection between this attempt on his life and that top-secret, encoded file Crash had received that very same morning.

"Come on, Lieutenant. Surely you can at least make a *guess.*"

"I'm sorry, sir, I've never found it useful to speculate in situations like this."

"Three of the men you brought into Admiral Robinson's house were operating under false names and identifications. Were you aware of that?"

Crash met the man's angry gaze steadily. "I feel sick about that, sir. I made the mistake of trusting my captain."

"Oh, so now it's your *captain's* fault."

Crash fought a burst of his own anger. Getting mad wouldn't do anyone any good. He knew that from the countless times he'd been in battle. Emotion not only made his hands shake, but it altered his perceptions as well. In a battle situation, emotion could get him killed. And Foster was clearly here to do battle. Crash had to detach. Separate. Distance himself.

He made himself feel nothing. "I didn't say that." His voice was quiet and calm.

"Whoever shot Robinson wouldn't have gotten past his security fence without your help. You brought them in, Hawken. You're responsible for this."

Crash held himself very still. "I'm aware of that." They—whoever they were—had used him to get inside Jake's home. Whoever had set this up had known of his personal connection to the admiral.

He'd barely been three hours stateside, three hours off the Air Force transport he'd taken back to D.C. when Captain Lovett had called him into his office, asking if he'd be interested in taking part in a special team providing backup security at Admiral Robinson's request.

Crash had believed this team's job was to protect the admiral, when in fact there'd been a different, covert goal. Assassination.

He should have known something was wrong. He should have stopped it before it even started.

He *was* responsible.

"Excuse me, sir." He had to check on Jake's condition. He had to sit in the waiting area and hope to hear continuous reports of his longtime mentor's improvement, starting with news of the admiral finally being moved out of ICU. He had to use the time to mentally sort through all the information Jake had passed to him in that file. And then he had to go out and hunt down the man who had used him to get to Jake.

But Tom Foster blocked the door. "I have a few more questions, if you don't mind, Lieutenant. You've worked with SEAL Team Twelve for how long?"

"On and off for close to eight years," Crash replied.

"And during those eight years, you occasionally worked closely with Admiral Robinson on assignments that were not standard SEAL missions, did you not?"

Crash didn't react, didn't blink, didn't move, carefully hiding his surprise. How had Foster gotten *that* information? Crash could count the number of people who knew he'd been working with Jake Robinson on one hand. "I'm afraid I can't say."

"You don't have to say. We know you worked with Robinson as part of the so-called Gray Group."

Crash chose his words carefully. "I don't see how that has any real relevance to your investigation, sir."

"This is information FInCOM has received from naval intelligence," Foster told him. "You're not giving away anything we don't already know."

"FInCOM takes part in its share of covert operations,"

Crash said, trying to sound reasonable. "You'll understand that whether I am or am not a part of the Gray Group is not something I'm able to talk freely about."

Reasonable wasn't on the list of adjectives Tom Foster was working with today. His voice rose and he took a threatening step forward. "An *admiral* has been shot. This is *not* the time to conceal *any* information *what*soever."

Crash held his ground. "I'm sorry, sir. I've already given you and the other investigators all the information I'm able to provide. The names of the deceased, as I knew them. An account of my conversation with Captain Lovett that afternoon. An account of the events that led to one of the men in the team opening fire upon the admiral—"

"What exactly is your reason for concealing information, Lieutenant?" Foster's neck was turning purple.

"I'm concealing nothing." Except for the shocking information Jake had sent him in a top-secret, high-level security-clearance file.

If Crash wanted to get to the bottom of this—and he *did*—it wouldn't help to go public with all that Jake had told him. Besides, Crash had to treat the information in that file with exactly the same care and secrecy as he treated every other file Jake had ever sent him. And that meant that even if he wanted to, he couldn't talk about it with anyone—except his Commander-in-Chief, the President of the United States.

"We know that Jake Robinson sent you some kind of information file on the morning of the shooting," Foster informed him tightly. "I will need you to turn that file over to me as soon as possible."

Crash met the man's gaze steadily. "I'm sorry, sir. You know as well as I do that even if I *did* have access to this alleged file from Admiral Robinson, I wouldn't be able to reveal its contents to you. The status of all of the work I did for the admiral was 'need to know.' My orders were to report back to Jake and to Jake only.''

"I *order* you to hand over that file, Lieutenant."

"I'm sorry, Commander Foster. Even if I had such a file, I'm afraid you don't have the clearance rating necessary to make such a demand." He stepped dangerously close to the shorter man and lowered his voice. "If you'll excuse me, I'm going to see how Jake's doing."

Foster stepped aside, pushing open the door with one hand. "Your concern for Robinson is heartwarming. At least, it would be if we didn't have indisputable evidence that proves *you* were the man who fired those first shots into Admiral Robinson's chest."

Crash heard the words Foster said, but they didn't make sense. The crowd of men standing outside the bathroom door didn't make sense, either. There were uniformed cops, both local and state police, as well as dark-suited FInCOM agents, and several officers from the shore patrol.

They were obviously waiting for someone.

Him.

Crash looked at Foster, the meaning of his words becoming clear. "You think *I'm*—"

"We don't *think* it, we *know* it." Foster smiled tightly. "Ballistic reports are in."

"Are you Lt. William R. Hawken, sir?" The shore-patrol officer who stepped forward was tall and young and humorlessly earnest.

"Yes," Crash replied. "I'm Hawken."

"By the way, the bullet taken from your arm was fired from Captain Lovett's weapon," Foster told him.

Crash felt sick, but he didn't let his reaction show. His captain had tried to kill him. His captain had been a part of the conspiracy.

"Lt. William R. Hawken, sir," the shore-patrol officer droned, "you are under arrest."

Crash stood very, very still.

"The ballistic report also shows that your weapon fired the bullets that were found in four of the five other dead men, as well as those removed from the admiral," Foster told him tightly. "Does that information by any chance clear up your foggy memory of who fired the first shots?"

"You have the right to remain silent," the shore-patrol officer chanted. "Anything you say can and will be used against you in a court of law. You have the right to an attorney—"

This was impossible. Bullets from *his* weapon...? That wasn't the way it had happened. He looked into the blandly serious eyes of the young officer. "What exactly am I being charged with?"

The young officer cleared his throat. "Sir. You have been charged with conspiracy, treason, and the murder of a United States Navy Admiral."

Murder?

Crash's entire world tilted.

"Admiral Robinson's wounds proved fatal one hour ago," Tom Foster announced. "The admiral is dead."

Crash closed his eyes. Jake was *dead.*

Disassociate. Detach. Separate.

The shore-patrol officer slipped handcuffs onto Crash's wrists, but Crash didn't feel a thing.

"Aren't you going to say *any*thing to defend yourself?" Foster asked.

Crash didn't answer. *Couldn't* answer. Jake was dead.

He was completely numb as they led him from the hospital, out to a waiting car. There were news cameras everywhere, aimed at him. Crash didn't even try to hide his face.

He was helped into the car, someone pushing down his head to keep him from hitting it on the frame. Jake was dead. Jake was dead, and Crash should have been able to prevent it. He should have been faster. He should have been smarter. He should have paid attention to the feeling he'd had that something wasn't right.

Crash stared out through the rain-speckled window of the car as the driver pulled out into the wet December night. He tried to get his brain to work, tried to start picking apart the information Jake had sent him in that file—the information that was recorded just as completely and precisely in his head.

Crash was no longer simply going to find the man responsible for shooting and killing Jake Robinson. He was going to find him, hunt him down and destroy him.

He had no doubt he'd succeed—or die trying.

Dear, sweet Mary. And he'd thought *last* Christmas had been the absolute pits.

Chapter 1

One year earlier

It was only two days after Thanksgiving, but the city streets were already decked with wreaths and bows and Christmas lights.

The cheery colors and festive sparkle seemed to mock Nell Burns as she drove through the city. She'd come into Washington, D.C. that morning to do a number of errands. Get a new supply of watercolor paper and paint for Daisy. Stop at the health food store and get more of that nasty seaweed stuff. Pick up the admiral's dress uniform from the dry cleaners near the Pentagon. It had been a week since Jake had been in to town, and it looked as if it would be a while before he returned.

Nell had saved the hardest, most unpleasant task for last. But now there was no avoiding it.

She double-checked the address she'd scribbled on a

Post-it note, slowing as she drove past the high-rise building that bore the same number.

There was a parking spot open, right on the street, and she slipped into it, turning off her engine and pulling up the brake.

But instead of getting out of her car, Nell sat there.

What on earth was she going to say?

It was bad enough that in just a few minutes she was going to be knocking on William Hawken's door. In the two years since she'd started working as Daisy Owen's personal assistant, she'd met the enigmatic Navy SEAL that her boss thought of as a surrogate son exactly four times.

And each time he'd taken her breath away.

It wasn't so much that he was handsome....

Actually, it was *exactly* that he was handsome. He was incredibly, darkly, mysteriously, broodingly, *gorgeously* handsome. He had the kind of cheekbones that epic poems were written about and a nose that advertised an aristocratic ancestry. And his eyes… Steely gray and heart-stoppingly intense, the force of his gaze was nearly palpable. When he'd looked at her, she'd felt as if he could see right through her, as if he could read her mind.

His lips reminded her of those old gothic romances she'd read when she was younger. He had decidedly cruel lips. Upon seeing them, she'd suddenly realized that rather odd descriptive phrase made perfect sense. His lips were gracefully shaped, but thin and tight, particularly since his default expression was not a smile.

In fact, Nell couldn't remember ever having seen William Hawken smile.

His friends, or at least the members of his SEAL team—she wasn't sure if a man that broodingly quiet actually *had* any friends—called him "Crash."

Daisy had told her that Billy Hawken had been given

that nickname when he was training to become a SEAL. His partner in training had jokingly started calling him Crash because of Hawken's ability to move silently at all times. In the same manner in which a very, very large man might be nicknamed "Mouse" or "Flea," Billy Hawken had ever after been known as Crash.

There was no way, *no* way, Nell would ever consider becoming involved with a man—no matter *how* disgustingly handsome and intriguing—whose work associates called him "Crash."

There was also no way she would ever consider becoming involved with a Navy SEAL. From what Nell understood, SEAL was synonymous with *superman*. The acronym itself stood for Sea, Air and Land, and SEALs were trained to operate with skill and efficiency in all three environments. Direct descendants from the UDTs or Underwater Demolition Teams of World War II, SEALs were experts in everything from gathering information to blowing things up.

They were Special Forces warriors who used unconventional methods and worked in small seven- or eight-man teams. Admiral Jake Robinson had been a SEAL in Vietnam. The stories he'd told were enough to convince Nell that becoming involved with a man like Crash would be sheer insanity.

Of course, she was failing to consider one important point as she made these sweeping statements. The man in question had barely even said four words to her. No wait— he'd said *five* words the first time they'd met. "Pleased to meet you, Nell." He had a quiet, richly resonant voice that matched his watchful demeanor damn near perfectly. When he'd said her name, she'd come closer to melting into a pathetic pool of quivering protoplasm at his feet than she'd ever done in her life.

The second time they'd met, *that* was when he'd said four words. "Nice seeing you again." The other times, he'd merely nodded.

In other words, it wasn't as if he was breaking down her door, trying to get a date.

And he certainly wasn't doing anything as ridiculous as not only counting the number of times they'd met, but adding up the total number of words she'd ever said to *him*.

With any luck, he wouldn't even be home.

But then, of course, she'd have to come back.

Daisy and her longtime, live-in lover, Jake Robinson, had invited Crash out to the farm for dinner several times over the past few weeks. But each time he'd cancelled.

Nell had made this trip into the city to tell him that he *must* come. Although he wasn't their child by blood, Crash was the closest thing to a son both Daisy and Jake had ever had. And from what Daisy had told her, Nell knew that Crash considered them his family, too. From the time he was ten, he'd spent every summer and winter break from boarding school with the slightly eccentric pair. From the time his own mother had died, Daisy had opened her home and her heart to him.

But now Daisy had been diagnosed with an inoperable cancer, and she was in the very late stages of the disease. She didn't want Crash to hear the news over the phone, and Jake was refusing to leave her side.

That had left Nell volunteering to handle the odious task.

Damn, what *was* she going to say?

"Hi, Billy, um, Bill, how are you? It's Nell Burns... remember me?"

Crash stared at the woman standing out in the hallway, aware that he was wearing only a towel. He held the knot together with one hand while he pushed his wet hair up and out of his eyes with the other.

Nell laughed nervously, her eyes skimming his near-naked body before returning to his face. "No, you probably don't know who I am, especially out of context this way. I work for—"

"My cousin, Daisy," he said. "Of course I know who you are."

"Daisy's your cousin?" She was so genuinely surprised, she forgot to be nervous for a moment. "I didn't realize you were actually related. I just though she was...I mean, that you were..."

The nervousness was back, and she waved her hands gracefully, in a gesture equivalent to a shrug.

"A stray she and Jake just happened to pick up?" he finished for her.

She tried to pretend that she wasn't fazed, but with her fair coloring, Crash couldn't miss the fact that she was blushing. Come to think of it, she'd started blushing the minute she'd realized he was standing there in only a towel.

A grown woman who still could blush. It was remarkable, really. And it was reason number five thousand and one on his list of reasons why he should stay far away from her.

She was too nice.

The very first time they'd met, the very first time Crash had looked into her eyes, his pulse had kicked into high gear. There was no doubt about it, it was a purely physical reaction. Jake had introduced him to Nell at some party Daisy had thrown. The instant he'd walked in, Crash had noticed Nell's blond hair and her trim, slender figure, somehow enhanced by a fairly conservative little black dress. But up close, as he'd said hello, he'd gotten caught in those liquid, blue eyes. The next thing he knew, he was fantasiz-

ing about taking her by the hand, pulling her with him up
the stairs, into one of the spare bedrooms, pinning her
against the door and just...

The alarming part was that Crash knew the physical attraction he felt was extremely mutual. Nell had given him
a look that he'd seen before, in other women's eyes.

It was a look that said she wanted to play with fire. Or
at least she *thought* she did. But there was *no way* he was
going to seduce this girl that Jake and Daisy had spoken
so highly of. She was too nice.

He couldn't see more than a trace of that same look in
her eyes now, though. She was incredibly nervous—and
upset, he realized suddenly. She was standing there, looking
as if she was fighting hard to keep from bursting into tears.

"I was hoping you'd have a few minutes to spare, to sit
down and talk," she told him. For someone so slight of
build, she had a deceptively low, husky voice. It was unbelievably sexy. "Maybe go out and get a cup of coffee
or...?"

"I'm not exactly dressed for getting coffee."

"I could go." She motioned over her shoulder toward
the bank of beat-up elevators. "I can wait for you downstairs. Outside. While you get dressed."

"This isn't a very good neighborhood," he said. "It'd
be better if you came inside to wait."

Crash opened the door wider and stepped back to let her
in. She hesitated for several long seconds, and he crossed
the idea that she was here to seduce him off his list of
possible reasons why she'd come.

He wasn't sure whether to feel disappointed or relieved.

She finally stepped inside, slipping off her yellow, flan-
nel-lined slicker, hanging it by the hood on the doorknob.
She was wearing jeans and a long-sleeved T-shirt with a
low, scooped collar that accentuated her honey-blond chin-

length hair and her long, elegant neck. Her features were delicate—tiny nose, perfectly shaped lips—with the exception of her jawline, which was strong and stubbornly square.

She wasn't conventionally beautiful, but as far as Crash was concerned, the intelligence and the sheer life in her eyes pushed her clear off the scope.

As he watched, she looked around his living room, taking in his garish purple-and-green-plaid sofa and the two matching easy chairs. She tried to hide her surprise.

"Rented furniture," he informed her.

She was startled at first, but then she laughed. She was outrageously pretty when she laughed. "You read my mind."

"I didn't want you thinking I was a purple-and-green-plaid furniture type by choice."

There was a glimmer of amusement in Crash's eyes, and his mouth quirked into what was almost a smile as Nell gazed at him. God, was it possible that William Hawken actually had a sense of humor?

"Let me get something on," he said as he vanished silently down a hallway toward the back of the apartment.

"Take your time," she called after him.

The less time he took, the sooner she'd have to tell him the reason she'd come. And she'd just as soon put that off indefinitely.

Nell paced toward the picture window, once again fighting the urge to cry. All of the furniture in the room was rented, she could see that now. Even the TV had a sticker bearing the name of a rental company. It seemed such a depressing way to live—subject to other people's tastes. She looked out at the overcast sky and sighed. There wasn't much about today, or about the entire past week and a half, that hadn't been depressing. As she watched, the clouds opened and it started to rain.

"Do you really want to go out in that?"

Crash's voice came from just over her shoulder and Nell jumped.

He'd put on a pair of army pants—fatigues, she thought they were called, except instead of being green, these were black—and a black T-shirt. With his dark hair and slightly sallow complexion, he seemed to have stepped out of a black-and-white film. Even his eyes seemed more pale gray than blue.

"If you want, I could make us some coffee," he continued. "I have beans."

"You *do?*"

The amused gleam was back in his eyes. "Yeah, I know. You think, rented furniture—he probably drinks instant. But no. If I have a choice, I make it fresh. It's a habit I picked up from Jake."

"Actually, I didn't really want any coffee," Nell told him. His eyes were too disconcertingly intense, so she focused on the plaid couch instead. Her stomach was churning, and she felt as if she might be sick. "Maybe we could just, you know, sit down for a minute and…talk?"

"Okay," Crash said. "Let's sit down."

Nell perched on the very edge of the couch as he took the matching chair positioned opposite the window.

She could imagine how dreadfully awful it would be if some near stranger came to *her* apartment to tell her that *her* mother had only a few months left to live.

Nell's eyes filled with tears that she couldn't hold back any longer. One escaped, and she wiped it away, but not before Crash had noticed.

"Hey." He moved around the glass-topped coffee table to sit beside her on the couch. "Are you okay?"

It was like a dam breaking. Once the tears started, she couldn't make them stop.

Silently, she shook her head. She *wasn't* okay. Now that she was here, now that she sitting in his living room, she absolutely couldn't do this. She couldn't tell him. How could she say such an awful thing? She covered her face with her hands.

"Nell, are you in some kind of trouble?"

She didn't answer. She couldn't answer.

"Did someone hurt you?" he asked.

He touched her, then. Tentatively at first, but then more firmly, putting his arm around her shoulders, pulling her close.

"Whatever this is about, I can help," he said quietly. She could feel his fingers in her hair, gently stroking. "This is going to be okay—I promise."

There was such confidence in his voice. He didn't have a clue that as soon as she opened her mouth, as soon as she told him why she'd come, it *wasn't* going to be okay. Daisy was going to die, and nothing ever was going to be okay again.

"I'm sorry," she whispered. "I'm so sorry."

"It's okay," he said softly.

He was so warm, and his arms felt so solid around her. He smelled like soap and shampoo, fresh and innocently clean, like a child.

This was absolutely absurd. She was *not* a weeper. In fact, she'd held herself together completely over the past week. There had been no time to fall apart. She'd been far too busy scheduling all those second opinions and additional tests, and cancelling an entire three-week Southwestern book-signing tour. Cancelling—not postponing. God, that had been hard. Nell had spent hours on the phone with Dexter Lancaster, Jake and Daisy's lawyer, dealing with the legal ramifications of the cancelled tour. Nothing about that had been easy.

The truth was, Daisy was more than just Nell's employer. Daisy was her friend. She was barely forty-five years old. She should have another solid forty years of life ahead of her. It was so damned unfair.

Nell took a deep breath. "I have some bad news to tell you."

Crash became very still. He stopped running his fingers through her hair. It was entirely possible that he stopped breathing.

But then he spoke. "Is someone dead? Jake or Daisy?"

Nell closed her eyes. "This is the hardest thing I've ever had to do."

He pushed her up, away from him, lifting her chin so that she had to look directly into his eyes. He had eyes that some people might have found scary—eyes that could seem too burningly intense, eyes that were almost inhumanly pale. As he looked at her searchingly, she felt nearly seared, but at the same time, she could see beneath to his all-too-human vulnerability.

"Just say it," he said. "Just tell me. Come on, Nell. Point-blank."

She opened her mouth and it all came spilling out. "Daisy's been diagnosed with an inoperable brain tumor. It's malignant, it's metastasized. The doctors have given her two months, absolute tops. It's more likely that it will be less. Weeks. Maybe even days."

She'd thought he'd become still before, but that was nothing compared to the absolute silence that seemed to surround him now. She could read nothing on his face, nothing in his eyes, nothing. It was as if he'd temporarily vacated his body.

"I'm so sorry," she whispered, reaching out to touch his face.

Her words, or maybe her touch, seemed to bring him back from wherever it was that he'd gone.

"I missed Thanksgiving dinner," he said, talking more to himself than to her. "I got back into town that morning, and there was a message from Jake on my machine asking me to come out to the farm, but I hadn't slept in four days, so I crashed instead. I figured there was always next year." Tears welled suddenly in his eyes and pain twisted his face. "Oh, my God. Oh, God, how's Jake taking this? He can't be taking this well...."

Crash stood up abruptly, nearly dumping her onto the floor.

"Excuse me," he said. "I have to... I need to..." He turned to look at her. "Are they sure?"

Nell nodded, biting her lip. "They're sure."

It was amazing. He took a deep breath and ran his hands down his face, and just like that he was back in control. "Are you going out to the farm right now?"

Nell wiped her own eyes. "Yeah."

"Maybe I better take my own car, in case I need to get back to the base later on. Are you okay to drive?"

"Yeah. Are *you?*"

Crash didn't answer her question. "I'll need to pack a few things and make a quick phone call, but then I'll be right behind you."

Nell stood up. "Why don't you take your time, plan to come out a few hours before dinner? That'll give you a chance to—"

Again, he ignored her. "I know how hard this must've been for you." He opened the door to the hallway, holding her jacket out for her. "Thank you for coming here."

He was standing there, so distant, so unapproachable and

so achingly alone. Nell couldn't stand it. She put her jacket down and reached for him, pulling him close in a hug. He was so stiff and unyielding, but she closed her eyes, refusing to be intimidated. He needed this. Hell, *she* needed this. "It's okay if you cry," she whispered.

His voice was hoarse. "Crying won't change anything. Crying won't keep Daisy alive."

"You don't cry for her," Nell told him. "You cry for *you*. So that when you see her, you'll be able to smile."

"I don't smile enough. She's always on my case because I don't smile enough." His arms suddenly tightened around her, nearly taking her breath away.

Nell held him just as tightly, wishing that he was crying, knowing that he wasn't. Those tears she'd seen in his eyes, the pain that had been etched across his face had been a slip, a fluke. She knew without a doubt that he normally kept such emotions under careful control.

She would have held him all afternoon if he'd let her, but he stepped back far too soon, his face expressionless, stiff and unapproachable once again.

"I'll see you back there," he said, not quite meeting her eyes.

Nell nodded, slipping into her raincoat. He closed the door quietly behind her, and she took the elevator down to the lobby. As she stepped out into the grayness of the early afternoon, the rain turned to sleet.

Winter was coming, but for the first time Nell could remember, she was in no real hurry to rush the days to spring.

Chapter 2

"What you want to do," Daisy was saying, "is not so much draw an exact picture of the puppy—what a camera lens might see—but rather to draw what *you* see, what you *feel*."

Nell looked over Jake's shoulder and giggled. "Jake feels an aardvark."

"That's not an aardvark, that's a *dog*." Jake looked plaintively at Daisy. "I thought I did okay, don't you think, babe?"

Daisy kissed the top of his head. "It's a beautiful, *wonderful…aardvark*."

As Crash watched from the doorway of Daisy's studio, Jake grabbed her and pulled her onto his lap, tickling her. The puppy started barking, adding canine chaos to Daisy's shouts of laughter.

Nothing had changed.

Three days had passed since Nell had told Crash about Daisy's illness and he'd gone out to the farm, dreading facing both Daisy and Jake. They'd both cried when they saw him, and he'd asked a million questions, trying to find what they might have missed, trying to turn it all into one giant mistake.

How could Daisy be dying? She looked almost exactly the same as she ever had. Despite being given a virtual death sentence by her doctors, Daisy was still Daisy—colorful, outspoken, passionately enthusiastic.

Crash could pretend that the dark circles under her eyes were from the fact that she'd been up all night again, painting, caught in one of her creative spurts. He could find an excuse for her sudden, sharp drop in weight—it was simply the result of her finally finding a diet that she stuck to, finally finding a way to shed those twenty pounds that she always complained were permanently attached to her hips and thighs.

But he couldn't ignore the rows of prescription medicines that had appeared on the kitchen counter. Painkillers. They were mostly painkillers that Crash knew Daisy resisted taking.

Daisy had told Crash that he and Jake and Nell would all have to learn to grieve on their own time. She herself had no time to spare for sad faces and teary eyes. She approached each day as if it were a gift, as if each sunset were a masterpiece, each moment of shared laughter a treasure.

It would only be a matter of time, though, before the tumor affected her ability to walk and move, to paint and even to speak.

But now, as Crash watched, Daisy was the same as always.

Jake kissed her lightly, sweetly on the lips. "I'm going to take my aardvark into my office and return Dex's call."

Dexter Lancaster was one of the few people who actually

knew of Daisy's illness. Dex had served in Vietnam when Jake had, but not as part of the SEAL units. The lawyer had been with the Marines, in some kind of support-services role.

"I'll see you later, babe, all right?" Jake added.

Daisy nodded, sliding off his lap and straightening his wayward dark curls, her fingers lingering at the gray at his temples.

Jake was the kind of man who just kept getting better-looking as he got older. He'd been incandescently, gleamingly handsome in his twenties and rakishly handsome in his thirties and forties. Now, in his fifties, time had given his face laugh lines and a craggy maturity that illustrated his intense strength of character. With deep blue eyes that could both sparkle with warmth and laughter or penetrate steel in anger, with his upfront, in-your-face, honestly sincere approach and his outrageous sense of humor, Crash knew that Jake could have had any woman, *any* woman he wanted.

But Jake had wanted Daisy Owen.

Crash had seen photos of Daisy that Jake had taken back when they'd first met—back when he was a young Navy SEAL on his way to Vietnam, and she was a teenager dressed in cotton gauze she'd tie-dyed herself, selling her drawings and crafts on the streets of San Diego.

With her dark hair cascading down her back in a wild mass of curls, her hazel eyes and her bewitching smile, it was easy to see how she'd caught Jake's eye. She was beautiful, but her beauty was far more than skin-deep.

And at a time when the people of the counterculture were spitting on the boots of men in uniform, at a time when free love meant that strangers could become the most intimate of lovers, then part never to meet again, Daisy gave Jake neither disdain nor a one-night stand. The first few times they'd met, they'd walked the city streets endlessly, sharing cups of hot chocolate at the all-night coffeehouses, talking until dawn.

When Daisy finally did invite Jake into her tiny apartment, he stayed for two weeks. And when he came back from Vietnam, he moved in for good.

During their time together, at least during all the summer vacations and winter breaks Crash had spent with the two of them, he had only heard Daisy and Jake argue about one thing.

Jake had just turned thirty-five, and he'd wanted Daisy to marry him. In his opinion, they'd lived together, unwed, for long enough. But Daisy's views on marriage were unswerving. It was their love that bound them together, she said, not some foolish piece of paper.

They'd fought bitterly, and Jake had walked out—for about a minute and a half. It was, in Crash's opinion, quite possibly the only battle Jake had ever lost.

Crash watched them now as Jake kissed Daisy again, longer this time, lingeringly. Over by the window, Nell's head was bent over her sketch pad, her wheat-colored hair hiding her face, giving them privacy.

But as Jake stood, Nell glanced up. "Is it my turn or yours to make lunch, Admiral?"

"Yours. But if you want I can—"

"No way am I giving up my turn," Nell told him. "You get a chance to make those squirrely seaweed barf-burgers every other day. It's *my* day, and *I'm* making grilled cheese with Velveeta and bacon."

"*What?*" Jake sounded as if she'd said "arsenic" instead of bacon.

"Vegetarian bacon," Daisy told him, laughter in her voice. "It's not real."

"Thank God," Jake clutched his chest. "I was about to

have a high-cholesterol-induced heart attack just from the thought.''

Crash took a deep breath, and went into the room.

''Hey,'' Jake greeted him on his way out the door. ''You just missed the morning art lesson, kid. Check this out. What do you think?''

Crash had to smile. Calling the object Jake had drawn an aardvark was too generous. It looked more like a concrete highway divider with a nose and ears. ''I think you should leave the artwork to Daisy from now on.''

''Tactfully put.'' Jake blew Daisy a kiss, then disappeared.

''Billy, are you here for the day or for longer?'' Daisy asked as Crash gave her a quick hug. She was definitely much too skinny.

Focus on the positive. Stay in the moment. Don't project into the future—there would be time enough for that when it arrived. Crash cleared his throat. ''I had the last of my debriefings this morning. My schedule's free and clear until the New Year, at least.'' Scooping the puppy into his arms, he glanced at Nell, changing the subject, not wanting to talk about the reasons why he'd arranged an entire month of leave. ''Is this guy yours?''

Nell was smiling at him, approval warming her eyes as she put away her sketch pad and pencils and stood up.

''This *guy* is a girl, and she's only here on loan from Esther, the cleaning lady, unfortunately.'' Nell reached out and scratched the puppy's ears. She moved closer—close enough that he could smell the fresh scent of her shampoo, and beneath it, the subtle fragrance of her own personal and very feminine perfume. ''Jake was afraid that you were going to be sent on another assignment right away.''

''I was asked, but I turned it down,'' Crash told her. ''It's been over a year since I've taken any leave. My captain had no problem with that.'' Especially considering the circumstances.

Nell gave the puppy a final pat and her fingers accidentally brushed his hand. "I better go get lunch started. You're joining us, right?"

"If you don't mind."

Nell just smiled as she left the room.

The puppy struggled in Crash's arms, and when he put her onto the floor, she scampered after Nell. He looked up to find Daisy watching him, a knowing smile on her face.

"'If you don't mind,'" she said, imitating him. "You're either disgustingly coy or totally dense."

"Since I don't know what you're talking about—"

"Totally dense wins. Nell. I'm talking about *Nell*." Daisy kicked off her shoes and pulled her legs up so that she was sitting tailor-style. "She's giving you all the right body-language signals. You know, the ones that say she wants you to jump her bones."

Crash laughed as he sat down on the window seat. "Daisy."

She leaned forward. "Go for it. She spends far too much time with her head in a book. It'll be good for her. It'll be good for you, too."

Crash looked at her. "You're actually serious."

"How old are you now?"

"Thirty-three."

She grinned. "I'd say it's definitely time for you to lose your virginity."

He couldn't help but smile. "You're very funny."

"It's not entirely a joke. For all *I* know, you *haven't* been with a woman. You've never brought anyone home. You've never mentioned so much as a name."

"That's because I happen to value my privacy—as well as respecting the privacy of the woman I'm seeing."

"I know you're not seeing anyone right now," Daisy said. "How could you be? You were away for four months, you got back for two days, and then you were gone again for another week. Unless you have a girlfriend in Malaysia or Hong Kong, or wherever it is you're sent..."

"No," Crash said, "I don't."

"So what do you do? Stay celibate? Or *pay* for sex?"

That question made Crash laugh out loud. "I've never paid for sex in my life. I can't believe you're asking me about this." Daisy had always been outrageous and shockingly direct, but she'd always steered clear from the subject of his sex life in the past. Some subjects were too personal—or at least they had been, before.

"I'm no longer worried about shocking anyone," she told him. "I've decided that if I want to know the answer to a question, dammit, I'm going to ask it. Besides, I love you, and I love Nell. I think it would be really cool if the two of you got together."

Crash sighed. "Daisy, Nell's great. I like her and I...think she's smart and pretty and...very nice." He couldn't help but remember how perfectly she had fit in his arms, how soft her hair had felt beneath his fingers, how good she'd smelled. "Too nice."

"No, she's not. She's sharp and funny and tough and she's got this real edge to her that—"

"Tough?"

Daisy lifted her chin defensively. "She can be, yeah. Billy, if you'll just take some time and get to know her, I *know* you'll fall in love with her."

"Look, I'm sorry, but I don't do 'in love.'" Crash wanted to stand up and pace, but there was no room. Besides, he knew without a doubt that Daisy would read some deep meaning into his inability to sit still. "The truth is, I don't even do long-term or permanent. I couldn't even if I wanted to—and I *don't* want to. You know that I'm never around for more than a few weeks at a time. And because I'm aware of those realities, I don't ever give anyone false hope by bringing them here to meet you.''

''All those *don'ts* are so negative. What *do* you do?'' Daisy asked. ''One-night stands? You know, that's dangerous these days.''

Crash looked out the window. The sky was overcast again. December in Virginia was wet and dreary and utterly depressing.

''What I do is, I walk into a bar,'' he told her, ''and I look around, see who's looking back at me. If there are any sparks, I approach. I ask if I can buy her a drink. If she says yes, I ask her to take a walk on the beach. And then, away from the noise of the bar, I ask her about her life, about her job, her family, her last scumbag of a boyfriend— whatever—and I listen really carefully to what she tells me because not many people bother to listen, and I know I'll win big points if I do. And by the time we've walked a quarter mile, I've listened so well, she's ready to make it with me.''

Daisy was silent, just watching him. Her expression was sad, as if what he was telling her wasn't what she'd hoped to hear. Still, there was no judgment and no disapproval in her eyes.

''Instead, I take her home and I kiss her good-night,'' Crash continued, ''and I ask her if I can see her again— take her to dinner the next night, take her someplace nice. She always says yes, so the next night we go out and I treat her really well. And then I tell her over dessert, right up front, that I want to sleep with her but I'm not going to be around for long. I lay it out right there, right on the table. I'm a SEAL, and I could be called away at any time. I tell her I'm not looking for anything that's going to last.

I've got a week, maybe two, and I want to spend that time with her. And she always appreciates my honesty so much that she takes me home. For the next week or however long it is until I get called out on some op, she cooks for me, and she does my laundry, and she keeps me very warm and very, very happy at night. And when I leave, she lets me go, because she knew it was coming. And I walk away— no guilt, no regrets.''

"Didn't you learn *any*thing from me at all? All those summers we spent together…''

Crash looked up. Daisy's eyes were still so sad. "I learned to be honest,'' he told her. "You taught me that.''

"But what you do seems so…cold and calculated.''

He nodded. "It's calculated. I don't pretend it's not. But I'm honest about it—to myself and to the woman I'm with.''

"Haven't you ever met anyone that you *burn* for?'' she asked. "Someone you just want to lie down in front of and surrender to? Someone you absolutely live and die for?''

Crash shook his head. "No,'' he said. "I'm not looking for that, and I don't expect to find it, either. I think most people go through life without that kind of experience.''

"That is so sad.'' There were tears in her eyes as she looked up at him. "It's crazy, too. I'm the one who's dying, but right now I feel so much luckier than you.''

Nell was moving at a dead run as she rounded the corner by the stairs and plowed smack into Crash.

Somehow he managed to catch her and keep them both from landing on the ground in a tangled pile of arms and legs.

"Sorry.'' Nell felt herself blushing as he made sure she was steadily on her feet again.

"Is everything all right?" he asked, finally letting go of her arms. "Is Daisy...?"

"She's fine," Nell said. "But she said *yes*."

He didn't bother to ask. He just waited for her to explain. He was dressed all in black again today, but because the chill of winter was in the air, he wore a turtleneck instead of his usual T-shirt.

Most men managed to look good in a simple black turtleneck. William Hawken looked incredible.

It hugged his shoulders and arms, accentuating his streamlined muscles. It was funny, Nell had always thought of him as somewhat thin—more lean and wiry than muscular—because most of the time he wore clothes that were just a little too large. His T-shirts were never tight and he always wore his pants just a little low on his hips and slightly loose.

But the truth was, he was built as solid as a rock.

Nell felt herself flush again as she realized she was standing there, staring at the man. "You look really good today," she admitted. "I like that shirt."

"Thank you," he said. If she'd surprised him, he didn't show it. But then again, he didn't show much of anything. With the exception of that one time in his apartment, he played all of his emotional cards extremely close to his chest.

"I'm going to need your help," Nell started toward the second-floor office she'd shared with Daisy. "What do you know about swing bands and health-food caterers? Or how about where I can find a florist specializing in poinsettias and holly?"

"Any florist should be able to handle a Christmas-style arrangement," Crash said, keeping pace. "Health-food caterers—I'm not the one to ask about that. As for swing bands, I've always preferred Benny Goodman."

"Benny Goodman's great, but unfortunately he's dead." Nell turned on the office lights and sat down at the desk with the computer, using the mouse and the keyboard to sign on to the Internet. "I need to find someone good who's alive, *and* ready to be booked for the evening before Christmas eve." She looked back at Crash. "Any idea where we can get a half dozen twelve-foot Christmas trees with root balls attached—delivered? And then there's lights and decorations... But we can't hire a decorator, because they do that 'monochromatic garbage'—that's a direct quote—all silver or all red, and that's not any good. We need *real* ornaments, all different colors and sizes."

Crash sat down on the other side of the desk. "Are we having a Christmas party?"

Nell laughed. And then, to her horror, her eyes filled with tears. She blinked them back, but she knew he saw them, because for a fraction of a second, a very peculiar mix of trepidation and an answering flash of pain crossed his face.

"I'm not going to cry," she told him, fiercely willing herself to do just that. "I'm just..." She forced a smile. "I feel so bad for Jake, you know? In a way, Daisy's got it easier, because Jake's the one who's going to have to go on living. And sometimes, when Daisy's not around, I see him, and he has this look in his eyes that just breaks my heart."

Nell sank down, resting her head on top of her desk.

Crash knew she was fighting tears again, and she didn't want him to see. Nell's loyalty impressed him. He understood loyalty. It was the one strong emotion he could relate to—and could allow himself to feel.

"You don't have to be here," he said.

She lifted her head and looked at him through a curtain of rumpled hair, her expression aghast. "Yes, I most certainly do. Daisy needs me now more than ever."

"This wasn't what you were hired to do."

"I was hired as her personal assistant."

"You were hired to take care of all the business aspects of Daisy's career," Crash pointed out, "so that she would have more time to paint."

"A good personal assistant does whatever's needed," Nell argued. "If the dishes need washing, I'll do the dishes. Or I'll clean the fish tank, or—"

"Most people would've given their notice weeks ago. Instead of that, you moved in."

"Yeah, well, the idea of Daisy having to go into a hospice was unacceptable." Nell swept her hair out of her face as she reached for a tissue and briskly blew her nose. "And she hated the thought of hiring some stranger to provide round-the-clock personal care. But she didn't want to dump all that responsibility on Jake, so…" She shrugged.

"So you volunteered."

"I haven't had any medical training, so when the time comes that she needs a nurse, someone's still going to have to come in, but at least she'll know I'll be there, too." Nell tossed the crumpled tissue across the room, sinking it expertly into the wastebasket. "It's no big deal." She took a deep breath and pretended to look at the computer screen.

"That's not true and you know it."

She looked up at him, gazing directly into his eyes. "Are you going to help me, Hawken, or what?"

Crash had to smile. He liked her direct approach. He liked *her*. He was definitely going to help with whatever it was that she was doing, but first he had to make something clear to her.

"I know we're all trying to be as upbeat as Daisy is," he said quietly, "but that gets hard sometimes. I don't want you to have to worry about what I'll say or do if you need to cry. You don't need *that* weighing you down, too. We're living with a lot of emotional upheaval here. There's nothing normal about this, and we can't expect each other to behave normally. So, let's make a deal, okay? You can cry whenever you want, but you can't hold it against me if I stand up and walk away when you do, because…everything that you're feeling…I'm fighting it, too.''

Nell just sat there, looking at him. Her eyes were rimmed with red, she wore no makeup, and she looked as if she'd slept about as much as he had in the past few days—which wasn't much at all.

Maybe they'd both sleep better if they shared a bed.

Crash gently pushed that thought away. He knew it would be true, but he also knew that the absolute, *absolute* last thing Nell needed in her life right now was to become intimately entangled with him.

She was the kind of woman he avoided like the plague when he walked into a bar. He'd recognized her on sight that first time they'd met. She was too sweet, too smart, too innocently full of life and hope and promise.

She was the kind of woman who wouldn't believe him when he said he wasn't looking for long-term or permanent. She was the kind of woman who would think that she could change him.

She was the kind of woman who would cry great big, silent tears as he packed his bag—the kind of woman who would beg him to come back.

No, under completely normal conditions, Crash wouldn't allow himself to get close to Nell. And right now she was a bubbling caldron of high-octane emotions. He knew—not with any sense of ego, but from that same flatly factual voice of experience—that it wouldn't take very much for her to fancy herself in love with him. He knew because he was experiencing the very same highs and lows himself.

But, like he'd told Daisy, he didn't do ''in love'' and he

knew himself well enough to recognize that the rush of emotions he was feeling wasn't real. It couldn't possibly be real. And giving in to this powerful physical temptation would be the worst thing he could do to this woman, no matter how badly he longed for something—for *someone*— to hold on to. No matter how badly he longed for the distraction of sexual release.

He liked Nell too much to use her that way. And knowing what he knew about her, he *would* be using her.

Crash forced himself to take a step back, to separate a little bit more from his emotions. He'd file his red-hot attraction for Nell in that mental holding area he'd created, right next to all the anger and grief and pain he felt over Daisy's impending death. All he needed was just a little more distance, a little more detachment.

But Nell finally moved, holding out her hand to him, stretching her arm across her desk. "I'll accept your deal," she said. "I want to state for the record, though, that I don't usually cry at the drop of a hat."

He took her hand. It was so much smaller than his, her fingers slender and cool. Her grip was firm, and that, along with the crooked smile she gave him, almost made him toss his resolve out the window.

He nearly asked her, point-blank, if she wanted to try to release some tension with him tonight. Daisy had purposely put them in bedrooms right next to each other. It wouldn't be difficult for him to slip into her room and...

Nell was looking at him, her eyes wide, as if she knew what he was thinking. But then he realized that he was still holding her hand. Quickly, he let it go.

Detach.

He cleared his throat. This entire conversation had started with evergreen trees, swing bands and poinsettias. "So, are Jake and Daisy throwing a Christmas party?"

Nell lifted an eyebrow. "Do you really think they'd do something *that* mundane or predictable—or easy to plan? No, this is not your average Christmas party. I was just up in the studio while Daisy was painting," she told him, "and Jake came in and asked her what she wanted to do tonight. He thought maybe she'd want to go to a movie. And she said that lately they only did what *she* wanted to do, and that wasn't fair. She thought that tonight they should do something that *Jake* wanted. And they got into this discussion about Daisy's list—the list of all the things she wants to do before...you know."

Crash nodded. He knew.

"So Daisy said she thought it would be fair if Jake made a similar list, and he said that he didn't need to. He said there was only one thing on *his* wish list—a wish that she would get well and live with him for another twenty years. And if he couldn't have that, then his only other wish would be for her to marry him."

Crash felt a lump forming in his throat. After all this time, Jake still wanted Daisy to marry him.

"So she said yes," Nell continued softly.

He tried to clear it, but it wouldn't go away. "Just like that?"

Nell nodded. "Yeah. She's finally giving in."

Poor Jake. He'd wanted forever, but all he was getting was a cheap illusion.

Crash felt helplessness and rage churning inside of him, fighting to break free and sweep him away like a tidal wave. It wasn't fair. He had to look away from the gentle blue of Nell's eyes, or, dammit, *he* was going to start to cry.

And once he started, he'd never be able to stop.

"Maybe," Nell said quietly, "maybe knowing that

Daisy loved him enough to give in and marry him will help. Maybe someday Jake will find some comfort in that.''

Crash shook his head, still unable to meet her gaze. He stood up, knowing that if he just walked away, she would understand. But she'd also asked for his help. He sat back down, willing himself to detach even more, to stop *feeling* so damn much. He took a deep breath and let it slowly out. And when he spoke, his voice was even. "So now we're planning a wedding."

"Yup. Daisy said yes, and then turned to me and asked if I could take care of the details—in exactly three weeks. Of course, I said yes, too." She laughed, and it came out sounding just on the verge of hysterical, just a little bit giddy. "Please, *please* say that you'll help me."

"I'll help you."

She briefly closed her eyes. "Thank God."

"But I don't have a lot of experience with weddings."

"Neither do I."

"In fact, I tend to avoid weddings like the plague," he admitted.

"All of my college friends who are married either eloped or got married on the other coast," Nell said. "I've never even *been* to a real wedding. The closest I've ever gotten was watching the TV broadcast of Princess Diana's wedding to Prince Charles when I was little."

"That probably had just a *little* bit more flash and fanfare than Daisy and Jake are going to want."

Nell laughed, and then stopped short. He'd just made a joke. That *had* been a joke, hadn't it?

He wasn't smiling, but there definitely was a glint of something in his eyes. Amusement. Or was it tears?

Crash turned his head and examined the toe of his boot. With his lids lowered, Nell couldn't see his eyes, and when he looked up again, he was carefully devoid of all expression.

"We should probably make a list of all the essential supplies for a wedding," he suggested.

"We've got the bride and the groom. They're pretty essential, and we can already cross them off the list."

"But they'll need clothes."

"A wedding gown—something funky that'll make Daisy feel as if she's still thumbing her nose at convention." Nell started an Internet search. "There must be some kind of wedding checklist somewhere that we can use—so we don't forget something important."

"Like wedding rings."

"Or—God!—someone to perform the ceremony." She looked up, pushing the phone and the yellow pages toward him. "Trees," she said. "A half a dozen twelve-foot Christmas trees. Live."

"Delivered ASAP," he said. "You can already cross it off your list." He reached for the phone, but she didn't let it go, and he looked up at her.

"Thanks," she said quietly. They both knew she was talking about more than just his help with this project.

Crash nodded. "You can cross that off your list, too."

"A prenuptial agreement?" Nell's voice was loaded with disbelief.

Crash paused in the kitchen doorway, looking in to find her sitting at the table across from Dexter Lancaster, Jake and Daisy's lawyer.

She'd made them both tea, and she sat with her hands wrapped around her cup, as if she were cold.

Lancaster was a big man. He had at least five inches and seventy pounds on Crash, but most of those pounds were the result of too many doughnuts and Danishes in the morning and too many servings of blueberry cheesecake at night. Age and a sweet tooth had conspired to take the sharp edges off Lancaster's WASP-y good looks and as a result, somewhat ironically, he was probably more handsome at age forty-nine than he'd been at thirty.

He was a friendly-looking bear of a man, with warm blue eyes that actually twinkled behind round, wire-framed glasses. His hair was sandy-blond and still thick and untouched by gray.

He sighed as he answered Nell. "Yeah, I know, it sounds crazy, but in a way, it'll clarify exactly which parts of Daisy's estate she wishes to leave to persons other than Jake. If it's in both the prenup *and* the will, it'll speed the process along after she's..." He shook his head, taking off his glasses and wiping his eyes with both hands. "Sorry."

Nell took a deep breath. "Don't be. It's coming, you know. Daisy faces it. She talks about it matter-of-factly. We should be able to do that, too." She made a sound that was half laughter, half sob. "Easier said than done, though, huh?"

Dex Lancaster set his glasses down and reached across the table to cover her hand with his. "You know, your being here is a godsend to both of them."

The exact same thought had crossed Crash's mind at least three times a day. But he'd never said it aloud. He'd figured that Nell surely knew.

She smiled at Lancaster. "Thanks."

The lawyer smiled back at her, still holding her hand.

The man liked her. He *more* than liked her.

Dexter Lancaster had a thing for Nell. The man was twenty years her senior, at *least,* but Crash knew from his subtle body language and from the way he was looking at her that he found her undeniably attractive.

Lancaster was no fool. And judging from the fact that

his law firm had one of the best reputations in the country, he also was not an underachiever. Any second now, he was going to ask Nell out to dinner.

"I was wondering…" Lancaster started.

Crash coughed and stepped into the room.

Nell slipped her hand out from beneath Lancaster's as she turned to look up at him. "You're back," she said, giving him a smile. It was a bigger smile than the one she'd given Dex Lancaster. "Did you have any problem getting the rings?"

Crash took the two jewelers' boxes from the inside pocket of his jacket and set them on the table in front of her. "None whatsoever."

"You know Dex, don't you?" she asked.

"We've met a few times," Crash said.

The lawyer stood up as he held out his hand, and the two men shook.

But their handshake wasn't a greeting. It was a not-so-subtle sizing up. It was more than obvious, from the once-over Lancaster was giving him, that he was trying to figure out what claim—if any—Crash had already staked out.

Crash met the older man's gaze steadily. And after the handshake was done, he moved slightly to stand closer to Nell, putting one hand on the back of her chair in a gesture that was clearly possessive.

What the hell was he doing?

He didn't want this girl.

He'd resolved to stay away from her, to keep his distance, both physically and emotionally.

But as much as he didn't want her, he didn't want to see her taken for a ride, either.

Crash didn't trust lawyers any farther than he could throw them, and Dexter Lancaster was no exception to his rule, despite the fact that his eyes twinkled like Santa Claus's.

Lancaster checked his watch. "I have to get going." He twinkled at Nell. "I'm sure I'll talk to you soon." He nodded at Crash as he slipped on his overcoat. "Nice seeing you again."

Like hell it was. "Take care," Crash lied in return.

"What was *that* all about?" Nell turned to ask as the door closed behind Dexter Lancaster.

Crash opened the refrigerator and pretended to be engrossed by its contents. "Just a little Army/Navy rivalry."

Nell laughed. "You're kidding. All that tension just because you're in the Navy and he was in the Army?"

Crash took a can of soda out and shut the refrigerator door. "Crazy, huh?" he said as he escaped into the other room.

Chapter 3

Nell glanced up from her computer to see Crash standing in her office. She jumped, nearly knocking over her cup of tea, catching it with both hands, just in time.

"God!" she said. "Don't *do* that! You're always sneaking up on me. Make some noise when you come in, will you? Try stomping your feet, okay?"

"I thought I'd made noise when I opened the door. I'm sorry. I didn't mean to scare you."

She took a deep breath, letting it slowly out. "No, *I'm* sorry. I've been…feeling sideways all day. There must be a full moon or something." She frowned at the half-written letter on her computer screen. "Of course, now I've got so much adrenaline raging through my system, I'm not going to be able to concentrate."

"Next time, I'll knock."

Nell looked up at Crash in exasperation. "I don't want you to *knock*. You've been working as hard as I have— this is your office, too. Just…clear your throat or play the bagpipes or whistle, or *some*thing.'' She turned back to the letter.

Crash cleared his throat. ''I've been ordered to tell you that after two days of rain, the sky's finally clear, and the sun's due to set in less than fifteen minutes,'' he said.

Sunset. Nell glanced at her watch, swearing silently. Was it really that time already?

''I'm waiting for a fax from the caterer, and Dex Lancaster's supposed to call me right back to tell me if Friday is okay to come out and discuss some changes Daisy wants to make to her will, but I guess he can leave a message on the machine,'' she told him, thinking aloud. ''I'm almost done with this letter, but I'll hurry. I'll be there. I promise.''

Crash stepped closer. ''I've been ordered to make sure you arrive on time, not five minutes after the sun has gone down, like last Monday. Daisy said to tell you that the rest of the week's forecast calls for total cloud coverage. In fact, the prediction is for snow—maybe as much as two or three inches. This could be the last sunset we see for a while.''

The last sunset. Every sunset they saw was one of Daisy's very last sunsets.

Every clear day for the past two weeks, Daisy had brought Nell's work to a screeching halt as they'd all met in the studio to watch the setting sun. But now there was less than a week before the wedding, and the list of things that needed to be done was *still* as long as her arm. On top of that, the sun was setting earlier and earlier as midwinter approached, cutting her workday shorter and shorter.

It was also reminding her that the passage of time was bringing them closer and closer to the end of Daisy's life.

Nell looked at her watch again, then up into the steely gray of Crash's eyes.

To her surprise, there was amusement gleaming there.

''I've been ordered not to fail,'' he told her, giving her

an actual smile, "which means I'm going to have to pick you up and carry you downstairs to the studio if you don't get out of that chair right now."

Yeah, sure he was. Nell turned back to the computer. "Just let me save this file. And wait—here comes that fax from the caterer now. I just have to— Hey!"

Crash picked her up, just as he'd said he would, throwing her over his shoulder in a fireman's hold as he carried her out of the door.

"Okay, Hawken, very funny. Put me down." Nell's nose bumped his back and her arms dangled uncomfortably. She wasn't sure where to put her hands.

He seemed to have no problem figuring out where to put *his* hands. He held her legs firmly with one arm, and anchored her in place by resting his other hand squarely on the seat of her jeans. Yet despite that, his touch seemed impersonal—further proof that the man was not even remotely interested in her.

And after two weeks of living in the same house, sleeping in a room one door down the hall from his, and working together twenty-four hours a day, seven days a week, on this wedding that had somehow grown from a small affair with forty guests into a three-hundred-person, Godzilla-sized event, Nell probably didn't need any further proof.

William Hawken *wasn't* interested.

Nell had given him all the full-speed-ahead signs—body language, lingering eye contact, subtle verbal hints. She'd done damn near everything but show up naked in his room at night.

But he'd kept at least three feet of air between them at all times. If he was sitting on the couch and she sat down next to him, he soon stood up on the pretense of getting something from the kitchen. He was always polite, always asking if he could get her a soda or a cup of tea, but when he came back, he was careful to sit on the opposite side of the room.

He never let her get too close emotionally, either. While she had babbled on about her family and growing up in Ohio, he had never, not even once, told her anything about himself.

No, he was definitely not interested.

Except whenever she turned around, whenever he thought she wasn't looking, he was there, looking at her. He moved so soundlessly, he just seemed to appear out of thin air. And he was always watching.

It was enough to keep alive that little seed of hope. Maybe he *was* interested, but he was shy.

Shy? Yeah, right. William Hawken might've been quiet, but he didn't have a shy bone in his body. Try again.

Maybe he was in love with someone else, someone far away, someone he couldn't be with while he was here at the farm. In that case, the careful distance that he kept between them made him a gentleman.

Or maybe he simply wasn't interested, but he didn't have anything better to look at, so he stared at her.

And maybe *she* should stop obsessing and get on with her life. So what if the most handsome, attractive, fascinating man she'd ever met only wanted to be friends? So what if every time she was with him, she liked him more and more? So what? She'd be friends with him. No big deal.

Nell closed her eyes, miserably wishing that he were carrying her to his room. Instead, he took her all the way down the stairs and into Daisy's art studio.

Jake had set up the beach chairs in front of the window that faced west. Daisy was already reclining, hands lazily up behind her head as Jake gently worked the cork free from a bottle of wine.

The last sunset. Crash's words rang in Nell's ears. One of these evenings, Daisy was going to watch her last sunset. Nell hated that idea. She *hated* it. Anger and frustration boiled in her chest, making it hard to breathe.

"Better lock the door before you put her down," Daisy told Crash. "She might run away."

"Just throw her down fast and sit on her," Jake recommended.

But Crash didn't throw her down. He placed her, gently, on one of the chairs.

"Watch her," Daisy warned. "She'll try to squeeze in just one more call."

Nell looked at the other woman in exasperation. "I'm here. I'm not going anywhere, okay? But I'm not going to drink any wine. I still have too much work to—"

Jake put a wineglass in her hand. "How can you make a toast if you don't have any wine?"

Daisy sat up to take a glass from Jake, who took the chair next to her. She leaned forward slightly to look across him to Nell. "I have an idea. Let's just let this wedding happen. No more preparations. We've got the dress, the rings, the band's set to come and nearly all the guest have been called. What else could we possibly need?"

"Food would be nice."

"Who eats at weddings, anyway?" Daisy said. Her cat-green eyes narrowed as she looked at Nell. "You look exhausted. I think you need a day off. Tomorrow Jake and I are going skiing over in West Virginia. Why don't you come along?"

Skiing? Nell snorted. "No thanks."

"You'd *love* it," Daisy persisted. "The view from the ski lift is incredible, and the adrenaline rush from the ride down the mountain is out of this world."

"It's really not my style." She preferred curling up in

front of a roaring fire with a good book over an adrenaline rush. She smiled tightly at Crash. "See, I'm one of those people who ride the Antique Cars in the amusement park instead of the roller coaster."

He nodded, pouring soda into the delicate wineglass Jake had left out for him. "You like being in control. There's nothing wrong with that." He sat down next to her. "But skiing's different from riding a roller coaster. When you ski, you've still got control."

"Not when *I* ski," Daisy said with a throaty chuckle.

Crash glanced at her, his mouth quirking up into one of his near smiles. "If you had bothered to learn how to do it instead of just strapping the skis on for the first time at the top of a mountain—"

"How could I waste my time on the bunny slope when that great huge mountain was sitting there, waiting for me?" Daisy retorted. "Billy, talk Nell into coming with us."

Crash's eyes met Nell's, and she wondered if he could tell just from looking how brittle she felt today. She'd been tense and out of sorts just a few minutes ago, but now she felt as if she were going to snap.

Crash on the other hand, looked exactly as he always did. Slightly remote, in careful control. That was how he did it, Nell realized suddenly. He stayed in control by distancing himself from the situation and the people involved.

He'd cut himself off from all his emotions. Sure, he probably didn't feel as if his rage and grief were going to come hurtling out of him in some terrible projectile vomit of emotion. But on the other hand, he didn't laugh much, either. Oh, occasionally something she or Daisy said would catch him off guard, and he'd chuckle. But she'd never seen him laugh until tears came.

He'd protected himself from the pain, but he'd cut himself off from the joy as well.

And that was another desperate tragedy. Daisy, so full of life, was dying while Crash willingly chose to go through life emotionally half-dead.

Nell was clinging to the very edge of the cliff that was her control, and the sheer tragedy of that thought made her fingernails start slipping.

Crash leaned slightly toward her. "I can teach you to ski, if you want," he said quietly. "I'd take it as slowly as you like—you'd be in control, I promise." He lowered his voice even further. "Are you all right?"

Nell shook her head quickly, jerkily, like a pitcher shaking off a catcher's hand signal. "I can't go skiing. I have *way* too much to do." She turned toward Daisy, unable to meet the other woman's eyes. "I'm sorry."

Daisy didn't say it in front of Jake and Crash, but Nell could see what she was thinking—it was clearly written on her face. She thought Nell was missing out. She thought Nell was letting her life pass her by.

But life was about making choices, dammit, and Nell was choosing to stay home, to stay warm instead of strapping slabs of wood onto her feet and risking broken arms and legs by sliding at an alarming speed down an icy slope covered with artificial snow. The only thing Nell was missing was fear, discomfort and the chance for a trip to the hospital.

She sat back in her chair, feeling as if the sudden silence in the room was the fault of her bitchiness. Her chest got even tighter and the suffocating feeling she was fighting threatened to overwhelm her. She looked at Crash. He was watching the sky begin to change colors as he sipped soda from his wineglass.

What did it look like to him? Did he look at the beautiful

pink and reddish-orange colors with as much detachment as he did everything else? Did he see the fragile lace of the high clouds only as a meteorological formation, only as cirrus clouds? And instead of the brilliant colors, did he see only the dust in the atmosphere, bending and distorting the sun's light?

"How come you're not required to drink wine?" Her words came out sounding belligerent, nearly rude. But if he noticed, he didn't take offense.

"I don't drink alcohol," he told her evenly, "unless I absolutely have to."

That didn't make sense. Nothing about her life right now made any sense at all. "Why would you *have* to?"

"Sometimes, in other countries, when I meet with…certain people, it would be considered an insult not to drink with them."

That was it. Nell boiled over. She stood up and set down her glass, sloshing the untouched contents on the tablecloth. "Could you possibly be *any* more vague when you talk about yourself? I mean, don't bother adding a single detail, please. It's not as if I give a damn."

Nell was furious, but Crash knew that her anger wasn't aimed at him. He'd just been caught in her emotional crossfire.

For the past two weeks, she had been in as carefully tight control as he was. But for some reason—and it didn't really matter what had triggered it—she'd reached her limit tonight.

She was staring at him now, her face ashen and her eyes wide and filled with tears, as if she'd realized just how terribly un-Nell-like she'd just sounded.

Crash got to his feet slowly, afraid if he moved too quickly she'd run for the door.

But she didn't run. Instead, she forced a tight smile.

"Well, I sure am the life of the party tonight, huh?" She glanced at the others, still trying hard to smile. "I'm sorry, Daisy. I think I have to go."

"Yeah, I have to go, too," Crash said, hoping that if he sounded matter-of-fact, Nell might let him walk with her. The stress she'd been under for the past few weeks had been hellishly intense. She didn't deserve to be alone, and he, God help him, was the only candidate available to make sure that she wasn't. He took her arm and gently pulled her with him toward the door.

She didn't say a word until they reached the stairs that led to the second floor of the rambling modern farmhouse. But then, with the full glory of the pink sky framed by the picture window in the living room, she spoke. "I ruined a really good sunset for them, didn't I?"

Crash wished that she would cry. He would know what to do if she cried. He'd put his arm around her and hold her until she didn't need him to hold her anymore.

But he didn't know what to do about the bottomless sorrow that brimmed like the tears in her eyes—brimmed, but wasn't released.

"There'll be other sunsets," he finally said.

"How many will Daisy get to see?" She turned to him, looking directly into his eyes as if he might actually know the answer to that question. "Probably not a hundred. Probably not even fifty. Twenty, do you think? Twenty's not very many."

"Nell, I don't—"

She turned and started quickly up the stairs. "I have to do better than this. This cannot happen again. I'm here to help her, not to be *more* of a burden."

He followed, taking the steps two at a time to catch up to her. "You're human," he said. "Give yourself a break."

She stopped, her hand on the knob of the door that led

to her room. "I'm sorry I said...what I said." Her voice shook. "I didn't mean to take it out on you."

He wanted to touch her, and knew that she wanted him to touch her, too. But he couldn't do it. He couldn't take that risk. Not without the excuse of her tears. And she still wasn't crying. "I'm sorry I...frustrate you."

It was a loaded statement—one that was true on a multitude of levels. But she didn't look up. She didn't acknowledge it at all, in *any* way.

"I think I have to go to sleep now," she whispered. "I'm *so* tired."

"If you want, I'll..." What? What could he possibly do? "I'll sit with you for a while."

At first he wasn't sure she heard him. She was silent for a long time. But then she shook her head. "No. Thanks, but..."

"I'll be right next door, in my room, if you need me," he told her.

Nell turned and looked up at him, then. "You know, Hawken, I'm glad we're friends."

She looked exhausted, and Crash was hit with a wave of the same fatigue. It was a nearly overwhelmingly powerful feeling, accompanied by an equally powerful sense of irrationality. It was all he could do to keep himself from reaching out and cupping the softness of her face, and lowering his lips to hers.

Instead, he stepped back, away from her. Detach. Separate. Distance.

And Nell slipped into her room, shutting the door tightly behind her.

At two in the afternoon, the trees were delivered.

As the huge truck rolled into the driveway, Nell pulled

her brown-leather bomber jacket on over her sweater and, wrapping her scarf around her neck, went out to meet it.

She stopped short before she reached the gravel of the drive.

Crash was standing next to one of the trucks.

What was he doing there?

He was wearing one of his disgustingly delicious-looking black turtlenecks, talking to the driver and gesturing back toward the barn.

It was starting to snow, just light flurries, but the delicate flakes glistened and sparkled in his dark hair and on his shirt.

What *was* he doing there?

The driver climbed back into the cab of the truck, and Crash turned as Nell came toward him.

"I thought you went skiing." She had to raise her voice to be heard over the sound of the revving engine and the gasping release of the air brakes.

"No," he said, watching as the truck pulled around the house, in the direction he had pointed. "I decided to stay here."

He started following the truck, but Nell stood still, glancing back at the house. "You should get a jacket." She was suddenly ridiculously nervous. After last night, he must think her an idiot. Or a fool. Or an idiotic fool. Or...

"I'm fine." He turned to face her, but he didn't stop walking. "I want to make sure the barn is unlocked."

Nell finally followed. "It is. I was out there earlier. I picked up the decorations in town this morning."

"I figured that's where you went. You left before I could offer to help."

Nell couldn't stand dancing around the subject of the night before one instant longer. "You didn't go skiing to-

day because you thought I might still need a baby-sitter,"
she said, looking him straight in the eye.

He smiled slightly. "Substitute *friend* for *baby-sitter,* and
you'd be right."

Friend. There was that word again. Nell had used it herself last night. *I'm glad we're friends.* If only she could
convince herself that friendship was enough. That was not
an easy thing to do when the very sight of this man made
her heart beat harder, when the fabric of his turtleneck
hugged the hard muscles of his shoulders and chest, clinging where she ached to run her hands and her mouth and...

And there was no doubt about it. She had it bad for a
Navy SEAL who called himself Crash. She had it bad for
a man who had cleanly divorced himself from all his emotions.

"I want to apologize," she started to say, but he cut her
off.

"You don't need to."

"But I *want* to."

"All right. Apology accepted. Daisy called while you
were out," he said, changing the subject deftly. They
walked around the now idling truck toward the outbuilding
that Jake and Daisy jokingly called the barn.

But with its polished wood floors, one wall of windows
that overlooked the mountains and another of mirrors that
reflected the panoramic view, this "barn" wasn't used to
hold animals. Equipped with heating and central air con-
ditioning, with a full kitchen attached to the ballroom-sized
main room, it was no ordinary stable. Even the rough, exposed beams somehow managed to look elegant. The previous owners had used the place as a dance studio and
exercise room.

Crash swung open the main doors. "Daisy said she and
Jake were getting a room at a ski lodge, and that they

wouldn't be back until tomorrow afternoon, probably on the late side.''

She and Crash would be alone in the house tonight. Nell turned away, afraid he would read her thoughts in her eyes. Not that it mattered particularly. He probably already knew what she was thinking—he had to be aware of what she wanted. She'd been far less than subtle over the past few weeks. But he didn't want the same thing.

Friends, she reminded herself. Crash wanted them to be friends. Being friends was safe, and God forbid he should ever allow anything to shake him up emotionally.

Crash stepped to the side of the room, gently pulling Nell with him as three workmen carried one of the evergreen trees into the building.

She moved out of his grasp, but not because she didn't want him to touch her. On the contrary. She liked the sensation of his hand on her arm too much. But she was afraid if she stood there like that, so close to him, it wouldn't be long before she sank back so that she was leaning against him.

But friends didn't do that.

Friends kept their distance.

And there was no need to embarrass herself in front of this man two days in a row.

Chapter 4

Crash held the stepladder while Nell positioned the angel on the top of one of the trees.

She'd brought a portable CD player into the barn, and Bing Crosby sang "White Christmas" over remarkably natural-sounding speakers. Nell sang along, right in Bing's octave, her voice a low, throaty alto.

She looked out the window as she came down the ladder. The snow was still falling. "I can't remember the last time it snowed for Christmas. Certainly not since I've lived in Virginia. And last year, I visited my parents in Florida. I was on the beach on Christmas Eve. The sand was white, but it just wasn't the same."

Crash was silent as he carried the stepladder to the last tree, as Nell removed the plastic wrapping from the final angel.

"You didn't make it out here to the farm last Christmas, did you?"

"No."

Nell glanced at him and he knew what she was looking for. She'd tossed him the conversational ball, and wanted him to run with it. She wanted him to tell her where *he'd* spent last Christmas.

He cleared his throat. "Last December, I was on a covert military op that is still so top secret, I can't even tell you which hemisphere of the globe I was in."

"Really?" Her eyes were wide. And very blue. Ocean blue. But not the stormy blue of the Atlantic, or even the turquoise of the Caribbean. Nell's eyes were the pure blue of the South China Sea. In fact, there was a beach there that— He cut his thought off abruptly. What was he doing? Allowing himself to submerge in the depths of this woman's eyes? That was insanity.

He turned away, making sure the stepladder was close enough to the tree. "Most of what I do, I can't talk about. Not to anyone."

"God, that must be really tough—considering the way you love to run off at the mouth."

She'd caught him off guard, and he laughed. "Yeah, well… What can I say?"

"Exactly." Nell paused on the rung of the ladder that brought them eye to eye. "Actually, I shouldn't be making jokes. It's probably really hard for you, isn't it?"

Malaysia. The beach was in Malaysia, and the ocean had been an impossibly perfect shade of blue. He'd sat there in the sand for hours, drinking it in, watching the sunlight dance across the water.

"It's my job," he said quietly.

Unlike in Malaysia, Crash forced himself to look away.

He could feel her gazing at him for several long moments before continuing on up the stepladder. She set the angel on the top branch of the tree, carefully adjusting its halo. "I know that part of what Jake does has to do with these…covert ops you're sent on. Although…they were called something else, weren't they? *Black* ops?''

Crash waited several beats before speaking. ''How do you know about that?''

Something in his voice must have been different, because she glanced down at him. ''Uh-oh. I wasn't supposed to know, was I? Now you're going to have to kill me, right?''

He didn't laugh at her joke. ''Technically, your having access to that information is a breach of security. I need to know what you saw or heard, to make sure it doesn't happen again.''

She slowly came back down the ladder. ''You're serious.''

''There are only five—now six—people in the world who know I work covert ops for Admiral Robinson,'' Crash told her. ''One of them is the President of the United States. And now one of them is *you*.''

Nell sat down on the second to last rung of the stepladder. ''Oh, my God, you *are* going to have to kill me.'' She looked up at him. ''Or vote me into office.''

He nearly laughed at that one. But in truth there was nothing funny about this. ''Nell, if you knew how serious…'' Crash shook his head.

''But that's just it,'' she said imploringly. ''I *don't* know. How can I know when you won't even finish your sentences? I know close to nothing about you. I'm friends with you almost entirely on faith—on vague gut instincts and the fact that Daisy and Jake think that the sun rises and sets with you. Do you know that in the past two weeks, you've told me *nothing* about yourself? We talk about books, and you tell me you're currently reading Grisham's latest, but you never say if you like it. You wouldn't even tell me your favorite color! I mean, what kind of friendship is *that?*''

The problem she had with him was nothing compared to the problem he currently had with her. He pinned her into place with his eyes. "Nell, this is extremely important. I need to know how you found out I was working with Jake. Have you mentioned this to anyone else? *Any*one at all?"

She shook her head, holding his gaze steadily. "No."

"Are you sure?"

"I'm positive," she said. "Look, I overheard Jake and Daisy talking. I didn't mean to, but they were being loud. They were...exchanging heated words. It wasn't quite an argument, but it was the closest to it that I've ever heard. Daisy accused Jake of sending you out on a black op. Those are the exact words she said. A black op. I remember because it sounded so spooky and dangerous. Anyway, Daisy wanted to know where you were. It was back when all that trouble was happening in the Middle East, and she was worried about you. She wanted Jake to stop using you for those dangerous covert missions—again, that's pretty much a direct quote—and he told her there was no one he trusted as much as you to get the job done. Besides, he said, you could take care of yourself."

Crash was silent.

"They both love you an awful lot," Nell told him.

He couldn't help himself. He started to pace. "You had a security check run on you before you started working for Daisy," he said, thinking aloud.

"No, I don't think so."

He shot her a look. "You probably didn't know about it, but you definitely have a FInCOM file with a copy at the NAVINTEL office. Think about it—you're working for Admiral Robinson's significant other. Believe me, you were checked out before you even met her." He took a deep breath. "I'm going to talk to Jake, and what's probably going to happen is we'll run a deeper, more invasive check.'' He stopped pacing and gazed down at her. "You'll be asked to make a complete list of people that you know. A *complete* list. Family, friends, lovers. Even casual acquaintances, so that—''

Nell laughed in disbelief. "My God, have you caught a whiff of the irony here? It positively reeks. I've been complaining because you never talk about yourself, but now *I've* got to give you a list of my lovers.'' She shook her head. "What's wrong with this picture?''

"You won't have to give those lists to me. You'll be contacted directly by FInCOM.''

"But you'll probably see it.'' She stood up. "You've probably already seen my current file, haven't you?''

Crash closed the stepladder, carefully hooking the two sides together. "Should I put this back?''

"Leave it out. We'll probably be using it again before the party.''

He set it against the wall by the kitchen. "How about we get a pizza delivered for dinner?''

"You're purposely not answering me.'' Nell slipped on her jacket and fastened her scarf around her neck. "You do that all the time—don't think I haven't noticed. You change the subject to avoid answering my questions. I *hate* that, you know.''

Crash might have sighed.

Or maybe Nell only imagined it. God, he gave *so* little away. She crossed her arms.

"Aren't you hungry?'' he asked. "I'm hungry.''

"I'm waiting,'' she said. "I believe the question was, you've already seen my current FInCOM file, *haven't you?*''

He turned off the overhead lights. In the dimness, the six trees they'd decorated looked spectacular. The colorful lights glistened and the ornaments gleamed.

"I'm not looking at the trees. I'm refusing to be distracted." She put her hands up around her eyes, like a horse's blinders. "I'm going to stand here until you answer my question."

Crash almost smiled, and for once she knew exactly what he was thinking. How could she even *dream* of winning this kind of contest of wills with him?

The answer to that was simple. She couldn't win. There was absolutely nothing she could do to force him to answer her question.

So she answered for him.

"Yes," she said. "You've seen it. I *know* you've seen my file. If you hadn't, you would have said so already. So what's the big deal, right? It's probably full of all kinds of boring details. Grew up in Ohio, just outside of Cleveland, oldest of three kids, attended NYU, graduated with a liberal-arts degree and without a clue. Stumbled into a personal assistant job for a Broadway-musical director who owned a chain of convenience stores on the side, went to work for Daisy Owens several years later. Any of this sound familiar?"

He didn't say a word. She hadn't really expected him to. "My personal life's been just as dull. In the past six years, I've dated three different men, all nice, respectable professionals with solid futures. Two proposed marriage. I think they thought they'd be getting some kind of bonus deal— a wife who worked as a personal assistant. I was like some kind of yuppie fantasy woman. Buy me some Victoria's Secret underwear, and I'd be perfect. I turned them both down. The one who *didn't* want me instantly became the one I wanted, and I pursued him—only to find out he was as boring as the rest of 'em. My mother is convinced I'm a victim of the fairy tales I read as a little girl. She thinks I suffer from 'Someday My Prince Will Come' syndrome, and I think she's probably right, although I'm not sure *that's* in my file.''

Crash finally spoke. ''Probably not in so many words. But all FInCOM files include psychological evaluations. Your reasons for remaining unmarried would have been touched on.''

Nell snorted. ''God, I can just see the fink-shrinks sitting around psychoanalyzing me. 'Subject is a complete chicken. Sits around reading books on her days off. Never does anything even remotely interesting, like skiing. Subject is a total loser who is afraid of her own shadow.''' Without looking at him she turned and walked out the door.

And then stopped short. It was still snowing. The sky was already dark, and the falling snow swirled around her face, reflecting the light from the lamps that lit the walkway to the house.

Nell looked up at the millions of flakes falling dizzily down from the sky. She could hear the softest, slightest hiss as the snow hit the frozen ground.

''It's beautiful,'' she whispered. if there was one thing she'd learned from these past few hellish weeks, it was to stop and take note of the sheer beauty of the world around her.

''It's been a while since I've seen snow.''

She turned to see Crash standing behind her. He'd actually made a somewhat personal comment without her dragging it out of him. And he didn't stop there.

''Being cautious doesn't mean you're a loser,'' he said.

Nell looked out at the field that went halfway up the hill back behind the barn before ending at a stone wall on the edge of the woods. It was covered with snow, so pristine and inviting.

''I used to like to do all sorts of things that scare me now,'' she admitted. ''When I was little, the sight of that hillside would've sent me running for my sled.'' She turned to face him. ''But now even the thought of doing something like skiing makes me break out in a cold sweat. When did I learn to be so afraid?''

''Not everyone was born to like the sensation of wind in their face.''

''Yeah, but that's where it gets really stupid. There's a part of me that *wants* that. A part of me is really ticked that I didn't go skiing with Daisy and Jake. There's a part of me that has these incredible fantasies....''

One of his eyebrows went up an almost imperceptible fraction of an inch, and Nell hastened to explain.

''Fantasies like riding a motorcycle. I've always secretly yearned for an enormous Harley. I've always wanted to come roaring up to some important meeting on a huge bike, with those long, black leather fringes coming out of the ends of the hand grips, wearing one of those helmets with the kind of visor you can't see through. I have this really vivid picture of myself taking off the helmet and shaking out my hair and unstrapping my briefcase from the back and...'' She shook her head. ''Instead, I drive a compact car and I can't even get up enough nerve to go skiing— and you're standing out here without a jacket on,'' she interrupted herself. ''We should go inside the house and order that pizza.''

''Large, extra cheese with sausage, peppers and onions,'' Crash told her. ''Unless you don't like sausage, peppers or onions, and then you get to pick what's on it. Go call from the barn while I get my jacket, then meet me out by the garage.''

The garage? ''You want to go pick it up?''

''No, have it delivered.''

''But—''

Crash was already gone, disappearing into the shadows as easily as he appeared.

"Why by the garage?" she called in the direction he'd vanished.

He didn't answer. She hadn't really expected him to.

Nell stopped short when she saw Crash holding the Flexible Flyer sled that he'd dug out of the garage.

"Oh, no," she said with a laugh. "No, no…"

The snow still fell with a whispering hiss around them. It was the perfect evening for sledding.

"The snow's supposed to turn to rain before midnight," Crash told her. "It'll probably all melt off by tomorrow."

"In other words, now or never, huh?"

Crash didn't answer. He just looked at her. The bright red scarf she was wearing accentuated the paleness of her face, and flakes of snow clung to her thick, honey-colored hair. On anyone else the combination of pale skin and not quite blond, not quite brown hair might have been drab, but her eyes were so blue and warm, and her smile was so perfect.…

Crash found her impossibly beautiful, and he knew that his attempt to take her sledding was nothing but an excuse to get close to her. He wanted to put his arms around this woman and he was resorting to subterfuge to do it.

"The pizza will be here in about thirty minutes," she told him. "We don't really have time to—"

"We have enough time to make at least a couple of runs down the hill."

She gestured up behind the barn. "*That* hill?"

"Come on." Crash held out his hand. He was wearing gloves and she had on mittens. It wasn't as if he would really be touching her.

But when she took his hand, Crash knew he was dead

wrong. It didn't matter. Touching her was touching her. But he couldn't stop now. He didn't *want* to stop. He pulled her up the hill, dragging the sled behind them.

It was slippery, but they finally reached the top.

Away from the lights of the house, the snow was even more beautiful as it fell effortlessly from the sky. And the snow that covered the ground seemed to glow in the darkness, reflecting what little light there was.

It was just dark enough. In this kind of shadow, Crash didn't have to worry about Nell seeing every little thought—every little desire—that flickered in his eyes.

"I'm not sure I can do this." Nell sounded breathless, her voice huskier than usual. "I'm not sure I remember *how* to do this."

"Sit on the sled and steer with your feet."

She sat gingerly down on the Flexible Flyer, but then looked up at him. "Aren't you coming, too?"

There was room for him—but just barely. They'd have to squeeze tightly together, with Nell positioned between his legs. Crash forced himself not to move toward her. "Do you want me to?"

"No way am I doing this without you." She inched forward a little. "Get your butt on this thing, Hawken."

"It helps if you start out by aiming the front of the sled *down* the hill."

Nell didn't move. "I thought we might take a more leisurely, zigzag path to the bottom."

Crash had to smile.

"All right, all right," she grumbled, swinging the front of the sled around. "If *you're* smiling at me, I must look pretty damn ridiculous. Get on the sled, Mona Lisa, and hold on tight. We're taking this sucker express, all the way to the barn."

Nell closed her eyes as Crash lowered himself onto the

sled behind her. He had to press himself tightly against her back—there was no way they could both sit on this thing without nearly gluing themselves together. His legs were much longer than hers, and with her boots on the outer part of the steering bar, he didn't have anywhere to put his feet.

She turned slightly to find that his face was inches from hers and she froze, trapped by his eyes. It might have been her imagination, or it might only have been a trick of the darkness, but he seemed almost vulnerable, almost uncertain. He smelled impossibly good, like coffee and peppermint. Her gaze dropped to the tight line of his gracefully shaped mouth. What would he do if she kissed him?

She didn't have the nerve. "Maybe you should steer."

"No. This is your ride. You're in control."

In control. God, if he only knew. She was shaking, but she wasn't sure if it was because she was afraid of falling off and breaking her leg or because he was sitting so close. She could feel his warmth against every inch of her back and she was nearly dying from the anticipation of feeling his arms around her. Because that was the only reason she was doing this. She wanted to feel his arms around her.

"Let me put my legs under yours," he continued.

Nell lifted her legs obediently and he set his boots against the metal bumper. She lowered her legs, resting her thighs on top of his, stretching around the outside for the steering bar. But it was no longer within reach.

"Move forward," he ordered.

She didn't want to move forward. She liked the sensation of his body against hers too much to want to move away from him. But when she hesitated, he pushed them both up closer to the front of the sled. Her feet reached the bar, and he was *still* pressed tightly against her.

He looped his arms around her, holding her securely. It was heaven. Nell closed her eyes.

"Ready?"

"God, no! What am *I* supposed to hold on to?" Her voice was breathy, betraying her. She couldn't reach the siderail—his legs were in the way.

"Hold on to me."

Nell touched his legs, tentatively sliding her hands down underneath his thighs. He was all muscle, all solid, perfectly male. She wondered if he could feel her heart hammering through all her layers of clothing.

"Ready?" he asked again. She could feel his breath against her neck, just underneath her ear.

Nell held him tighter and closed her eyes. "Yeah."

"You're in control." His voice was just a whisper. "Get us started by rocking forward a little..."

She opened her eyes. "Can't you just give us a push?"

"I could, but then you'd only have survived the ride. You wouldn't have *taken* it, if you know what I mean. Come on. All you have to do is rock us forward."

Nell looked down the hill. The barn seemed so far away, and the hill suddenly seemed dreadfully steep. She was having trouble breathing. "I'm not sure I can."

"Take your time. I can wait—at least until the pizza-delivery man comes."

"If we sit here much longer, we'll be covered with snow."

"Are you cold?" he asked. His breath warmed her ear and his arms tightened slightly around her.

Cold? Nell couldn't remember her name, let alone a complicated concept like *cold.* "Maybe we can take this in steps," she said. "You know. Just sit here on the sled for a while. I mean, I made it all the way up the hill, and I actually got *on* the sled. That's a solid start. I should be really proud of myself. And then maybe by the next time it snows, I'll be ready to—"

"This is Virginia," he reminded her. "This may be all the snow we get this year. Come on, Nell. Just rock us forward."

Nell stared down the hill. She couldn't do it. She started to get up, but he held her in place.

"Blue," he said quietly. "My favorite color is blue. The color of the South China Sea. And I didn't really like the latest Grisham book as much as I liked his other stuff."

Nell turned her head and stared at him.

"And you're right, I've seen your FInCOM file," he continued. "I helped gather the information that's in it."

She knew what he was doing. She knew *exactly* what he was doing. He was showing her that he, too, could take little risks. Maybe he wasn't afraid to sled down a hill, but talking about himself was an entirely different story. She knew he never, *ever* willingly volunteered any information about himself.

True, he wasn't telling her anything terribly personal, but Nell knew that saying anything at all had to have been incredibly difficult for him.

At least as difficult as riding a Flexible Flyer down a relatively gentle hill. If she fell off, she wouldn't break her leg. She'd only bruise her bottom and her pride. This was no big deal.

She rocked the sled forward.

"I knew you could do it," Crash said softly into her ear as the sled teetered and then went over the edge of the hill.

It went slowly at first, nearly groaning under their weight, but then it began to pick up speed.

Nell screamed. The runners of the sled swished as the ground sped past, as the falling snow seemed to scatter and swirl around them.

Faster and faster they went, until it seemed as if they were almost flying. Nell clung to Crash's legs as they hit a bump and for a moment they *did* leave the ground, and when they landed, the sled wasn't quite underneath them.

She felt rather than heard the giddy laughter that left her throat as they skidded off the sled and slid for a moment on the slippery hillside without it, a tangle of arms and legs, Crash still holding her tightly.

She was still laughing as they slowed to a stop, and she realized that Crash was laughing too. "You screamed all the way down the hill," he said.

"No, I didn't! God, did I really?" She was half on top of Crash, half sprawled in the snow, and she lay back, relaxing against him as she caught her breath, gazing up at the falling snowflakes.

"You sure did. Are you okay?" he asked.

"Yeah." In fact, she couldn't remember having been better. His arms were still around her and one of his legs was thrown casually across hers. Yes, she was very much okay. "That almost was…fun."

"You want to go again?"

Incredulous, Nell turned her head to look at him.

He smiled at her expression.

He was an outrageously good-looking man in repose, but when he smiled, even just a little smile like that one, he was off the charts.

He got to his feet, holding out his hand for her.

She must have been insane or hypnotized because she reached for him, letting him pull her to her feet.

He released her and ran, skidding in the snow, to collect the sled, then came back up the hill, catching her by the hand again and pulling her along with him.

This time he didn't ask. This time he got on behind her, holding her around the waist with an easy familiarity.

Nell couldn't believe she was doing this again.

"This time try to steer around that bump," he said, his breath warm against her ear.

Nell nodded.

"You're in control," he said.

"Oh, God," she said, and rocked the sled forward.

Chapter 5

"I remember when I was a kid," Crash said softly, "Jake showed me how to make angels in the snow."

They were lying closer to the bottom of the hill this time, looking up at the snow streaking down toward them. It looked amazing from that perspective. The sensation was kind of like being in the middle of a living computer screen-saver or a *Star Wars* style outer-space jump to light-speed.

This time they'd skidded off the sled in different directions. This time they weren't touching, and Crash tried rather desperately not to miss Nell's softness and warmth.

Nell pushed herself up on one elbow. "Jake? Not Daisy?"

"No, it was Jake. It was Daisy's birthday, and Jake and I made snow angels all over the yard and…" He glanced over to find her watching him, her eyes wide.

"From what Daisy's said, I've gathered that you spent

some of your summer and winter vacations from boarding school with her and Jake," she said softly.

Crash hesitated.

But this was Nell he was talking to. Nell, who'd trusted *him* enough to take not one or two but five separate trips down this hill on his old sled. His friend Nell. If they were lovers he wouldn't dare tell her anything, but they were *not* going to become lovers.

"I spent all of my vacations with them," he admitted. "Starting when I was ten—the year my mother died. I was scheduled to go directly from school to summer camp. I didn't even go home in between. My father was away on business and—" He broke off, realizing how pathetic he sounded.

"You must've been miserable," she said softly. "I can't imagine having been sent away to boarding school when I was only ten. And you went when you were what? *Eight?*"

Crash shook his head. "It wasn't that bad."

"I think it must've been awful."

"My mother was dying—it was a lot for my father to deal with. Imagine if Jake and Daisy had an eight-year-old."

Nell snorted. "You can bet your ass Jake Robinson wouldn't send *his* kid away to boarding school. You were deprived of your mother two years before you absolutely had to be. And your poor mother…"

"My mother was so loaded on painkillers, the few times I was allowed to see her, she didn't even know me and… I don't want to talk about this." He shook his head, swearing softly. "I don't even want to *think* about it, but…"

"But it's happening all over again, with Daisy," Nell said quietly. "God, this must be twice as hard for you. I know *I* feel as if I'm stretched to the absolute end of my emotional rope as it is. What are we going to do when the tumor affects her brain to the point that she can't walk?''

Crash closed his eyes. He knew what he *wanted* to do. He wanted to run, to pack up his things and go. It would only take one phone call, and an hour later he'd be called in on a special assignment, his leave revoked. Twenty-four hours after that, he'd be on the other side of the world. But running away wouldn't really help him. And it wouldn't help Daisy, either. If there'd ever been a time that she needed him—that *Jake* needed him—it was now.

And God knew Daisy and Jake had been there for him. They'd *always* been there for him.

Nell was still watching him, her eyes filled with compassion. ''I'm sorry,'' she whispered. ''I shouldn't have brought that up.''

''It's something we're both going to have to deal with.''

Tears brimmed in her eyes. ''I'm terrified that I'm not going to be strong enough.''

''I know. I'm afraid that—'' Crash broke off.

''What?'' She moved closer, almost close enough to touch him. ''Talk to me. I know you're not talking to Jake or Daisy about any of this. You've got to talk to *some*one.''

Crash looked toward the house, squinting slightly, his mouth tighter than Nell had ever seen it. When he spoke, his voice was so low, she had to lean closer to hear him. ''I'm afraid that when the time comes, when the pain gets too intense, when she can't walk anymore, she's going to ask me to help her die.'' When he glanced up at her, he didn't bother to hide the anguish in his eyes. ''I know she'd never ask Jake to do that.''

Nell drew in a shaky breath. ''Oh, God.''

''Yeah,'' he said.

Nell couldn't stand it any longer. She put her arms around him, knowing full well that he would probably push

her away. But he didn't. Instead, he pulled her close. He
held her tightly as, around them, the snow began to thicken
and turn to freezing rain.

"I remember the day she came to get me from summer
camp like it was yesterday," he said softly, his face buried
in her hair, his breath warm against her neck. "I'd only
been there two days when I got a message from the head
counselor that Daisy was coming to see me." He lifted his
face, resting his cheek against the top of her head. "She
hit the place like a hurricane. I swear she came up the path
to the camp office like Joan of Arc marching into battle.
She was wearing a long skirt that just kind of flowed around
her when she walked and about twenty bangles on her arm
and a big beaded necklace. Her hair was down—it was long
back then, it went down past her waist, and she was carrying her sandals. Her feet were bare and I remember there
was bright red polish on her toenails."

He was talking about the year he was ten, Nell realized.
The year his mother had died and his father had sent him
directly to summer camp from boarding school.

"I was waiting for her on the porch of the office, and
she stopped and gave me a big hug and she asked me if I
liked it there. I didn't, but I told her what my father had
told me—that there was no place else for me to go. I didn't
really know her that well—she was my mother's cousin
and they hadn't been particularly close. But she stood there,
and she asked me if I would like to spend the summer out
in California with her and Jake. I didn't know what to say
and she told me that I didn't have to go with her if I didn't
want to, but…" he cleared his throat, "that she and Jake
very much wanted me to come stay with them."

Nell could hear his heart beating as he was silent for a
moment.

"I guess I didn't really believe her, because I didn't go

to my cabin to pack when she went into the office. I stayed on the porch, and I heard her talking to the administrator. Without my father's permission, he refused to let me leave. Daisy called my father—he was in Paris—right from the camp office, but she couldn't get through. He was in negotiations. He wasn't taking any calls until after the weekend. No one would interrupt him. He was...pretty formidable.

"So Daisy came back outside and she gave me another hug and told me she'd be back tomorrow at dinnertime. She said, 'When I get here, be packed and ready to go.'"

He was quiet again for a moment. "I remember feeling disappointed when she left without me. It was a strange feeling because I'd gone so long without any expectations at all. And that night I actually packed my stuff. I felt really stupid doing it, because I really couldn't believe she was going to come back. But something made me do it. I guess—even though most of it had been shaken out of me by then—I still had some hope left. I wanted her to come back so much I could barely breathe."

It was raining harder now, but Nell was afraid to move, almost afraid to breathe herself for fear she would break the quiet intimacy and he would stop talking.

But he was silent for so long, she finally lifted her head and looked at him. "Was she able to get in touch with your father?"

"She couldn't get anyone to interrupt his meetings, so she flew to Paris." Crash laughed ruefully, his mouth curving up into a half smile. "She just walked in on him with a letter for him to sign, giving her permission to take me out of the camp. I remember doing the math, adding up the hours, and realizing that she must have been traveling continuously from the time she left the camp to make it to Paris and back in a single day.

"It was so amazing to me," he continued quietly. "The fact that someone actually *wanted* me that badly. And Daisy really did. Both she and Jake actually wanted me around. I think about all the time Jake spent with me, that summer in particular, and it *still* amazes me. They really wanted me. I wasn't in the way."

Nell couldn't keep the tears that were filling her eyes from overflowing and mixing with the rain that was falling.

Crash gently touched her cheek with one knuckle. "Hey, I didn't mean to make you cry."

She pulled away from him slightly, using her hands to wipe her face. "I'm not crying," she insisted. "I never cry. I'm not a crier, I swear it. I just... I'm so glad you told me."

"I would do anything for Daisy and Jake," Crash said simply. "Anything." He paused. "Watching Daisy die is hard enough, though. If I have to help her to..." He shook his head. "It's raining—and our pizza's here."

It was. The delivery truck was pulling into the driveway.

Nell stood up and followed Crash the rest of the way down the hill. She put the Flexible Flyer back inside the garage as he paid for the pizza.

Unfortunately, her appetite was completely gone.

"Today we're doing *what?*"

"Learning to tap-dance," Daisy said, taking a sip of her orange juice.

Nell glanced up. The look on Crash's face was nearly as good as the look on Jake's.

"I don't think SEALs are allowed to tap-dance," Crash said.

Daisy set down her glass. "The instructor should be here in about an hour. I told her to meet us in the barn."

"She's kidding," Jake said. He looked at Daisy. "You *are* kidding?"

She just smiled.

Nell drained the last of her coffee and set the mug on the breakfast table with a thump. "I already know how to tap-dance," she announced. "And since I have four million phone calls to make, I'm going to excuse myself from this morning's activity."

Crash actually laughed out loud. "Oh, not a chance," he said.

"You know how to tap-dance?" Daisy was intrigued. "How come you never told me that?"

"Oh, come on, Daisy, she's bluffing," Crash said. "Look at her."

"I never mentioned it because it's not something that usually comes up in normal conversation," Nell said. "I don't go around introducing myself to people and saying, 'Hi, I'm Nell Burns—oh, by the way, I know how to tap-dance.'"

"I don't buy it." Crash shook his head. "No way. She's just trying to get out of this."

He was teasing. There was a light in his eyes that told Nell he was teasing. Ever since the evening they went sledding, the evening he'd actually *talked* about himself, their relationship had continued to grow. But only in one direction. They only continued to be friends.

It was driving her nuts.

"You just think because you're helping FInCOM do an advanced security check, you know everything there is to know about me," Nell countered. "I'm glad you don't believe me. This proves that I'm still capable of having secrets. God knows everyone needs at least *one* little secret— even if it's only that they know how to tap-dance."

The truth was, Nell had more than one secret. And one

of those secrets she was keeping was enormous. She was falling for Crash. With every moment that passed, she was falling harder for this man who was determined to be no more than her friend.

She glanced at Daisy, who was watching her with a smile. Strike that. The way Nell felt about Crash was apparently quite obvious to *some* people in the room.

"I believe you," Jake told her. "But there's only one way you're going to convince Lieutenant Skeptic here. You're going to have to tap dance for him."

"That's right." Crash gestured toward the spacious kitchen floor. "Come on, Burns. Knock yourself out."

"Right *here?* In the kitchen?"

"Sure." He leaned back in his chair, waiting.

Nell shook her head. "I...don't have tap shoes."

"I bought us each a pair," Daisy said helpfully. "They're out in the barn."

Nell stared. "You bought four pairs of—"

Crash stood up. "Let's go."

"Now?"

He started for the door. "Jake was right. The only way I'll let you get out of the required beginners' class is if you walk your talk, so to speak."

Nell rolled her eyes at Daisy, then followed Crash out to the barn. She shivered as he unlocked the door.

He glanced at her. "Where's your jacket?"

"You didn't take yours."

"I usually don't need one."

"You usually work in the jungles of Southeast Asia where the average December temperature is a steamy eighty degrees."

"You aren't supposed to know that." He held the door open for her and then closed it behind them. "It's cold in here, too. I'll turn up the heat."

"Don't. It's not good for the trees to be really warm until they absolutely *have* to be," Nell explained. "If we keep 'em inside at seventy-two degrees for a week, and then put them outside when it's in the twenties…it blows their minds."

"They're trees," Crash pointed out dryly. "They don't have minds."

"That's not what my mother thinks. She talks to all her plants. And I think it works. My parents' entire house is like a botany experiment gone wild."

"I hate to break it to you, Burns, but that says more for the power of CO_2 than anything else."

"Yeah, yeah," Nell said. "Be that way." The morning was gray and she turned on the overhead lights.

Four shoe boxes were neatly stacked underneath one of the Christmas trees that she and Crash had decorated.

Tap shoes. Two pairs of men's shoes, and two pairs of women's. They were all black leather, and the women's had a sturdy two-inch heel.

Somehow Daisy had known Nell's exact shoe size. She sat on the floor and pulled off her boots. "It's been a while," she said, looking up at Crash as she strapped on the shoes. "I learned to tap back when I was in high school. I was a theater-major wanna-be—you know, in the chorus of all the school musicals, never good enough to get a lead role. I was an okay dancer, but not talented enough to get into a performing-arts program at any college. At least not any college *I* wanted to go to."

She stood up. Trust Daisy to spend the money on quality shoes that fit comfortably.

Nell caught sight of herself in the wall of mirrors. Dressed in jeans and a turtleneck, she felt odd in fancy black heels. She felt odder still about Crash, leaning against the wall, arms crossed, waiting to watch her dance. She knew he wouldn't laugh at her—at least not out loud.

She glanced over her shoulder at him. "You know, I really shouldn't have to do this," she said. "We're friends. You should believe me. You should take on faith what I've told you is true."

He nodded. "Okay. I believe you. Dance."

"No, what you should say is that you believe me, and because you believe me you don't have to see me dance."

"But I want to see you dance."

"All right, but I'm warning you. It's been years, and even back when I was taking lessons I wasn't very good."

Crash turned toward the windows. "What's that?"

"What?"

He straightened up, pushing himself off the wall. "A siren."

"I don't hear…" She heard it then. In the distance, moving closer.

Nell went toward the door, but Crash was even faster. He pulled it open and went outside at a run. Her tap shoes clattered on the macadam as she followed. Somehow the kitchen door had gotten locked, and they raced around to the front of the house, arriving just as an ambulance bounced over the speed bump and up into the main part of the driveway.

God, what had happened? It hadn't been more than fifteen minutes since they'd left Daisy and Jake in the kitchen.

"Jake!" Crash burst into the house.

"In the studio," the admiral bellowed back.

Nell held the door for the paramedics. "Down the hall on the left," she instructed them, standing back to let them go first. They were moving fast and she raced after them.

Please God… Nell stopped in the studio doorway as the three paramedics crowded around Daisy.

She was on the floor, as if she'd fallen, with Jake beside her, and Crash crouched beside him. Nell hung back, suddenly aware that she was not a member of the family.

"She blacked out," Jake was telling the paramedics. "It's happened before, but not like this. This time I couldn't rouse her." His voice broke. "At first I thought…"

"I'm okay," Nell heard Daisy murmur. "I'm all right, baby. I'm still here."

Nell shivered, holding on to herself tightly. She knew what Jake had thought. Jake had thought that Daisy had slipped into a coma. Or worse.

The paramedics were deep in discussion with both Jake and Daisy. They wanted to take Daisy to the hospital, to run some tests.

"Nell."

She looked up to find Crash gazing at her. He'd straightened up and now held out his hand to her—a silent invitation to come stand beside him.

She took both his invitation and his hand, lacing their fingers tightly together.

"Your hand is cold," he whispered.

"I think my heart stopped beating for a minute."

"She's okay, you know," he told her.

"For now." She felt her eyes fill with tears.

Crash nodded. "Now is all we've got. It stinks, but it's better than the alternative, which is *not* to have now."

Nell closed her eyes, willing her tears away.

To her surprise, he touched her, gently pulling a strand of her hair free from where it had caught on her eyelashes, pushing it back, dragging his fingers lightly through her hair. "But remember that line of thinking doesn't apply to every situation," he said quietly. "Sometimes taking advantage of now doesn't do anyone any good."

He was talking about…them? Was it possible…? Nell

looked up at him, but he'd let go of her hand, all of his attention on Jake, who was pushing himself to his feet.

As she watched, Jake backed away to let the paramedics put Daisy on a stretcher.

"She didn't agree to go in for tests, did she?" Crash asked incredulously.

Jake gave him a you've-got-to-be-kidding look. "No chance. She's only letting them help her into the bedroom. She's still feeling kind of dizzy." He forced himself to smile as Daisy was carried past. "I'll be in in a sec, babe," he told her before turning back to Nell. "I know this is asking a lot, but... What are the chances of moving the wedding up a few days?"

Nell glanced from Jake to Crash then back. "How many days?"

"As many as possible. To tomorrow, if you can swing it."

Tomorrow. Oh, God.

"I'm afraid..." Jake cleared his throat and started again. "I'm afraid we're running out of time."

She would have to call the pastor, see if he could change his schedule. And the caterer was going to have a cow. It wasn't a weekend, so the band might be open to switching the dates. But—the guests! She'd have to call them individually. That meant close to two hundred phone calls. But first she'd have to *find* all those phone numbers and...

Crash touched her shoulder. When she looked up at him, he nodded, as if he could read her mind. "I'll help."

Nell took a deep breath and turned back to Jake. "Consider it done."

Chapter 6

As far as weddings went, this one had been perfect.

Or rather, it *would* have been perfect, had the bride not been dying.

Crash closed his eyes. He didn't want to go there. All day long, he'd avoided that dark place.

The barn sparkled and glistened with the decorations he'd helped Nell hang. It rang with laughter and music. It glowed with warmth and light.

The band was great, the food was first-rate, the guests were bemused by the bride and groom's sudden change of plans—because none of them knew the truth.

And amidst all the sparkle and joy, Crash could almost pretend that he was just as ignorant.

The champagne he'd had hadn't hurt much, either.

The crowd was really thinning out as it approached eleven o'clock. Crash watched Nell from across the room as she spun around the dance floor in the arms of a man he'd met just that evening. He blanked on the name. Tall, dark and distinguished-looking, whoever he was had just been elected to the U.S. Senate. Mike something. From California. Garvin. That was it. Senator *Mark* Garvin.

Garvin said something to Nell and she laughed.

Crash was certain that Garvin—along with the other 299 wedding guests—couldn't tell that Nell hadn't had more than two hours of sleep in the past forty-eight. The only reason he knew that she hadn't slept much was because in the past two days he hadn't had time to catch more than a short combat nap himself.

Of course, *he* was used to going without sleep. He was trained to be able to stay alert and functioning under severe conditions.

Nell was running on adrenaline and sheer grit.

"She's great, isn't she?"

Crash looked up to see Dexter Lancaster standing beside him, following his gaze. He was talking about Nell.

"Yeah," Crash agreed. "She's great."

"I figured you out, you know." Lancaster took a sip of his drink. "I've danced with Nell four times tonight. Garvin over there has danced with her twice. A collection of other gentlemen have taken her around the floor this evening as well. But you, my friend, have not danced with her at all."

"I don't dance."

Lancaster smiled and his blue eyes twinkled warmly. "She doesn't have a clue that you're hung up on her, does she?"

Crash met the man's gaze steadily. "She's my friend," he said quietly. "I happen to know that she's emotionally vulnerable right now. She doesn't need me—or anyone else—taking advantage of her."

The lawyer nodded, setting his empty glass down on a nearby table. "Fair enough. I'll wait to call her until spring or early summer."

Crash gritted his teeth and forced himself to nod. By spring or early summer, unless there was some kind of miracle and Daisy went into remission, he'd be on the other side of the world. "Fair enough."

"Say good-night to her for me," Lancaster said.

Across the room Mark Garvin gallantly kissed the back of Nell's hand before releasing her. What was it about Nell that attracted older men like flies to honey? Garvin was Jake's age—maybe even older. He was a walking ad for Grecian Formula.

Nell seemed unaffected by the blazing-white flash of Garvin's perfectly capped teeth as she turned and approached a group of women who were putting on their coats.

She looked incredible.

She was wearing a long gown, befitting the black tie formality of the evening wedding. It was long-sleeved, with something Crash had heard Daisy describe as a sweetheart neckline that dipped elegantly down between her breasts. It was a rich shade of emerald, which—Daisy claimed— was Nell's duty to wear as maid of honor, because it accentuated the bride's green eyes.

The gown was made of some kind of stretchy velvet material that clung to Nell's slender figure, and drew Crash's attention—along with Garvin's and Lancaster's apparently—away from the bride's eyes.

As Crash watched, Nell laughed at something one of the women said. And as she laughed, she looked up and directly over at him.

He was in trouble. He knew that everything he'd tried for so long to hide from her was written clearly on his face. He knew everything he was feeling, all of his longing and desire, was burning in his eyes. But he couldn't look away.

Nell's smile slowly faded as she stared across the room

at him, trapped by his gaze, just as he was by hers. He could see the hint of a blush rising in her cheeks.

Any second now, she would look away. Crash knew it. Any second, she'd turn and...

She didn't turn. She walked toward him. She came right across the dance floor.

Yes, he was in trouble here. He *knew* he was in *big* trouble. But he still couldn't bring himself to look away.

"I owe you a dance."

Bad idea. If he took her in his arms, if he touched the soft velvet of her dress, felt it warmed by the heat of her body beneath...

"I know it's not the same as tap-dancing," Nell said, "but for now it'll have to do."

She took his hand and led him onto the dance floor. And just like that, he was holding her. He wasn't sure exactly what she'd done, but he knew it wasn't entirely her doing that had put her in his embrace. He'd surely done something stupid, like hold open his arms.

And now that she was there, now that they were dancing, his instinct was confirmed. This was a *very* bad idea. He'd had way too much to drink to be doing this. "I'm not a very good dancer."

"You're doing fine." The fingers of her right hand were looped gently around his thumb, and her left hand was resting comfortably on his shoulder. He was holding her loosely, his hand against the small of her back, against the warm softness of her dress. Her legs brushed against his as they moved slowly in time to the music. She smelled deliciously sweet. Her face was tilted up, her mouth close enough to kiss. "How are you holding up?" she asked, looking up into his eyes.

He was dying. "I'm hanging in," he said.

She nodded. "I noticed you broke your no-drinking-unless-you-have-to rule tonight."

Crash gazed down into the calming blue of her eyes. "No, I didn't. Tonight, I had to."

"'Til death do us part,'" Nell said quietly. "That was what really got to me."

"Yeah." Crash nodded. He desperately didn't want to talk about that. "Do you think if I kissed you tonight, we could both pretend it never happened tomorrow?"

Her eyes widened.

"I didn't really mean that," he said quickly. "I was only trying to change the subject to an allegedly less emotional topic. It was a bad attempt at an even worse joke."

She wasn't laughing. "You know, Hawken—"

"I don't want to go there, Nell. I shouldn't have said that. Look, I don't know what I'm doing here, dancing with you like this. I'm a lousy dancer, anyway." He forced himself to let go of her, to step back, away. Distance. Separation. Space. Please God, don't let him kiss her....

He turned to walk away. It was the best possible thing he could do for her. He knew that. He believed it with all of his heart. But she put her hand on his arm, and he hesitated.

He who hesitates is lost....

He turned and looked into her eyes, and indeed, he was lost.

"This whole night's been like some kind of fairy tale," Nell whispered. "Like some kind of fantasy. If I close my eyes, I can pretend that Daisy's going to be all right. Give me a break, will you, and let me have my dance with Prince Charming. My world's going to turn back into a rotten pumpkin soon enough."

"You've got it wrong," he said harshly. "I'm no prince."

"I never said you were. Not really. This is just a fantasy, remember? I just want to hold someone close—and pretend."

Somehow she was back in his arms again, and he was holding her even closer this time. He could feel the entire length of her, pressed against the entire length of him. Her hand was no longer on his shoulder but instead was wrapped around his neck, her fingers entwined in the hair at the nape of his neck. It felt impossibly good.

He was no longer dying. He *had* died—and gone to heaven.

"You know what's really stupid?" she whispered.

He was. He was impossibly stupid and certifiably insane. He should've walked away. He should do it now. He should just turn and walk out of the barn and stand for several long minutes in the bracing cold. And then he should walk into the house, up the stairs and into his bedroom, and lock himself in until his sanity returned with the rising sun.

Instead he bent his head to brush his cheek and nose against the fragrant softness of Nell's hair. Instead, he let his fingers explore the velvet-covered warmth of her back. Please God, he absolutely *couldn't* let himself kiss her. Not even once. He knew one taste would never be enough.

"It's really stupid, but even after all these weeks, I never know what to call you," she murmured.

He could feel her breath, warm against his skin, her lips a whisper away from his throat. Her words didn't seem to make any sense.

Not that *any* of this made any sense at all.

"I don't know what you mean." His voice was hoarse. She felt so good pressed against him, her breasts full against his chest, the softness of her stomach, the tautness of her thighs...

She lifted her head to look up at him. "I don't know

what name to use when I talk to you," she explained. "Crash seems so...well, strange."

He was hypnotized by her eyes, drugged by the scent of her perfume, held in thrall by the beautiful curves of her lips.

"I mean, what am I supposed to say? 'Hi, Crash. How are you, Crash?' It sounds like I'm talking to one of the X-Men. 'Excuse me, Crash, would you and your buddy Cyclops mind carrying this tray into Daisy's office?'" She shook her head. "On the other hand, I find it nearly impossible to call you Billy, the way Jake and Daisy do. Calling you Billy is kind of like calling a Bengal tiger *Fluffy*. I guess there's always Bill, but you don't seem very much like a Bill." She narrowed her eyes, still gazing up at him. "Maybe William..."

Crash *still* didn't walk away. "No, thanks. My father always called me William."

"Ew. Forget *that*."

"I guess you could always call me 'The SEAL Operative Formerly Known as Billy.'"

She laughed. "And I suppose I'd have to call you 'The SEAL Operative' for short."

"It works for me."

Nell's eyes sparkled. "God, if that's my choice, I'm going to have to rethink this 'Crash' thing. Maybe after a decade or two, I'll get used to it."

Crash didn't kiss her. For one instant, he thought he'd totally lost control and was going to do it. He'd even lowered his head, but somehow he'd stopped himself. He felt sweat bead on his upper lip, felt a trickle slide down past his ear. For someone who had a reputation of always keeping cool, he was losing his, fast.

Nell didn't seem to notice. "What's the latest word on my security check?"

"So far, so good. After this is over, you'll be able to get a job working at FInCOM Headquarters, if you want." As soon as he said the words, he realized how awful they sounded. "I meant, after the security check is over," he amended. "I didn't mean…"

But the sparkle had already left her eyes. "I know," she said quietly. "I'm just… I'm not letting myself think that far into the future. I know it's coming, but…" She shook her head. "Damn. And we were doing so well."

The song had ended. Crash gently stepped away from her and led her off the dance floor. "I'm sorry."

"It's not your fault. I'm just…so tired." Nell laughed softly. "God, am I tired."

He put his hands in his pockets to keep himself from reaching for her again. "Is there anything else you need to do tonight? I could handle it for you."

"No, I'm mostly done. Jake slipped the band God knows how much extra to play another hour, even though most of the guests have gone home. The caterer packed up hours ago. The only thing I have to remember is to turn the heat down in the barn so the trees don't bake all night long."

"I can take care of that," Crash told her. "Why don't you go to bed? Come on, I'll walk you back to the house."

She didn't protest, and he knew she was more exhausted than she'd admitted.

Jake and Daisy were still on the dance floor, wrapped in each other's arms, oblivious to anyone else. Crash opened the door, holding it for Nell, then followed her out into the crisp coldness of the December night.

She didn't have a jacket and he quickly slipped off his tuxedo coat and put it around her shoulders.

"Thanks."

Even as tired as she was, her smile made his stomach do flips. He had to get her inside, and then he had to get himself away from her. He'd walk her to the kitchen, no further. He'd unlock the door, and he'd close it behind her.

But the stars were brilliant, Orion's belt glittering like jewels against the black-velvet backdrop of the night sky. Nell was looking up at them, standing completely still, not hurrying toward the kitchen door. "It's beautiful, isn't it?"

What could he possibly say? "Yeah."

"Now might be a really great time for you to kiss me." She glanced at him, and in the darkness, her eyes seemed colorless and unearthly. "Just as a tonight kind of thing, like you said, you know? The grand finale to the perfect fantasy evening."

Crash's lips were dry, and he moistened them. "I'm not sure that's such a good idea." Christ, what was he saying? He wasn't *sure?* He was certain that kissing her was a very, very *bad* idea.

Nell looked back up at the sky. "Yeah, I thought you might think that. It's all right. It's been a nice fantasy anyway."

God, he wanted to kiss her. And he also wanted her to go inside so he wouldn't be faced with such an incredibly hellish temptation.

She took a deep breath and let it out in a rush as she turned again to look at him. "Tell me, 'The SEAL Operative Formerly Known as Billy,' do you believe in God?"

Her blunt question caught him even more off guard than her talk about kissing, but fortunately her somewhat unorthodox delivery gave him time to recover. "You're not really going to call me that, are you?"

She smiled.

His stomach flipped again.

"Do you?" she asked.

"Are you?" he countered.

"Yes. But if you want, I'll call you Billy for short. But

you better believe I'll be thinking the whole thing." Another smile.

This time his entire heart did a somersault. Crash nodded. "Yes."

"Yes, you want me to call you Billy for short, or yes, you believe in God?"

"Yes for Billy, and… Yes, I believe in something that could probably be called God." He smiled ruefully. "I've never admitted that to anyone before. Of course, no one's ever dared to ask me that question. I think they've all assumed I'm soulless—considering the kind of work I sometimes do."

"What kind of work do you sometimes do?"

Crash shook his head. "I couldn't tell you even if I wanted to, but believe me, I don't want to—and you don't want to know."

"But I *do*."

He stood there for a moment, just looking at her.

"I really, *really* do," she said.

"There are certain…covert ops," he said slowly, carefully choosing his words, "in which a team might target—and eliminate—known confessed terrorists. The key word there is *confessed*. The kind of scumbags who take out an entire 747 of innocent civilians, then take credit—boast about it."

Nell's eyes were wide. *"Eliminate…?"*

He held her gaze steadily. "Still want me to kiss you?"

"Are you telling me that *Jake* asks you to—"

Crash shook his head. "No, I'm telling you nothing. I've already said way too much. Come on. It's cold out here. Let's get you inside before you catch the flu."

She stepped directly in front of him. "Yes," she said. "I still want you to kiss me."

Crash had to pull up short to keep from knocking her over. "No, you don't. I promise you, you don't."

She just laughed. And she went up on her toes, and she brushed her lips across his, and Crash's world went into slow motion.

One heartbeat.

He couldn't move. He knew that the smart thing to do would be to go for the kitchen door. He knew he should get it unlocked, push this woman inside, then lock it tightly again, with him on the outside.

Instead he stood there, holding his breath, waiting to see if she'd do it again.

Two heartbeats. Three. Four.

And then she did kiss him once more, slowly this time. She stared into his eyes as she stood on her toes again, her gaze finally flickering down to his mouth and back, before she touched her lips to his again—her lips, and the very tip of her tongue. She tasted him, softly, lightly, and the last of his control shattered.

He pulled her close and kissed her, *really* kissed her, lowering his head and claiming her lips, sweeping his tongue deeply inside of her sweet mouth, his heart pounding crazily.

Crash felt her fingers in his hair as she kissed him back just as fiercely, just as hungrily. She pressed herself against him even as he tried to pull her closer and he knew without a doubt that she wanted far more than a kiss. All he had to do was ask, and he knew he could spend the night in her bed.

She was a sure thing. He could sate himself, with Nell as a willing participant. He could bury himself inside her. He could lose himself completely in her sweetness.

And tomorrow, she would wake him up with a kiss, her

hair tangled charmingly around her pretty face, her eyes sleepy and smiling and…

And the light and laughter would fade from her eyes as he quietly tried to explain why he couldn't become a permanent fixture there in her bed. Not couldn't—*didn't want to*. He didn't really want her. He'd just wanted *someone*, and she'd been there, willing and ready and…

And he knew he couldn't do that to Nell.

Crash found the strength to push her gently away. She was breathing hard, her breasts rising and falling rapidly beneath her dress, her eyelids heavy with passion. Dear God, what was he doing? What was he giving up?

"I'm sorry," he said. He'd been saying that far too often lately.

Realization dawned in her eyes. Realization and shocked embarrassment. "Oh, God, *I'm* sorry," she countered. "I didn't mean to attack you."

"You didn't," he said quickly. "That was me. That was my fault."

Nell stepped even farther back, away from him. "It was just, um, part of tonight's fantasy, right?"

She was searching his eyes, and Crash knew that she was more than half hoping he'd deny her words. But instead, he nodded. "Yeah," he said. "That's all it was. We're both tired, and…that's all it was."

Nell hugged his jacket more tightly around her, as if she'd suddenly felt the cold. "I better get inside."

Crash went up the stairs and unlocked the kitchen door, holding it open. She slipped out of his jacket, handing it back to him.

"Good night," he said.

To his surprise, she reached out and touched the side of his face. "Too bad," she said softly.

And then she was gone.

Crash locked the door behind her. "Yeah," he said. "Too bad."

Out in the barn, the band was finally packing up. But as Crash watched from the shadows beyond the doorway, Jake and Daisy still danced to music only they could hear.

Admiral and Mrs. Jacob Robinson.

The evening had been one of laughter and celebration. Jake had accepted the congratulations of friends and colleagues. He'd smiled through the toasts that wished the two of them long life and decades more of happiness. He'd laughed as friends had joked, trying to guess exactly how he'd finally convinced his long-time lover to willingly accept the chains of matrimony.

Jake had finally gotten what he'd always wanted, but Crash knew he would trade it all for a miracle cure.

As Crash watched them dance, Jake wiped his eyes, careful to keep Daisy from seeing that he was crying.

Jake was crying.

All evening long, Crash had fought to keep the constant awareness of Daisy's mortality at bay.

But now death's shadow was back.

Crash waited until the band had left, until Jake and Daisy slowly made their way out to the house.

He turned down the heat and locked the barn door, then went to his room.

Nell's door was closed, and as he passed it, it stayed tightly shut.

He was glad for that. Glad she was asleep, glad she hadn't been waiting for him. He didn't think he would have had the strength to turn her down again.

He hesitated outside his own bedroom door, looking back down the hall toward Nell's room.

Yes, he was glad. But he was also achingly disappointed.

Chapter 7

Nell sat numbly on her bed, next to her suitcase. She was aware that she was going to have to stand up and walk over to her dresser if she wanted to transfer her socks and underwear from the drawer into that suitcase.

It couldn't have happened so quickly, it didn't seem possible. But yet it had.

Two days after the wedding, Daisy had had another of her fainting spells. It had taken even longer for her to be roused, and when she was conscious, she'd found that she could no longer walk unassisted.

The doctor had come out to the house, leaving behind a final, chilling prognosis—the end was near.

Yet Daisy and Jake had continued to celebrate their newlywed status. They'd sipped champagne while watching the sunset from Daisy's studio. Jake had carried Daisy wherever she wished to go, and when he grieved, he did it out of her sight.

And then, three days after Christmas, Daisy and Jake

went to sleep in their master-bedroom suite, and only Jake had awakened.

Just like that, in the blink of an eye, in the beat of a heart, Daisy was gone.

The evening before, they'd all been together in the kitchen. Nell had been making a cup of tea, and Jake, with Daisy in his arms, had stopped in to say good-night. Crash had come in from outside, wearing running clothes and a reflective vest. Even though Nell had offered to make him some tea as well, he'd gone upstairs shortly after Daisy and Jake. Ever since the night of the wedding, he'd been careful not to spend any time alone with her.

But he'd come into her room the next morning, to wake her up and tell her that Daisy had died, peacefully, painlessly, in her sleep.

That day and the next had passed in a blur.

Jake grieved openly, as did Nell. But if Crash had cried at all, he'd done it in the privacy of his own room.

The wake had been filled with many of the same people who'd come to the wedding barely a week before. Senators. Congressmen. Naval Officers.

Washington's elite.

Four different people had given Nell their card, knowing that she had not only lost a friend but was suddenly out of work. It was a gesture of kindness and goodwill, Nell tried to tell herself. But still, she couldn't shake the image of herself in the middle of a feeding frenzy. Good personal assistants were hard to find, and here she was, suddenly available.

Senator Mark Garvin had talked for ten minutes about how his fiancée was seeking a personal assistant. With their wedding only a few months away, she was hard-pressed to keep her social schedule organized. Nell had stood there uncomfortably until Dex Lancaster had come to her rescue and pulled her away.

Still, despite that, the wake had been lovely. As at the wedding, laughter resounded as everyone told of their own special memories of Daisy Owen Robinson.

The funeral, too, had been a joyous celebration of a life well lived. Daisy definitely would have approved.

But through it all, Crash had been silent. He'd listened, but he hadn't responded. He didn't tell a story of his own, he didn't laugh, he didn't cry.

Several times, Nell had been tempted to approach him and take his pulse, just to verify that he was, indeed, alive.

He'd distanced himself so completely from all of the grief and turmoil around him. She didn't doubt for a minute that he'd distanced himself from everything he was feeling inside as well.

That was bad. That was really bad. Did he honestly expect to keep everything he was feeling locked within him forever?

Nell stood up, took her socks from the drawer and tossed them into her suitcase. Just as quickly as Daisy had died, other changes were happening, too. She was leaving in the morning. Her job here was finished.

As much as she wanted to stay, she couldn't help but hope that once he was alone with Jake, Crash would be able to come to terms with his grief.

Her favorite pair of socks had rolled out of the suitcase, and as Nell picked them up off the floor, she noticed the heels were starting to wear through. The sight made her cry. For someone who never, *ever* used to cry, nearly everything made her burst into tears these days.

She lay back on her bed, holding the rolled-up ball of socks to her chest, staring at the familiar cracks in the ceiling, letting her tears run down into her ears.

She'd loved it here at the farm. She'd loved working here, and she'd loved living here. She'd loved Daisy and Jake, and she loved...

Nell sat up, wiping her face with the back of her hand. No. She definitely didn't love Crash Hawken. Even *she* wouldn't do something as foolish as fall in love with a man like him.

She put the socks in her suitcase and went back to the dresser for her underwear.

Sure, she loved Crash, but only in a non-romantic way— only the way she'd loved Daisy, the way she loved Jake. They were friends.

Yeah, right. She sat down on her bed again. Who was she trying to kid? She wanted to be friends with Crash about as much as she wanted to sign on to be personal assistant to oily California Senator Mark Garvin's pampered debutante fiancée. In a single word—*not*.

What she *wanted* was to be Crash Hawken's lover. She wanted him to kiss her again, the way he'd kissed her on the night of the wedding. She wanted to feel his hands against her back, pulling her close.

She wanted to tear off her clothes and share with him the hottest, most powerful sexual experience of her entire life.

But those feelings weren't necessarily based on love. They were the result of attraction. Lust. Desire.

There was a knock on her door, and Nell nearly fell off her bed. Heart pounding, she went to open it.

But it was Jake, not Crash. He looked exhausted, his eyes rimmed with red. "I just wanted to let you know that I'm going to be sleeping downstairs again tonight."

Nell had to clear her disappointment out of her throat before she could speak. "Okay." Had she honestly thought that it might be Crash knocking on her door? What was she thinking? In the entire month that they'd slept under the same roof, with the sole exception of the night of Jake and Daisy's wedding, Crash had never made a move on her. He'd never done anything at all that even *remotely* suggested that he was interested in anything but her friendship. So why on earth had she thought he would knock on her door now?

"What time are you leaving tomorrow?" Jake asked.

She was going home to Ohio for a week or two. "First thing in the morning. Before seven. I want to try to miss the rush-hour traffic."

He reached into his jacket pocket and drew out an envelope. "I better give this to you now, then. I want to sleep as long as I can in the morning." His mouth twisted into an approximation of a smile. "Like, until April." He handed her the envelope. "Severance pay. Or a bonus. Call it whatever you like. Just take it."

Nell tried to give it back. "I don't want this, Jake. It's bad enough that Daisy left me all that money in her will."

Somehow Jake managed a more natural smile. "Yeah, well, she *really* wanted to give you Crash. She was sorry that didn't work out."

Nell felt herself blush. "It didn't *not* work out," she said. "It just... There was nothing there. No spark."

Jake snorted. "You really don't think Daisy and I didn't notice the two of you staring when you didn't think the other was looking? Yeah, right, there were no sparks— there were nuclear-powered *fireworks*."

She shook her head. "I don't know what you think you saw." She lowered her voice. "I did everything but throw myself at him. I'm telling you, he's not interested in me that way."

"What he *is* is scared to death of you." Jake pulled her in close for a quick hug. "You know I'll never be able to thank you enough for all you did, but right now I have to go lie down and become unconscious. Or least attempt it.''

''Admiral, are you sure you want to be alone? I could get Billy, and we could all have something to eat and—''

''I've got to get used to it, you know? Being alone.''

''Maybe tonight's not the night to start.''

''I just want to sleep. The doctor gave me something mild to help me relax. I'm not proud—if I need to, I'll take it.'' Jake gave her a gentle noogie on the top of her head. ''Just give me a call when you get to your mom and dad's so that I know you made it to Ohio safely.''

''I will,'' Nell promised. ''Good night, sir.'' She was still holding the envelope he'd given her. ''And thank you.''

Jake was already gone.

She turned and looked at Crash's door.

It was tightly shut, the way it always was when he was inside his bedroom.

What he is is scared to death of you.

What if Jake was right? What if the attraction Nell felt for Crash really was mutual?

If she didn't do *something* now, if she didn't walk over to that tightly shut door and knock on it, if she didn't get up the courage to look Crash in the eye and tell him exactly how she felt, she could very well lose the opportunity of a lifetime—a chance to start a very real relationship with a man who excited her on every level. Emotionally, physically, intellectually, spiritually—there was no doubt about it, William Hawken turned her on.

When she woke up in the morning, he'd probably already be downstairs, coming back inside from his morning run. She would load up her car, then shake his hand and that would be it. She would drive away, and probably never see him again.

She stood a chance at making a royal fool of herself, but

if she wasn't going to see him ever again, what did that matter?

As she stood there, gazing at Crash's closed door, she could almost hear Daisy whispering in her ear, "Go for it."

Nell tossed the envelope Jake had given her into her suitcase and, straightening her shoulders, she went back into the hall, heading for Crash's room.

Crash sat in the dark, fighting his anger.

He'd sat through the funeral as if he were watching it from a distance. It didn't seem possible that Daisy was dead. Part of him kept looking around for her, waiting for her to show up, listening for her familiar laughter, watching for her brilliant smile.

He didn't know how Jake could possibly stand it. But for the past two days, Jake had accepted condolences with a graciousness and quiet dignity that Crash couldn't imagine pulling off.

The anger Crash felt was something he could manage. He was good at controlling his anger. He was practiced in distancing himself from it. But the grief and the pain he was feeling—they were threatening to overpower him.

He'd found he could stomp down the grief, controlling it with his stronger feelings of anger. But after two solid days, the anger was getting harder and harder to control.

And so he sat in the dark with his hands shaking and his teeth clenched, and he silently let himself rage.

Nell was leaving in the morning. The thought made him even angrier, the feeling washing over him in great, thick waves.

He heard a sound in the hallway. It was Jake, knocking on Nell's door. He heard the door open, heard the two of them talking. He could hear the murmur of voices, but he couldn't make out the words. Still, he managed to get the gist. Jake and Nell were saying their goodbyes. Then he heard Jake walk away.

Crash closed his eyes, listening even harder, but he didn't hear Nell's door close. A board creaked in the hall, and his eyes opened. She was standing right outside of his room.

Dear, sweet Mary, how was he supposed to fight the temptation that Nell brought as well as all his grief and pain?

He closed his eyes, again, willing her to walk away. Walk away.

She didn't. She knocked on his door.

Crash didn't move. Maybe if he didn't answer, she would just go away. Maybe...

She knocked again.

And then she opened the door a crack, peering in, looking in the direction of his bed. "Billy? Are you asleep?"

He didn't answer, and she stepped further into the room. "Hawken...?" The light from the hallway fell onto the bed, and he saw when she realized it was empty. "Crash, are you even in here?"

He spoke then. "Yes."

Nell jumped, startled by his voice coming from the other side of the room.

"It's dark in here," she said, searching for him in the shadows. "May I turn on the light?"

"No."

She flinched at the flatness of his reply. "I'm sorry. Are you... Are you all right?"

"Yes."

"Then why are you sitting in the dark?"

He didn't answer.

"This all must seem like some terrible kind of déjà vu to you," she said quietly.

"Have you come to psychoanalyze me, or did you have something else in mind?"

It was too dark to see her clearly, even with the light from the hall, but he could picture the slight flush rising in her cheeks.

"I came because I'm leaving in the morning and I wanted to...say goodbye."

"Goodbye."

She flinched again, but instead of turning and walking out of the room the way he hoped she would, she moved toward him.

He was sitting on the floor with his back against the wall, and she sat down right next to him. "You're not alone in what you're feeling," she said. "There was nothing any of us could do to keep her from dying."

"So you *are* here to psychoanalyze. Do me a favor and keep it to yourself."

He couldn't see her eyes, but he could tell from the silhouette of her profile that she was not unaffected by the harshness of his words.

"Actually," she started. Her voice wobbled and she stopped and cleared her throat. When she spoke again, her voice was very, very small. "Actually, I'm here because *I* didn't want to be alone tonight."

Something clenched in Crash's chest. It was the same something that tightened his throat and made tears heat his eyes. It made his bitter anger start to fade, leaving behind a hurt and anguish that was too powerful to keep inside. There was no way he could detach and move far enough away from the pain he was feeling. It was too strong.

"I'm so sorry," he whispered. "What I said was rude and uncalled-for."

Crash tried to get mad at himself. He'd been a son of a bitch from the moment she walked in, a jerk, a complete ass, a total bastard. He tried to get good and angry—because that anger was the only thing that was going to keep him from breaking down and crying like a baby.

Nell moved in the darkness beside him, and he knew she was wiping her eyes on the sleeve of her shirt. ''That's okay,'' she said. ''I'd rather have you mad at me than have to watch you do your zombie impression.''

''Maybe you should go,'' Crash said desperately. ''Because I'm not feeling very steady here, and—''

She interrupted, turning in the darkness to face him. ''I came to your room because I wanted to tell you something before I left.'' She reached out, touching him on the arm. ''I wanted to—''

''Nell, I'm not sure I can—''

''Make sure that you knew that—''

''—handle sitting here like this with you.'' He'd meant to shake her hand off, but somehow he'd reached for her instead, gripping her tightly by the elbow.

''I've wanted to be your lover since the first time we met,'' she whispered.

Oh, Lord.

All of the intense feelings—the wanting, the guilt, the desire, the relentless pain—of the past few days, the past few *weeks,* spun together inside of him, in a great, huge tornado of emotion.

''I just wanted you to know that before I left,'' she said again, ''in case you maybe felt something similar and, even though we've only got one night—''

Crash kissed her. He had to kiss her, or everything inside of him, this churning maelstrom of despair and heartache and guilt and grief would erupt from him, tearing him apart, leaving him open and exposed.

He kissed her—and he didn't have to cry. He pulled her

close—and he didn't need to break things, he didn't lash out in anger, he didn't fall apart with grief.

She nearly exploded in his arms, clinging to him as desperately as he clung to her, matching the fury of his kisses, the ferociousness of his embrace.

He pulled her onto his lap so that her legs straddled him, her heat pressed tightly against him.

Sweet God, he'd wanted her for *so* long.

This was wrong. He knew it was wrong, but he no longer cared. He needed this. He *needed* her—just as she needed him tonight.

And Lord, how she needed him.

Her fingers were running through his hair, her hands skimming down his back as if she couldn't get enough of touching him. She kissed him as if she wanted to inhale him. She pressed herself against him as if she would die if he didn't fill her.

Nothing else existed. For right now, for this time, there was no past, no future—only this moment. Only the two of them.

As still they kissed, he touched her just as greedily, slipping one hand between them to cup the sweet fullness of her breast. She made a low, unbearably sexy noise deep in the back of her throat, then pulled her lips away from his, just long enough to grab the hem of her shirt and pull it quickly over her head.

And then she kissed him again, as if the few seconds they'd been apart had been an eternity.

Her skin was so smooth, so perfect beneath his hands. She reached between to unfasten the front clasp of her bra. The sensation was nearly unbearable then and, as she tugged at his own shirt, he knew that feeling her naked against him would drive him mindlessly past the point of no return.

"Is this really what you want?" he breathed, pushing her hair back from her face, trying to see her eyes in the dimness.

"Oh, yes." She kissed the palm of his hand, catching his thumb between her teeth, touching him with her tongue, damn near sending him through the roof.

When she pulled at his shirt again, this time he helped her, yanking it off.

And then she was touching him, her hands skimming his shoulders as she kissed his throat, his neck, her delicate lips driving him mad.

He pulled her close, crushing his mouth to hers, crushing the softness of her breasts to the hard muscles of his chest.

Skin against skin.

Crash wanted to take his time. He wanted to pull back and look at her, to taste her, to fill his hands with her, but he couldn't slow down without that emotional tornado inside of him breaking free and wreaking havoc.

But there was no way in hell he was going to take her here on the floor.

He swept his hands to the soft curve of her rear end and stood, pulling himself to his feet with Nell still in his arms.

Two long strides brought him close enough to kick the door closed. Two more took them both to his bed.

He put her down and pulled away to rid himself of his boots, and when he turned back, he found she'd opened the curtains on the window over the bed.

Pale winter moonlight filtered in, giving Nell's beautiful skin a silvery glow.

Crash reached for her, and she met him halfway, kissing him and pulling him back with her onto the bed. He felt her hands at the waistband of his pants even as he unfastened the top button of her jeans.

"Please tell me you've got a condom," she breathed as

she helped him pull her jeans down the long, smooth lengths of her legs.

"I've got a condom."

"Where?"

"Bathroom."

She slid off the bed as he wrestled with his own pants, but even so, he still managed to beat her into the attached bath. He always kept protection in his toilet kit on the counter next to the sink, and he searched for a foil-wrapped square without even turning on the light.

She pressed herself against him, her breasts soft against his back, reaching around him to slide both hands down past the waistband of his shorts. As he found what he was looking for, she did, too. Her fingers closed around him and it was all he could do to keep from groaning aloud.

Never in his wildest dreams had he imagined sweet Nell Burns would be so bold.

He could have had this for an entire month. He could have…

She took the foil packet from his hands, tore it open, and began to guide the condom onto him.

But she took too long, touched him too lightly, and he pulled away, breathing hard, quickly finishing the task himself as she dragged his shorts down his legs. When he turned to face her, he saw that she'd taken off her own panties as well.

She was beautiful, standing there naked in the moonlight, all silvery-smooth skin and shining hair, like some kind of goddess, some kind of faerie queen.

Crash reached for her, and she was there, filling his arms, kissing him hungrily. He reached between them, touching her intimately, finding her more than ready for him.

She turned them around, backing herself up against the sink counter. He knew by now that she was far from shy when it came to sex, but when she lifted herself up onto the counter, opening herself to his exploring fingers, pressing him more deeply inside of her, he thought his heart would stop.

But then he stopped thinking as she wrapped her legs around his waist and pulled him toward her. She kissed him hard, and with one explosive thrust, he was inside her.

Crash heard himself cry out, his voice mixing with hers.

It was too good, too incredible. He could feel her fingernails sharply against his back as she gripped him, as her legs tightened around him. She wanted him hard and fast and he wasn't about to deny her anything.

She moved beneath him, meeting each of his thrusts with a wild abandon, a savage passion that left him breathless. And he knew that this was more than mere sex for her, too. This was a way for them both to take comfort. This was a way to reaffirm that they were both still very much alive. It wasn't so much about pleasure as it was about trying to drive away the pain.

He'd always been a considerate lover, always taking his time, giving slow, leisurely pleasure to the woman he was with, making certain that she was satisfied several times over before he allowed himself his own release. He'd always been in careful control.

But tonight, his control had gone out the window with his good judgment. Tonight, he was on fire.

He lifted her off the counter, still kissing her, still moving inside her. He carried her toward the bed, stopping to press her back against the bathroom wall, the closet door, the bedroom wall, stopping to drive himself inside her as deeply as he possibly could.

She strained against him, her head thrown back and her breath catching in her throat as he roughly took first one, then the other of her breasts into his mouth, drawing hard on her deliciously taut nipples.

It was there, against the wall that separated his room from hers, that he felt her climax. It was there, as she cried out, as she shook and shattered around him, that he lost all that remained of his shredded control. He exploded, his release like a fiery rocket scorching his very soul.

And then it was over, but yet it wasn't. Nell still gripped him, still clung to him as if he were her only salvation. And he was still buried deeply inside of her.

Crash stood, his forehead resting on the wall above her shoulder, more than just physically spent. He was emotionally exhausted.

One minute slid into two, two into three and Nell didn't move either, didn't shift, didn't stir, didn't do more than hold him and breathe.

He kept his eyes closed, afraid to open them, afraid to *think*.

Dear God, what had he done?

He'd used her. She'd come to him for comfort, offering her own sweet comfort in return, and he'd done little more than use her to vent his anger and frustration and grief.

He lifted his head and somehow the Jell-O that had once been his legs made it over to the bed. He sank down, pulling himself free from Nell. He immediately missed the intimacy of that connection, but who was he kidding? They couldn't stay joined that way for the rest of their lives. He leaned back on the mattress, pulling her down with him, so that her back nestled against his chest, so that he wouldn't have to meet her gaze.

She lifted her head only slightly—not far enough to look into his eyes. "May I sleep in here with you tonight?"

She sounded so uncertain, so afraid of what he might

say. Something in his chest tightened. "Yeah," he said. "Sure."

"Thank you," she whispered, shivering slightly.

He shifted them both so he could cover them with the sheet and blanket. He pulled her closer, wrapping her tightly in his arms, wishing he could make her instantly warm, wishing for a lot of things that he knew he couldn't have.

He wished that he could keep her safe from the rest of the world. But how could he? He hadn't even been able to keep her safe from himself.

Chapter 8

Crash sat up in bed. "What time is it?"

One second, he'd been sound asleep, and the next his eyes were wide open, as if he'd been awake and alert for hours.

"It's nearly six." Nell resisted the urge to dive back under the sheet and blanket and cover herself. Instead, she sat on the edge of the bed with her back toward him, briefly closing her eyes, feeling her face heat with a blush.

Her jeans were here on the floor. Her shirt and bra were across the room. Her underpants…in the bathroom, she remembered suddenly, with a dizzying surge of extremely vivid memory.

She slipped into her jeans, forsaking her underpants. There was no way she was going to walk naked all the way across this room with Crash watching. Yes, he'd seen her naked last night, but that had been last night. This was the morning. This was very different. She was leaving for Ohio today, and if he shed any tears at her departure, they were surely only going to be tears of relief.

Nell knew with a certainty that could have gotten her hired by one of those psychic hotlines, that what had happened between herself and William Hawken last night had been a fluke. It had been a result of the high emotions of the past few days, of Daisy's death and the wake and funeral that had quickly followed.

It had been an incredible sexual experience, but Nell knew that a single episode of great sex didn't equal a romantic relationship. When it came down to it, nothing had changed between them. They were still only friends—except now they were friends who had shared incredibly great sex.

She stood up, fastening the button on her jeans, knowing that she couldn't keep her back to him as she went across the room in search of her shirt and bra. She was just going to have to be matter-of-fact about it. That's all. She had breasts, he didn't—big deal.

But Crash caught her arm before she could take a step, his fingers warm against her bare skin. ''Nell, are you all right?''

She didn't turn to face him, wishing that he would prove her wrong. Right now, he could do it—he could prove her entirely, absolutely wrong. He could slide his hand down her arm in a caress. He could pull her gently to him, move aside her hair and kiss her neck. He could run those incredible hands across her breasts, down her stomach, and unfasten the waistband of her pants. He could pull her back into the warmth of his bed and make love to her slowly in the gray morning light.

But he didn't.

''I'm...'' Nell hesitated. If she said *fine,* she would sound tense and tight, as if she *weren't* fine. His hand dropped

from her arm, and her last foolish hopes died. She crossed
the room and picked up her shirt.

It was inside out, of course, and she turned away from
him as she adjusted it. She slipped it over her head and
only then could she turn and look at him.

Bed head. He had bed head, his dark hair charmingly
rumpled, sticking out in all different directions. He looked
about twelve years old—except for the fact that even the
simple act of sitting up in bed had made many of his powerful-looking muscles flex. God, he was sexy, even with
bed head.

Nell used all her limited acting skills to sound normal.
"I'm…still pretty amazed by what happened here last
night."

"Yeah," he said. His pale blue eyes were unreadable.
"I am, too. I feel as if I owe you an apology—"

"Don't," she said, moving quickly toward him. "Don't
you *dare* apologize for what happened last night. It was
something we both needed. It was really *right*—don't turn
it into something wrong."

Crash nodded. "All right. I just…" He glanced away,
closing his eyes briefly before he looked back at her. "I've
been so careful to stay away from you all this time," he
said, "because I didn't want to hurt you this way."

Nell slowly sat down at the foot of the bed. "Believe
me, last night didn't hurt at all."

He didn't smile at her poor attempt at a joke. "You know
as well as I do," he said quietly, "that it wouldn't work,
right? A relationship between us…" He shook his head.
"You don't really know me. You know this…kind of
PG-rated, goody-two-shoes, Disney cartoon version of
me."

Nell wanted to protest, but he wasn't done talking and
she held her tongue, afraid if she interrupted, he would stop.

''But if you really knew me, if you knew who I really am, what I do...you wouldn't like me very much.''

She couldn't hold it in any longer. ''How can you just make that kind of decision *for* me?''

''Maybe I'm wrong. Maybe you have some kind of sick thing for cold-blooded killers—''

''You are *not* cold-blooded!''

''But I *am* a killer.''

''You're a soldier,'' she argued. ''There's a difference.''

''Okay,'' he said levelly. ''Maybe you could get past that. But being involved with a SEAL who specializes in black ops is not something I'd wish on my worst enemy.'' His usually quiet voice rang with conviction. ''I certainly wouldn't wish it on you.''

''Again, you're just going to decide that for me?''

He threw off the covers, totally unembarrassed by his nakedness. He found his pants, but they were the ones he'd worn to the funeral. Dress pants. He tossed them over a chair and pulled a pair of army fatigues from the closet.

Nell closed her eyes at a sudden vivid image from last night. His hands around her waist, his mouth locked on hers, his *body*...

''Here's the deal with black ops,'' he said, zipping his fly and fastening the button at his waist. ''I disappear— literally—sometimes for months at a time. You would never know where I was, or for how long I'd be gone.''

He ran his fingers back through his hair in a failed attempt to tame it, the muscles in his chest and arms standing out in sharp relief. ''If I were KIA—killed in action—you might never be told,'' he continued. ''I just wouldn't come back. Ever. You'd never find out about the mission I was on. There'd be no paper trail, no way to know how or why I'd died. It would be as if I'd never existed.'' He shook his head. ''You don't need that kind of garbage in your life.''

"But—"

"It wouldn't work." He gazed at her steadily. "Last night was…nice, but you've got to believe me, Nell. It just wouldn't work."

Nice.

Nell turned away. *Nice?* Last night had been wonderful, amazing, fantastic. It hadn't been *nice*.

"I'm sorry," he said softly.

She looked out the window. She looked at the rug. She looked at a painting that hung on the wall. It was one of Daisy's—a beach scene from her watercolor phase.

Only then did she look up at him. "I'm sorry, too. I'm sorry you think it wouldn't work," she finally said. "You know, I knew most of what you were going to say before you even said it. And I was going to pretend to agree with you. You know, 'Yeah, you're right, it would never work, different personalities, different worlds, different lives, whatever.' But to hell with my pride. Because the truth is, I *don't* agree with you. I think it *would* work. *We* would work. I think we'd be great together. Last night could be just the beginning and I'm…saddened that you think otherwise."

Crash didn't say anything. He didn't even look at her.

Nell bolstered the very last of her rapidly fading courage and tossed the final shred of her pride out the door. "Can't we at least *try?*" Her voice broke slightly—her final humiliation.

Crash didn't speak, and again she found the courage to go on.

"Can't we see what happens? Take it one day at a time?"

He looked up at her, but his eyes were so distant, it was as if he wasn't quite all there.

"I'm sorry," he said again. "I'm not looking for any

kind of a relationship at all right now. I was wrong to give in to this attraction between us. I wanted the comfort and the instant gratification, and the real truth is, I used you, Nell. That's all last night was. You came along, and I took what you offered. There's nothing for us to try. There's nothing more to happen.''

Nell stood up, trying desperately to hide her hurt. ''Well,'' she said. ''I guess that clears *that* up.''

''It's my fault, and I *am* sorry.''

She cleared her throat as she moved toward the door. ''No,'' she said. ''I knew last night...I mean, it was clear that's what it was. Comfort, I mean. It was that way for me, too, sort of, at first anyway, and...I was just hoping...Billy, it's *not* your fault.''

She opened the door and stepped into the hall. Crash hadn't moved. She wasn't even sure if he'd blinked.

''Happy New Year,'' she said quietly, and shut the door behind her.

Chapter 9

A year later

Someone opened fire.

Someone opened fire, and the world went into slow motion.

Crash saw Jake pushed back by the force of the gunshots, arms spread, face caught in a terrible grimace as an explosion of bright red blood bloomed on the front of his shirt.

Crash heard his own voice shouting, saw Chief Pierson fall as well, and felt the slap as a bullet hit his arm. His years of training kicked in and he reacted, rolling down onto the office floor, taking cover and returning fire.

He shut part of his brain down as he always did in a firefight. He couldn't afford to think in terms of human beings when he was spraying lead around a room. He couldn't afford to feel anything at all.

He analyzed dispassionately as he evaded and struck

back. Jake had pulled out the compact handgun he always wore under his left arm, and even though the glimpse Crash had had of the other man's chest wound made him little more than a still-breathing dead man, the admiral somehow found the strength to pull himself to cover, and to fight back.

There could be as few as one and as many as three possible shooters.

Crash noted emotionlessly that his captain, Mike Lovett, and Chief Steve Pierson, a SEAL known as the Possum, were undeniably dead as he efficiently took down one of the shooters.

Not a man. A shooter. The enemy.

At least two other weapons still hiccuped and stuttered.

He could hear the rush of blood in his ears as he tipped what had once been Daisy's favorite table on its side and used it as a shield to work his way around to an angle where he could try to take out another of the shooters.

Not men. Shooters.

In the same way, Mike and the Poss weren't his teammates anymore. They were KIAs. Killed in action. Casualties.

Crash could do nothing for them now. But Jake wasn't dead yet. And if Crash could eliminate the last of the shooters, maybe, just maybe Jake could be saved....

Crash wanted Jake to live. He wanted that with a ferocious burst of emotion that he immediately pushed away. Detach. He had to detach more completely. Emotion made his hands shake and skewed his perception. Emotion could get him killed.

He separated himself cleanly from the man who wanted to rage and grieve over the deaths of his teammates. He set himself apart from the man who was near frantic from wanting to rush to Jake's side, to stanch the older man's wounds, to force him to fight to stay alive.

Crash felt clarity kick in as he looked at himself from the outside. He felt his senses sharpen, felt time slow even further. He knew the last of the shooters was circling the room, looking for a chance to finish off Jake, and then take Crash out as well.

One heartbeat.

He could hear the sound of the admiral's FInCOM security team, shouting as they pounded on the outside of the locked office door.

Two heartbeats.

He could hear the almost inaudible scuff as the shooter moved into position. There was only one left now, and he was going for the admiral first. Crash knew that without a doubt.

Three heartbeats.

He could hear Jake struggling for breath. Crash knew, also dispassionately, that Jake's wounds had made at least one lung collapse. If he didn't get medical help soon, the man was definitely going to die.

Four heartbeats.

Another scuff, and Crash was able to pinpoint precisely where the shooter was.

He jumped and fired in one smooth motion.

And the last shooter was no longer a threat.

"Billy?" Jake's voice was breathy and weak.

With a pop and a skip as jarring as a needle sliding across a phonograph record, the world once again moved at real time.

"I'm still here." Crash was instantly at his old friend's side.

"What the hell happened...?"

Jake's shirtfront was drenched with blood. "That's just

what I was going to ask you," Crash replied as he gently tore the shirt to reveal the wound. Dear sweet Mary, with an injury like this, it was a miracle Jake had clung to life as long as he had.

"Someone…wants me…dead."

"Apparently." Crash had been trained as a medic—all SEALs were—but first aid wasn't going to cut it here. His voice shook despite his determination to maintain his usual deadpan calm. "Sir, I need to get you help."

Jake clutched Crash's shirt, his brown eyes glazed with pain. "You need…to *listen*. Just sent you…file… incriminating evidence…last year's snafu in Southeast Asia…six months ago… You were…there. Remember?"

"Yes," Crash said. "I remember." A civil war had started in a tiny island nation when two rival drug lords had pitted their armies against each other. "Two of our marines were killed—Jake, please, we can talk about this on the way to the hospital."

But Jake wouldn't let him go. "The military action…was instigated by an American…a U.S. Navy commander."

"*What?* Who?"

The door burst open and Jake's security team swarmed inside the room.

"I need an ambulance *now!*" the security chief bellowed after just one look at the admiral.

"Don't know…who," Jake gasped. "Some…kind of…cover-up. Kid, I'm counting…on you…"

"Jake, don't die!" Crash was pushed back, out of the way, as a team of paramedics surrounded the admiral.

Please, God, let him make it.

"For God's sake, what happened?"

Crash turned to find Commander Tom Foster, Jake's security chief, standing behind him. He took a deep breath and let it out in a rush of air. When he spoke, his voice was calm again. "I don't know."

"How the hell could you not know what happened?"

He didn't let himself react, didn't let himself get angry. The man was understandably shaken and upset. Crash could relate. Now that the shooting was over, his own hands were shaking and he was dizzy. He hunkered down, sliding his back against the wall of Jake's private office as he lowered his rear end all the way to the floor.

He realized then that his arm was bleeding pretty profusely, and had been since the battle had started. He'd lost quite a bit of blood. He set down his weapon and applied pressure with his other hand. For the first time since he was hit, he noticed the searing pain. He looked up. "I didn't see who fired the first shots," he said evenly.

He turned to watch as the paramedics carried Jake from the room. *Please, let him make it.*

The security chief swore. "Who would want to kill Admiral Robinson?"

Crash shook his head. He didn't know *that* either. But he sure as hell was going to find out.

Dex Lancaster kissed her good-night.

Nell knew from his eyes, and from the gentle heat of his lips, that he was hoping that she would ask him to come inside.

It wasn't that outrageous a hope. They'd had dinner seven or eight times now, and she honestly liked him.

He lowered his head to kiss her again, but she turned her head and his mouth only brushed her cheek.

She liked him, but she wasn't ready for this.

She forced a smile as she unlocked her door. "Thanks again for dinner."

He nodded, resignation and amusement in his blue eyes.

"I'll call you." He started down the steps, his long overcoat fanning out behind him like an elegant cape, but then he stopped, turning back to look up at her. "You know, I'm not in any real big hurry either, so take as long as you need. I've decided that I'm not going to let you scare me off." With a quick salute, he was gone.

Nell smiled ruefully as she locked her door behind her, turning on the light in the entryway of her house. The single women in her exercise class would have been lining up for a chance to invite a man like Dexter Lancaster into their homes.

What was wrong with her, anyway?

She had just about everything she'd ever wanted. A house of her own. A great job. A handsome, intelligent, warmhearted man who wanted to spend time with her.

Thanks to the money Daisy Owen had bequeathed her, she'd bought her own house, free and clear—a drafty old Victorian monster with prehistoric plumbing and ancient wiring that still ran on a fuse box. Nell was fixing the place up, little by little.

And she'd found a new job that she really loved, working part-time for the legendary screen actress, Amie Cardoza. Amie had had most of her successes on film in the seventies and eighties, but as she approached and then passed middle age, the better roles had disappeared, and she'd turned to the stage. She'd started an equity theater in the heart of Washington D.C., her hometown. She'd really needed a personal assistant—the theater company was still struggling and Amie was becoming politically active as well.

Dex had introduced Nell to Amie, and Nell had liked the famous actress instantly. She was outspoken and funny and passionate—much like Daisy in many ways. With the life of her theater hanging by a thread, Amie couldn't afford to pay as much as Daisy had, but Nell didn't mind. She'd used the remainder of the money from Daisy to make investments that were already making her a profit. With that, and her house fully paid for, Nell was more than happy to be able to work for someone she admired and respected at a little bit less than the going rate.

She'd only been with Amie for the past four months, but her days had settled into a comfortable routine. On Monday mornings, she'd work at the actress's home, dealing with her day-to-day household affairs. On Tuesday and Wednesday afternoons, they'd meet at the theater. Thursdays and Fridays depended on what additional projects Amie had going. And there was always *something* additional going.

Dex often dropped in. He was a member of an organization called Volunteer Lawyers for the Arts, and he did pro bono work for the theater. Although he was older than the men Nell had dated in the past, she liked him. And when he'd asked her out to dinner several months ago, she couldn't think of a single reason why she shouldn't go.

It had been almost a year since her last romantic entanglement. Or rather, her last *non*-romantic entanglement. She'd tangled, so to speak, with Crash Hawken, a man she should have accepted as a friend. Instead, she'd pushed for more, and she'd lost that friendship.

Crash had never called her. He'd never even dropped her a postcard in response to the letters she'd written. When she'd spoken to Jake and asked, he'd told her the SEAL had been spending a great deal of time out of the country. Jake had also told her very clearly that if she were waiting for Crash to come back, she shouldn't hold her breath.

Well, she wasn't holding her breath. But sometimes, when her guard was down, she still dreamed about the man.

And even now, the nearly year-old memory of his kisses was stronger and more powerful than the two-minute-old memory of Dex's lips.

Nell briefly closed her eyes, willing that particular memory away. She refused to waste her time consciously letting her thoughts stray in that direction. It was bad enough when she did it *sub*consciously.

She hung her coat in the front closet and went into the kitchen to fix herself a cup of tea.

The next time Dex asked her out to dinner, she'd invite him in. She had been wrong. It *was* time. It was definitely time to exorcise some old ghosts.

The phone rang, and she glanced at the clock on the microwave. It was eleven. It had to be Amie with something urgent she'd forgotten about—something that needed to be done first thing in the morning.

"Hello?"

"Thank God you're home!" It *was* Amie. "Turn on the TV right now!"

Nell reached for the power button on the little black-and-white set that sat on her kitchen counter. "What channel? Is there something on the news about the theater?"

"Cable channel four. It's not the theater. Nell, my God, it's something about that man you used to work for—that Admiral Robinson?"

"There's…a commercial playing on channel four."

"They showed one of those previews," Amie imitated a TV announcer's voice. "'Coming up at eleven.' They said something about an *assassination!*"

"*What?*" The commercial ended. "Wait, wait, it's on!"

The credits rolled endlessly and finally a news anchor gazed seriously into the camera. "Tonight's top story— Navy spokesmen have released confirmation that a gun battle raged three nights ago at the home of U.S. Navy Admiral Jacob Robinson, injuring the admiral and killing several others. Early reports indicate that four or five people are dead. All are believed to be members of the admiral's security team. Let's go to Holly Mathers, downtown.''

Nell couldn't breathe. *A gun battle.* At the farm?

The picture changed to a chilled-looking young woman, standing outside a brightly lit building. ''Thanks, Chuck. I'm here outside of the Northside Hospital. A number of additional statements have just been released, the first and most tragic of which is that Jake Robinson has *not* survived. I repeat, the fifty-one-year-old U.S. Navy admiral was declared dead from gunshot wounds to the chest, here at Northside, just one hour ago.''

''Oh, my God.'' Nell reached blindly behind her for a chair, but couldn't find one, and sank down onto the kitchen floor instead. Jake was dead. How could Jake be *dead?*

''Navy spokesmen have stated that the suspected assassin is in custody, also here at Northside Hospital,'' the reporter continued, ''where it's speculated that he was being treated for minor wounds. They have not yet released the name of this man, nor the names of the men—apparently a team of Navy SEALs—who gave their lives attempting to protect Robinson.''

Navy SEALs. Nell went hot and then cold. Please dear God, don't let Crash be dead, too.

She wasn't aware she had spoken aloud until Amie's voice asked. ''Crash? Who's Crash?''

Nell was still holding the phone, the line open. ''Amie, I'm sorry, I have to go. This is…terrible. I've got to go and…''

What? What could she do?

''I'm so sorry, sweetie. I know how much you liked Jake. Do you want me to come out there?''

''No, Amie, I have to…'' Call someone. She had to call someone and find out if Crash was one of the men who had died today at the farm.

"I won't expect to see you for the next few days. Take as much time as you need, all right?"

Nell didn't answer. She couldn't. She just pressed the power button on the cordless phone.

She tried to think. Tried to remember the names of Jake's high-powered friends—people she'd called both to tell about the change in wedding plans, and then about Daisy's death. There were several other admirals that Jake knew quite well. And what was the name of that FInCOM security commander? Tom something. He'd come out to the farm a few times to double-check the security fence....

On the television, the reporter was talking with the anchor, discussing Jake's career in Vietnam, his long-term relationship with popular artist Daisy Owen, their marriage and her relatively recent death.

The reporter touched her earpiece. "I'm sorry," she said, interrupting the anchor in midsentence. "We've just received word that the alleged assassin, the man believed to be responsible for Admiral Jake Robinson's murder and the murders of at least five members of his security team, is being brought out of the hospital, being transferred to FInCOM Headquarters to await arraignment."

The camera jiggled sickeningly as the cameraman rushed to get into position. The hospital doors opened, and a crowd of police and other uniformed men came out.

Nell got to her knees, still holding the telephone as she moved closer to the TV set, wanting a glimpse of the face of the man who had killed her friend.

That man was in the center of the crowd, his long, dark hair parted in the middle and hanging slackly down to his shoulders. The picture was still wobbling, though, and Nell could see little more than the pale blur of his face.

"Admiral Stonegate!" the reporter called to one of the

men in the crowd. "Admiral Stonegate, sir! Can you identify this man for our viewers?"

The camera zoomed in on the murder suspect, and the cordless phone dropped out of Nell's hands and clattered on the kitchen floor.

It was Crash. The man being led to the police cars was Crash Hawken.

His hair was long and stringy—parted in the middle and hanging around his face in a style that was far from flattering. But Nell would have known that face anywhere. Those cheekbones, that elegant nose, the too-grim mouth. His pale gray eyes were nearly vacant, though. He seemed unaware of the explosion of questions and cameras focusing on him.

The relief that flooded through Nell was so sharp and overpowering, she nearly doubled over.

Crash was alive.

Thank God he was alive.

"I've been authorized to release the following statement. The man in our custody is former Navy Lieutenant William R. Hawken," a raspy male voice said.

On the screen, Crash was pushed into the back seat of a car. The camera focused for a moment on his hands, cuffed at the wrist behind his back, before once again settling, through the rain-streaked window of the car, on his seemingly soulless eyes.

"The charges include conspiracy, treason, and first-degree murder," the male voice continued. As the car pulled away, the camera moved to focus on the reporter, who was one of a crowd surrounding a short, white-haired navy admiral. "With the evidence we have, it's an open-and-shut case. There's no question in my mind of Hawken's guilt. I was a close friend of Jake Robinson's and I intend, personally, to push for the death penalty in this case.''

The *death* penalty.

Nell stared at the TV as the words being spoken finally broke through her relief that Crash was alive.

Crash was being arrested. His hands had been cuffed. He'd been charged with conspiracy, the man had said. And treason. And *murder*.

It didn't make sense. How could anyone who claimed to be a friend of Jake's possibly believe that Crash could have killed him? Anyone who knew them both would have to know how ridiculous that was.

Crash could no more have killed Jake than she could have gone to the window, opened it, and flown twice around the outside of her house before coming back inside. It was ridiculous. Impossible. Totally absurd.

Nell pushed herself up off the kitchen floor and went into the little room she'd made into her home office. She turned on the light and her computer. Somewhere, in some forgotten file deep in the bowels of her hard disk, she must still have the names and phone numbers of the people she'd invited to Jake and Daisy's wedding. *Someone* would be able to help her prove that Crash was innocent.

She wiped her face and went to work.

Crash had to shuffle when he walked. Even for the short trip from his cell to the visiting room, he had to be hand-cuffed and chained like a common criminal. His hands and feet were considered to be deadly weapons because of his martial-arts skills. He couldn't raise his hands to push his hair out of his face without a guard pointing a rifle in his direction.

He couldn't imagine who had come to see him—who, that is, had the pull and the clout and the sheer determination to request and be granted a chance to talk one-on-one to a man charged with conspiracy, treason and murder.

It sure wasn't any of the members of his SEAL Team. His *former* SEAL Team. He'd been stripped of his commission and rank upon his arrival here at the federal prison. He'd been stripped of everything but his name, and he was almost certain that they would've have taken that as well, if they could have.

But no, there was no one in his former SEAL Team who would want to sit down and talk to him right now. They all thought he'd killed Captain Lovett and the Possum—Chief Steven Pierson—in the gun battle at Jake Robinson's house.

And why shouldn't they believe that? The ballistics report showed that Crash's bullets had been found in both of the SEALs' bodies—despite the fact Crash had been standing right next to the Possum when the man was hit.

It was quite possible that the only reason Crash was still alive today was because the chief had fallen in front of him when he'd gone down, also taking the bullets that had been meant for Crash.

No, Crash's mysterious visitor wasn't a member of SEAL Team Twelve. But it *was* possible he was a member of SEAL Team Ten's elite Alpha Squad. Crash had worked with Alpha Squad this past summer, helping to train an experimental joint FInCOM/SEAL counterterrorist team.

Crash had worked with Alpha Squad on the same operation in Southeast Asia that Jake had believed was the cause of this entire hellish tragedy. It had been that very op that Jake had been investigating right before his death—and had detailed in the encoded file he had sent Crash. Crash couldn't deny that that particular operation had gone about as wrong as it possibly could. Jake had believed that the snafu had not been accidental, and that the mistakes made were now being covered up.

And Jake never could abide a cover-up.

But was a cover-up of a botched op enough reason to kill an admiral?

Crash had had little else to think about day and night during the past week.

But right now, he had a visitor and he turned his thoughts toward wondering who was sitting on the other side of the wired glass window in the visitors' room.

It might be his swim buddy, Cowboy Jones—the man with whom he'd gone through the punishingly harsh SEAL training. Cowboy wouldn't condemn him. At least not before talking to him. And then there was Blue McCoy. Last summer Crash had come to know and trust Alpha Squad's taciturn executive officer.

He liked to think that Blue would want to hear Crash's version of the story first, too.

Still, it was odd to imagine that someone he had met only six months earlier would take the time to question him about what had happened, when his own teammates, men he'd worked with for years, had clearly already judged and found him guilty as charged.

Crash waited while one of the guards unlocked the door. It swung open and…

It wasn't Cowboy and it definitely wasn't Blue McCoy.

Out of all the people in all the world, Nell Burns was the *last* person Crash had expected to see sitting in that chair on the other side of that protective glass.

Yet there she was, her hands tightly clasped on the table in front of her.

She looked almost exactly the same as she had the last time he'd seen her—the morning she'd walked out of his room after they'd spent the night together.

It had been nearly a year, but he could still remember that night as if it had been yesterday.

Her hair was cut in the same chin-length style. Only her clothes were different—a severely tailored business suit with shoulder pads in the jacket, and a stiff white shirt that did its best to hide the soft curves of her breasts.

But she didn't have to wear sexy, revealing clothes. It didn't matter what she wore—boxy suit or burlap sack. The image of her perfect body was forever branded in his memory.

God, he was pathetic. After all this time, he still wanted Nell more than he'd ever wanted any woman.

The guard pulled out his chair and Crash sat, refusing to acknowledge just how much he'd missed her, refusing to let himself care that the glass divider kept him from breathing in her sweet perfume, refusing to care that she had to see him like this, chained up like some kind of animal.

But he *did* care. God, how he cared.

Separate. Detach. He had to start thinking like the kind of man he was—a man with no future. A man on a final mission.

Crash had a single goal now—to hunt down and destroy the man responsible for Jake Robinson's death. He had lost far more than his commanding officer when he'd been unable to save Jake's life. He'd lost a friend who'd been like a father to him. And he'd lost everything else that was important to him as well—the trust of his teammates, his rank, his commission, his status as a SEAL. Without those things he was nothing. A nonentity.

He was as good as dead.

But it was that very fact that gave him the upper hand against the unknown man who was behind his fall from grace. Because with everything that mattered to him gone,

Crash had nothing more to lose. He was going to succeed at his mission if it was the last thing he ever did. He was determined to succeed, even at the price of his own worthless life.

As Crash sat and gazed at Nell through the protective glass, he was struck by the irony of the situation. He'd worked hard to make sure that Nell wasn't his to have—or his to lose. Yet here he was, having lost everything else in his life, except, it appeared, her trust.

Yeah, the irony was incredible. His one ally, the only person who believed he didn't kill Jake Robinson, was a woman who by all rights should want nothing more to do with him.

And he knew Nell didn't believe that he'd killed Jake. Even after a year apart, he could still read her like a first-grade primer.

See Nell.

See Nell refuse to run.

See Nell's loyalty blazing in her eyes.

Crash sat in the chair and waited for her to speak.

She leaned forward slightly. "I'm so sorry about Jake."

It was exactly what he'd expected her to say. He nodded. "Yeah. Me, too." His voice came out sounding harsh and raspy, and he cleared his throat.

"I tried to go to his funeral, but apparently he'd requested it be private and…they didn't let you go either, did they?"

Crash shook his head no.

"I'm sorry," she whispered.

He nodded again.

"I would've come sooner," she told him, "but it took me nearly a week to talk my way in here."

A *week.* His chest felt tight at the thought of her going

to bat for him day after day for an entire week. He wasn't sure what to say to that, so he didn't say anything.

Her gaze slipped to the bandage he still had on his arm. "Are you all right?"

When he didn't answer, she sat back, closing her eyes briefly. "I'm sorry. Stupid question. Of course you're not all right." She leaned forward again. "What can I do to help?"

Her eyes were so intensely blue. For a moment he was back in Malaysia, gazing out at the South China Sea.

"Nothing," he said quietly. "There's nothing you can do."

She shifted in her seat, clearly frustrated. "There must be *something*. Are you happy with your lawyer? It's important to have a good defense lawyer that you trust."

"My lawyer's fine."

"This is your life that's at stake, Billy."

"My lawyer's fine," he said again.

"Fine's not good enough. Look, I know a really good criminal defense lawyer. You remember Dex…"

"Nell, I don't need another lawyer, particularly not—" He cut himself off short. Particularly not Dexter Lancaster. Crash knew he had no right to be jealous, especially not now. An entire year had passed since he'd willingly given up his right to be jealous. But there was no way he was going to sit down with Dexter Lancaster and plan a defense he wasn't even going to need. He'd spend the entire time torturing himself, wondering if Dex was planning to leave their meeting and head over to Nell's house and…

Don't go there, don't go there, don't go there….

God, he was on the verge of losing it. All he needed was Nell finding out that he'd been keeping track of her this past year, that he knew she was seeing Lancaster socially. All she needed was to know that he'd made an effort to find out if she was okay—made a gargantuan effort, since he'd had to do it from some godforsaken corner of the world.

And then she would read some deep meaning into it. She would think he'd kept track of her because he'd cared. And he would have to explain that it was only responsibility that had driven him to check up on her, and once again, she would be hurt.

What he needed to do was make her leave. He'd done it before, he could do it again.

"What *really* happened at the farm last week?"

That was one question he could answer honestly. "I don't know. Someone started shooting. I wasn't ready for it, and…" He shook his head.

Nell cleared her throat. "I was told that the ballistics reports prove that you killed Jake and most of the other men. That's pretty damning evidence."

It was damning evidence, indeed. It proved to Crash that this "Commander" that Jake had spoken about, this man Jake himself had believed was responsible for setting up the assassination, was someone with lots of clout in Washington. He was a powerful man with powerful connections. He *had* to be, in order to have had the results of those ballistics tests falsified. And those test results *had* been falsified.

Crash was being framed, and he was going to find out just who was framing him. He knew when he found that out, he'd also find the man responsible for Jake's death.

It was possible whoever had framed him was watching him, even now. They surely would be aware Nell had come to see him. It was important for her own safety that she not make a habit of this.

Nell leaned even closer to the protective glass. "Billy, I

can't believe that you killed him, but…isn't it possible that in the chaos, your bullets accidentally hit Jake?''

"Yeah, right. That must've been what happened," he lied. He stood up. The last thing he needed was her brainstorming alternatives and coming up with the theory that he'd been framed. If she *did* come up with that, and if she was vocal about it, she'd be putting herself in danger. "I've got to go."

She stared at him as if he'd lost his mind. "Where?"

He moved very close to the microphone that allowed her to hear him on the other side of the glass. He spoke very softly, very quickly. "Nell, I don't want or need your help. I want you to stand up and walk out of here. And I don't want you to come back. Do you understand what I'm saying?"

She shook her head. "I still think of you as my friend. I can't just—"

"Go away," he said harshly, enunciating each word very clearly. *"Go away."*

He turned and shuffled toward the guards at the door, aware that she hadn't moved, aware that she was watching him, hating his chains, hating himself.

One guard unlocked the door as the other held his rifle at the ready.

Crash went out the door and didn't look back.

Chapter 10

People had turned out in droves to see the freak show.

Crash's chains clanked as he was led into the courtroom for his hearing. He tried not to look up at all the faces looking down at him from the gallery.

Tried and failed.

The surviving members of his SEAL Team—his *former* SEAL Team—were sitting in the back, arms crossed, venom in their eyes.

They thought he was responsible for Captain Lovett and the Possum's death. They believed the ballistics report. Why shouldn't they? Everyone else did.

Except Nell Burns. God, she was sitting there as well. Crash felt a rush of hot and then cold at the thought that she hadn't stayed away. What was wrong with her? What did he have to say or do to make her stay away from him for good?

Crash didn't want to waste any time at all worrying about Nell running around, proclaiming his innocence, stirring things up and catching the attention of a man who'd killed an admiral to keep his identity hidden.

He would rather picture Nell safe at home. Sweet Mary, he'd rather picture Nell having breakfast in bed with Dexter Lancaster than have to worry about her becoming another target for a man with no scruples.

He purposely didn't meet her eyes, even though he made it clear that he saw her. He purposely, coldly, turned his back on her, praying that she would leave.

But as he turned, he saw another familiar face in the crowd.

Lt. Commander Blue McCoy of Alpha Squad was sitting in the front row of the side balcony.

Crash hadn't expected Blue McCoy to come to gape at him, to sit there mentally spitting at him, ready to cheer when the court expressed its desire to impose the death sentence.

He'd liked working with Blue. He'd trusted the quiet man almost immediately. And he'd thought that Blue had trusted him as well.

He tried not to look in Blue's direction, either, but a flash of movement caught his eye.

He turned and Blue did it again. Moving quickly, almost invisibly, he hand-signaled Crash. *Are you okay?*

There were no accusations in Blue's eyes—no hatred, no animosity. Only concern.

Crash turned to face the judge without responding. He couldn't respond. What could he possibly say?

He closed his hand around the bent piece of metal he had concealed in his palm, feeling its rough edges scrape against his skin. He couldn't wait to be free of these chains. He couldn't wait to see the sky again.

He couldn't wait to find the man who had killed Jake, and send the bastard straight to hell.

It was only a matter of minutes now.

He sat through the procedure, barely hearing the droning of the lawyers' voices. He could feel his former SEAL Team members' hot eyes on his back. He could feel Blue watching him as well.

And if he closed his eyes and breathed really deeply, he could pretend that he could smell Nell's sweet perfume.

As the two guards escorted Crash from the courtroom, Nell willed him to turn his head and acknowledge that she was there.

She didn't expect him to smile, or even to nod. All she wanted was for him to look into her eyes.

She'd dressed in a bright red turtleneck so that she would stand out among all the drab winter coats and business suits. She *knew* he'd seen her. He'd looked straight at her when he came in—he just hadn't met her gaze.

But he went out the door without so much as a glance in her direction, his actions echoing the words he'd said three days ago. *Go away.*

But Nell couldn't do that.

She wasn't going to do that.

She stood up, squeezing past the knees of the people still in their seats, people who'd settled in to wait for Crash's bail hearing—which had quickly been set for later in the afternoon.

That was going to be over before it even started. Crash's lawyer was going to request bail—after all, his client had pleaded not guilty.

But then the judge was going to take a look at Crash sitting there, chained up like some monster because his hands and feet were considered deadly weapons. The judge was going to realize that as a former SEAL, Crash could disappear, leaving the country with ease, never to be seen again. And the judge was going to deny bail.

Nell hiked her bag higher up on her shoulder and, carrying her leather bomber jacket over one arm, went out into the hallway.

Crash's lawyer, Captain Phil Franklin, a tall black man in a heavily decorated Navy uniform, was around somewhere, and she was determined to talk to him.

She went out of the courtroom and into the hallway, spotting the captain stepping into an elevator.

There were too many people waiting to go up or down, so Nell could only watch to see which direction the elevator was heading.

Down. Directly down four flights, all the way to the basement. There was a coffee shop down there. With any luck, she'd find the Navy lawyer there.

Nell opened the door to the stairwell. As she stepped inside, she was nearly knocked over by a man coming down from the floor above. He was taking two and three steps at once and wasn't able to stop himself in time.

He recognized her at the same instant she recognized him. Nell knew because he froze.

And she looked up into Crash's light blue eyes. He was alone—no guards, and his chains were gone.

She knew instantly what had happened. He'd broken free. She thrust her jacket at him. "Take this," she said. "My car keys are in the pocket."

He didn't move.

"Go!" she said. "Take it and *go!*"

"I can't," he said, finally moving. He backed one step away from her, and then two. "I'm not going to let you go to jail for helping me."

"I'll tell them you grabbed my jacket and ran."

The corner of his mouth twitched. "Right. Like they'd believe that, considering our history."

"How will they know? I never told anyone about that night."

Something flickered in his eyes. "I was referring to our friendship," he said quietly. "The fact that we lived in the same house for an entire month."

Nell felt her cheeks heat with a blush. "Of course."

Crash shook his head. "You've got to stay away from me. You've got to walk out of this courthouse and go home and not look back. Don't think about me, don't talk about me to anyone. Pretend that you never knew me. Forget I ever existed."

She closed her eyes. "Just *go*, all right? Get out of here, dammit, before they catch you."

Nell didn't hear him leave, but when she opened her eyes, he was gone.

Four hours. It had been nearly four hours, and no one was allowed to enter or exit the federal courthouse.

An alarm had sounded not more than thirty seconds after Crash had vanished in the stairwell, and within five minutes, the entire building had been locked up tight as the police searched for the fugitive.

It didn't seem possible that he hadn't been caught, but Crash was indisputably gone. It was as if he'd simply turned to smoke and drifted away.

Crash's lawyer had been questioned extensively by FInCOM agents but now Captain Phil Franklin sat alone in the coffee shop, reading a newspaper.

Nell slipped into the seat across from him. "Excuse me, sir. My name is Nell Burns, and I'm a friend of your missing client's."

Franklin looked at her over the top of his paper, his dark brown eyes expressionless. "A friend?"

"Yes. A *friend*. I know for a fact that he didn't kill Admiral Robinson."

Franklin put his paper down. "You know for a fact, hmm? Were you there, Miss…I'm sorry, what did you say your name was?"

"Nell Burns."

"Were you there, Miss Burns?" he asked again.

Nell shook her head. "No, but I was there last year. I was Daisy Owens's—Daisy *Robinson's*—personal assistant right up until the day she died. I lived in the same house with Jake and Daisy—and William Hawken—for four weeks. There's no way Billy could have conspired to kill Jake. I'm sorry, sir, but the man I came to know loved Jake. He would've died himself before harming the admiral."

Franklin took a sip of his coffee, studying her with his disconcertingly dark eyes. "The prosecution has witnesses who overheard Admiral Robinson and Lieutenant Hawken arguing this past January," he finally said, "before Hawken left the country for an extensive length of time. Apparently my client…your friend, Billy, and the victim had a rather heated disagreement."

"I just don't see how that could have been," she countered. "Those witnesses had to have been mistaken. In the entire time I lived with Crash—I mean, we didn't *live* together," she corrected herself quickly. "What I meant to say was that during the time that we lived under one roof…" She was blushing now, but she staunchly kept going, "I never heard Lieutenant Hawken raise his voice. Not even once."

"The witnesses claim the two men were arguing over a woman."

"What?" Nell snorted, her embarrassment overridden by her disbelief. "That's impossible. The only woman in both of their lives was Daisy, and she died a few days after Christmas." She leaned forward. "Captain, I want to take the stand—be a character witness, isn't that what it's called?"

"That's what it's called. But when the defendant does something like jump his guards, pick the locks on his chains with the equivalent of a paper clip..." Franklin shook his head. "The man ran away, Miss Burns. If they ever catch him, if we ever *do* go to trial, I'm not sure a character witness is going to do your Billy-boy much good. Because when a man runs, he looks pretty damn guilty in the eyes of a judge and jury."

"He's not running away." There was no doubt about that in Nell's mind. "He went to find the person who's really responsible for Jake's death."

Franklin gazed at her. "Do you know where he is?"

"No. But I don't think they're going to find him until he comes back on his own. And you better believe that when he *does* come back, he's going to have the admiral's *real* killer in tow."

"It is possible that he'll try to contact you?"

Nell wished that he would. She shook her head. "No. He's been pretty adamant about me staying out of this."

Franklin's eyebrows lifted. "And this is what you call staying out of it?"

She didn't answer that.

He was silent for several long moments. "To be honest with you, Miss Burns, in the conversations I've had with Lieutenant Hawken, I didn't get a real strong sense that he cared a whole lot about this hearing. He seemed very...distant and...odd, I guess would be the best word for it. When I asked, he told me he didn't conspire to kill

Admiral Robinson. But the evidence those ballistic reports provides is damning. And I can't help but wonder if perhaps this man didn't suffer some kind of breakdown, or—''

"No," Nell said.

"...post-traumatic stress syndrome, or—"

"No," she said more loudly.

"It's just that he was positively strange."

"That's just his way. When things get hard to deal with, he shuts himself down. He loved Jake," she said again, "and these past few weeks must've been hell for him. To lose a man he loved like a father, and then be accused of killing that man?" Nell held his gaze steadily. "Look, Captain, I've been thinking. Whoever *did* kill Jake knew about his relationship with Billy. They used him to get the assassins into Jake's house. That's the only reason Billy— Crash—was there that night."

Franklin didn't hide his skepticism. "And the ballistic reports are totally wrong...?"

"Yes," Nell agreed. "They're wrong. I think someone made a mistake in the lab. I think the tests should be run again. In fact, as Crash's lawyer, you should *demand* that the guns be tested again."

The captain just looked at her. Then he sighed. "You really don't think Hawken did this, do you?"

"I don't just think it, I *know* it," she said. "Billy did *not* kill Jake."

Franklin sighed again. And then he pulled a notepad and a pen from his inside jacket pocket. He took a business card with his name and phone number on it and slid it across the table toward her. "That's my number," he said. "You better give me yours. Address, too. And spell your last name for me while you're at it."

"Thank you." Nell felt almost weak with relief as she

pocketed his card and gave him all the information he needed.

"Don't thank me yet," he said. "I'll talk to the judge about the possibility of getting those weapons retested. It's a long shot. There's no guarantee the court will foot the bill for that kind of redundant expense."

"I'll pay," she told him. "Tell the judge that I'll pay to have the ballistic tests redone. I don't care what it costs, I'll take care of it."

Captain Franklin closed his pad and slipped it back into his pocket. As he got to his feet, he held out his hand for Nell to shake.

"Thank you, Captain," she said again.

He didn't release her hand right away. "Miss Burns, God forbid I should ever get into the kind of trouble Lieutenant Hawken is in right now, but if I do, I sincerely hope I'd have someone who believed in me the way you believe in him." He smiled. "I can't believe I'm saying this, but he's a lucky man to have a friend like you."

"Please call the judge, Captain," Nell said. "The sooner the better."

Nell couldn't sleep.

It was 2:00 a.m. before she finished writing a grant proposal seeking funds for the theater, but even after she E-mailed a copy of the draft to Amie, she still was far too restless to sleep.

Crash was out there somewhere. For the first night in weeks, Nell didn't know exactly where he was.

She prowled around the kitchen once, opening the refrigerator door but, of course, finding nothing exciting inside. She then pulled on her sneakers and leather jacket. Dunkin' Donuts was calling. Five blocks away, there was a very exciting honey-dipped donut with her name on it.

Nell turned out the light and locked the door, ready to walk, but the air was so sharply cold, she hurried to her car instead. There had been a real cold spell like this last December, too, she remembered. It had even snowed. Crash had forced her to go sledding and...

And he hadn't kissed her. Yeah, that had been just another of the many, *many* nights that he *hadn't* kissed her.

She pulled out from the curb, gunning the engine, hoping her car would warm up soon so she could turn on the heat.

That lawyer, Captain Franklin, had been really impressed by her loyalty to Crash. But the truth was, she was an idiot. She was a certified fool.

There was nothing, *nothing* that bound the two of them together, except for her own, misguided wishful thinking.

Nearly a year ago, she'd had sex with the man. That's all it had been. Sex. Period, the end. All the intensity and seemingly high emotions of the moment had nothing to do with his feelings for her. All the emotion of that night had been about Daisy's death. When Crash had kissed her so fiercely, when he'd driven himself hard inside her, it wasn't because he wanted to join himself emotionally with Nell. No, what they'd done had been purely physical. He'd been using sex as a release for his pain and anger. He'd been taking temporary comfort in surrounding himself with her warm body. She could have been any warm body, any nameless, faceless woman. Her identity truly hadn't mattered.

The stupid thing was, Nell had been more hurt by the fact that Crash had ended their friendship than by his honest admission that the sex had been nothing more than sex.

She'd written him letters. She'd been brutally honest, too, telling him that she hoped that what had happened between them wouldn't affect their friendship. She'd asked him to call her when he was in town.

He hadn't called.

And he hadn't written.

And if this mess hadn't happened, Nell knew that she never would have so much as *seen* Crash Hawken again.

As she approached, she saw that the orange-lettered Dunkin' Donuts sign was dark. The all-night shop was inexplicably closed, and Nell said all of the absolutely worst bad words that she knew. She even said some of them twice. And then she kept driving. Somewhere in the District of Columbia there was a donut shop that was open right now, and dammit, she was going to find it.

Nell took a right turn, suddenly aware that she was driving the still-familiar route from the city to the Robinson farm.

She knew for a fact that there were no donut shops between here and there, but she kept going, pulled in that direction.

The interstate was empty except for a few truckers.

She kept the radio off during the twenty-minute drive, waiting for the hum of the tires to lull her into a state of fatigue.

It didn't happen. When she pulled off at the exit for the farm, she was as wide awake as ever.

It was more than six months since she'd come out here to pick up a painting of Daisy's that Jake had wanted her to have for the new house. It had been summer then, but now the trees were bare, their branches reaching up toward the sky like skinny arms with clawed hands, tormented by the cold wind.

God, she hated winter. Why on earth had she bought a house here in D.C., rather than down in Florida? What had she been thinking?

She hadn't *really* been thinking that sooner or later Crash would come back and knock on her door. She hadn't actually believed that he'd just appear in her bedroom one night, although for a while, she'd gotten a lot of mileage out of *that* fantasy.

No, he'd made it more than clear that he didn't want her. And she wasn't the type to face that kind of rejection more than once.

But despite the fact that he clearly felt otherwise, she was still his friend. She had been his friend before that one night they'd slept together. And she could be a grown-up about the whole thing, and still be his friend.

But not if he didn't want to be hers.

Slowing to a stop as she finally approached the gates of the farm, her eyes filled with tears.

The Robinsons' farm had always buzzed with life. Even in the dead of night, there had been an intensity about the place—the lights were always on, there was a sense of someone being home.

But now the place was deserted. The dark windows of the house looked mournfully empty. Sagging yellow police tape flapped pathetically in the wind.

And there already was a For Sale sign on the gate.

Her first reaction was outrage. Jake had been dead less than two weeks, and already someone was selling off his beloved farm.

But then reality crept in.

The farm meant nothing to Jake now. Whichever of his distant relatives who'd inherited the place obviously realized that holding on to the property wouldn't do anyone any good. It wouldn't bring Jake back from wherever he'd gone—that was for sure.

Wherever he'd gone…

Wherever he was, she hoped he'd found Daisy again.

When Nell closed her eyes, she could picture Jake dancing with Daisy. The image was so clear, so real. In her mind's eye, they were both alive, vibrant and laughing.

It was bitterly ironic. Even as ghosts Jake and Daisy were more alive than either Nell or Crash.

The two who had survived were the ones who wouldn't let themselves live. They were quite a pair—one who willingly deadened himself by stepping back from his emotions, and one who was too afraid to live life to its fullest.

Except Nell wasn't afraid anymore.

She'd stopped being afraid on the night she'd found out Jake had died, but Crash was still alive. He was still alive, and dammit, she was going to be his friend, whether he liked it or not.

He was still alive, and she was going to fight for him. She was going to do whatever she had to in order to tell the entire world that he was an innocent man, that he'd been falsely accused.

In fact, she was going to go home and first thing in the morning, she was going to call every single reporter and news contact that she had in her media file. She was going to hold a press conference.

And she was going to make *damn* sure those ballistic tests were redone.

Hell, she was even feeling brave enough to ski down Mount Washington with a banner proclaiming Crash's innocence if that would help.

Nell turned her car around and headed for home.

It was 4:00 a.m., but there was a traffic jam on Nell's street.

There was a traffic jam totally blocking the road, caused by four different fire trucks and three TV-news vans.

And they were blocking the road because Nell's house was on fire.

Her *house* was on *fire*.

She didn't bother to park. She just turned off the engine right there in the middle of the road and got out of her car.

She could feel the heat of the blaze from where she was standing. She could see flames licking out every single window.

"You better move that car!" one of the firemen shouted to her.

"I can't," she said dazedly. "My garage is on fire."

"Are you the owner?"

She nodded. She was the owner—but what she owned was going to be little more than a charred pile of ashes before this was over.

"Hey, Ted, we found the lady who lives here!"

Another, shorter man approached. His hat identified him as the fire chief. "Is there anyone else inside?" he asked.

Nell shook her head, staring at the flames. "No."

"Thank God." He raised his voice. "There's no one inside. Everyone get out of there, pronto!"

"How could this have happened?"

"It's probably an electrical fire," the chief told her. "It probably started small, but an old place like this'll go up like a tinderbox, especially this time of year. We'll have a better idea of how it started after it's out and we can go in and look around. Whatever the case, you're lucky you weren't home, or we'd probably be pulling your body out of there right now."

She was lucky.

She was *incredibly* lucky. Nell couldn't remember the last time she'd not only been awake this late, but had left the house as well. She was *damned* lucky.

She tried very hard to feel lucky as she stood in the early morning darkness and watched everything she owned but her car and the clothes on her back go up in smoke. There were things that were burning right now that couldn't be replaced. Photographs. She'd had a really great photo of her and Crash and Jake that Daisy had taken. All of her books and CDs, the dishes her grandmother had given her, Daisy's irreplaceable watercolor painting. It was all gone. She'd been out of the house for only two hours, and just like that, nearly everything she'd cherished was gone.

Tears filled her eyes, and she fought them. She *was* lucky, dammit. She could have died.

It was dawn before the fire was down to a smolder, mid-morning before the insurance forms were filled out and the paperwork was filed.

Nell drove to the Ritz-Carlton—one of the fanciest hotels in town—and checked herself into a very expensive room. She deserved it.

She was exhausted, but she took the time to call Captain Franklin's office, leaving the hotel phone number with the lawyer's administrative staff, with a message asking him to call if he heard any news of Crash's whereabouts.

Tired to the bone, Nell peeled off her clothes, climbed into bed and fell almost instantly into a deep, dreamless sleep.

Chapter 11

The curtains were hanging open an inch or two, and Crash quietly slid them all the way closed.

They were effective in shutting out the last streaks of light in the late afternoon sky. He moved silently through the now complete darkness of the room, toward the bathroom that was next to the door.

He closed the bathroom door all but an inch, and turned on the bathroom light.

It was dim, but no longer pitch-black. He went back into the other room. Yeah, it was bright enough for him to be able to see Nell's face as she slept.

She was curled up in the middle of the hotel room's king-size bed. The blankets covered all but her face and the very top of her head. She slept fiercely, eyes tightly shut.

Crash stood for a moment, just watching her, wishing he didn't have to disturb her, wishing for things he couldn't have. But there was no time now to let her sleep, and there'd never been time for the other things he wanted.

"Nell," he said quietly.

She didn't move.

He nudged the bed with his leg. "Nell, I'm sorry, but you've got to wake up."

Nothing.

He sat down on the bed, leaning over to gently shake her shoulder. "Nell."

Her eyes opened and widened in fear.

Crash knew at that moment that he'd made a mistake. With the bathroom light shining dimly behind him, she couldn't see his face. All she could see was a big, dark figure looming menacingly over her.

She took a deep breath to scream, and he quickly put his hand over her mouth. "Nell, shhh! It's me. Crash. *Billy.*"

She sat up, shaking herself free from his hand, all but launching herself into his arms. "Billy! God! You scared me to death! Thank God you're all right!" She pulled back to look at him in the darkness. "*Are* you all right?"

She smelled so good. Crash wanted nothing more than to bury his face in her hair and just sit on that bed with his arms around her. But that wasn't why he'd come.

And after that one initial hug, Nell seemed as eager as he was to put distance between them.

She let go of him quickly when he released her, wrapping her arms around her knees as he stood up. "I can't believe you came here. How did you find me?"

Her low, husky voice was so familiar, so warm. God, how he'd missed her. He had to keep distance between them, or he was going to be tempted to do something that he'd later regret.

Again.

Crash turned on the desk lamp. "It wasn't that hard."

"My house burned down last night. I went out for a doughnut, and when I came back, my house was on fire."

"I know." When he'd seen the picture in the newspaper and realized it was Nell's house that had burned, his heart had stopped beating. And when he'd read that no one had been killed or injured, he'd gotten dizzy with relief.

And even though he'd had plenty of other things to do in his quest to find the man responsible for Jake's death, Crash had spent the entire afternoon tracking Nell down. There was no way, no *way* he was going to let her die, too.

She ran one hand back through her hair as if she was suddenly conscious of the fact that it was rumpled from sleep. And she pulled the blanket up a little higher around her neck.

Crash saw that her jeans and shirt were in a pile on the floor. Under those covers she was wearing only her underwear. Or less. He had to turn away from her. He couldn't let his thoughts move in that direction.

"I can't believe you came to me for help," she said quietly.

He couldn't keep himself from turning back to look at her. Was that really what she thought? That he'd come here because he wanted or needed her help?

"I spoke to your lawyer about having the ballistic tests repeated," Nell told him.

She looked far too good in the soft, romantic light, sitting there, possibly naked beneath the covers of an Olympic-event-sized bed. Crash turned on another lamp, and then another, trying to make the room as glaringly bright as possible. "So that's what it was."

She squinted slightly in the brightness. "That's what *what* was?"

"That's why they tried to kill you."

She stared at him. "Excuse me?"

He couldn't keep himself from pacing. "You don't really think that fire was an accident, do you?"

"According to the experts in the fire department, it was an electrical malfunction. The wiring was ancient, there was a power surge and—"

"Nell, someone tried to kill you. That's why I'm here. To make sure that when they try again, they don't succeed."

She was so completely blown away she almost dropped the blanket. "Billy! God! Who would want to kill *me?*"

"Probably the same person who killed Jake and framed me," Crash told her. "Did you tell anyone you were coming to this hotel?"

Nell shook her head. "No. Wait. Yes. I called your lawyer and left this phone number in case he needed to get in touch with me."

He swore softly and Nell realized how infrequently she'd heard him use that kind of language. Even words like *damn* or *hell*—they just weren't part of his normal working vocabulary.

He picked up her clothes and put them next to her on the bed. "I'll go into the bathroom while you get dressed. And then we have to get out of here. Fast."

Nell quickly pulled on her shirt and slipped into her jeans before he'd even closed the bathroom door. "Billy, wait! You honestly think that whoever killed Jake is somehow privileged to your Navy lawyer's phone messages? Doesn't that sound just a *little* paranoid...?"

He pulled open the bathroom door and looked at her. He was dressed entirely in black. Black fatigues, black boots, black turtleneck, black winter jacket. Underneath the jacket he was wearing what looked to be some kind of equipment vest—also black. His preference for wearing black had nothing to do with fashion, she realized. He was dressed to blend with the shadows of the night.

"Here's what we know about the man we're after,"

Crash told her. "We believe him to be a U.S. Navy commander with a lot of connections. Whether he's that or not, we *do* know for certain that... *We*. God, listen to me." His voice shook. "I'm talking as if Jake is still alive."

He swiftly turned away from her, and for a minute Nell was certain that he was going to put his fist through the bathroom door. Instead he stopped himself, and slowly, carefully laid the palm of his hand against the wood instead. He took a deep breath, and when he spoke again, his voice was steady.

"*I* know for sure that this son of a bitch has got something to hide, something he was afraid Jake was about to uncover. And that something—whatever it is—is *so* important to him, he'd risk his eternal soul to keep it secret. He had Jake killed, and set me up to take the fall. Whoever he is, he's powerful enough to falsify the results of those ballistic tests and believe me, that couldn't have been easy to do." Crash turned to face her. "Since he's already killed once, I wouldn't put it past him to decide that it'd be easier to kill you than to do whatever he'd had to do to fake those test results all over again. So, yes, it sounds paranoid, but I can't assume that someone that powerful *won't* have access to the information coming into and out of Captain Franklin's law office."

His hair was pulled back into a ponytail, and the severe style emphasized his high cheekbones, making his face look starkly handsome. And his eyes... The burning intensity in those eyes had haunted her dreams.

"Come on, Nell," he said softly as her silence stretched on. "Don't quit believing in me now."

As crazy as his theory was, it was clear that *he* believed it.

"You didn't come here to ask me to help you," Nell realized. "You came because you think *I* need *your* help."

He didn't answer. He didn't have to answer.

"What if I said I didn't want your help?" she asked.

It was clear from the look on his face that he knew where she was going. She was revisiting the words he'd said to her. "This is different."

"No, it's not. We both think the other needs saving." Nell crossed her arms. "You want to save me? You better be ready to let me help save you."

"Maybe we can argue about this in the car."

She nodded, feeling lighter in spirit than she had in a long time. He may not have written. He may not have called. But he'd put in an appearance when he thought her life was in danger. Despite everything he'd said and done, he cared—he was still her friend.

Friend, she repeated to herself firmly. He'd jumped back as if her touch had burned him. It was clear that he had no intention of letting their relationship move past the friendship stage ever again. And that was good because she felt that way, too. She had absolutely no intention of making the same mistake twice.

"I'll put on my boots, and we can go." She turned back to look at him. "Do we have a destination in mind?"

"I'll tell you in the car."

A loud knock sounded on the hotel-room door, and Nell jumped. She hadn't seen Crash move, but suddenly he had a gun in his hand. He motioned for her to be silent, and to back away from the door.

Whoever was out there knocked again. "Room service. I have complimentary hors d'oeuvres and a bottle of non-alcoholic Chablis for Ms. Burns."

Crash moved back toward her and spoke almost silently into her ear.

"Tell him to leave it outside the door. Tell him you're

just about to take a shower. Then get under the bed, do you understand?''

She nodded, unable to pull her eyes away from his gun. It was enormous and deadly-looking. This was the closest she'd ever come to that kind of weapon. And it was amazing in more than one way—despite the fact that Crash was the subject of the biggest manhunt of the decade, he'd somehow managed to arm himself.

He was holding her arm, and he gave her a quick squeeze before he released her. He moved quickly around the room, turning off all the lights that he'd turned on earlier.

Nell cleared her throat, raising her voice so that the person on the other side of the door could hear her. ''I'm sorry, you caught me at a bad time. I'm just about to step into the shower. Can you leave it outside the door?''

''Will do,'' the voice cheerfully replied. ''Have a good evening.''

Crash motioned for her to move. As she slid underneath the bed, she saw him go to into the bathroom and heard the sound of the shower going on.

It all seemed kind of silly. The person who'd knocked on the door was probably a room-service waiter, just as he'd said.

She lifted the dust ruffle and saw Crash come back out of the bathroom. *He* sure didn't seem to think it was at all silly. He stood in the shadows, out of sight of the door, his gun held at the ready. Holding the gun that way, with his mouth set in equally grim resolve, he looked incredibly dangerous.

Crash had told her once that she didn't really know him, that he had only let her see a small, very whitewashed part of him.

Nell had a feeling that if she was wrong and there really was someone outside her door who wanted to hurt her, in the next few minutes she was going to get a good look at the other side of Crash. She was going to see the Navy SEAL in action.

And then she saw the door to her room open. The sound of the bolt being drawn back was drowned out by the noise from the shower. The bathroom door was ajar, and in the light that came through it, she saw a man come into the room.

He wasn't carrying a plate of cheese or a bottle of wine. Instead, he held a gun like Crash's.

Nell's heart was pounding. Crash had been right. This man *had* come here to kill her.

The intruder gently closed the door behind him, careful not to make any noise.

He was smaller than Crash, more wiry than Crash, and he had less hair on the top of his head than Crash.

But his gun looked just as deadly.

As Nell watched, he pushed open the bathroom door.

That was when Crash moved. One moment he was in the shadows, and the next he was almost on top of the man, his gun pressed against the back of his head. Even his voice sounded different—harsher, rougher. "Drop it."

The man froze but only for a second.

Crash knew when the man didn't instantly drop his weapon that this guy was not going to go down easily. The gunman's hesitation only lasted a fraction of a second, but it was enough for Crash to anticipate his next move.

He was, rightly, calling Crash's bluff. It didn't take the brain of a rocket scientist to figure out that, at this point, this gunman was the only potential link Crash had to the mysterious commander. The only real reason Crash had to shoot this man was to protect Nell.

The gunman, on the other hand, had no reason whatso-ever not to shoot Crash.

But Crash was a nanosecond ahead of him. He hit the man hard on the side of the head with the barrel of his weapon, even as he disarmed him with a well-placed kick.

The man's handgun hit the door frame and bounced back, skittering across the rug and into the center of the room.

The blow to the head that Crash had delivered would have taken damn near anyone else in the world down, and down hard, but this guy wasn't about to call it a day.

Pain exploded as the gunman smashed his fist back into Crash's face and elbowed him hard in the ribs. The man tucked his chin against his chest, bending over in an attempt to throw the SEAL over his shoulder. But pain or no pain, Crash anticipated that move, too, and instead, the gunman hit the floor.

But he went down willingly, diving out into the room, going for his weapon.

The gun wasn't there.

Crash silently blessed Nell as he leapt on top of the man. The bastard fought as if he was possessed by the devil, but Crash would have taken on Satan himself in order to keep Nell safe. He hit the man again and again and again until finally, *finally* he delivered a knockout punch and the son of a bitch sagged.

Searching the gunman quickly, Crash came up with a smaller automatic and a large combat knife. Both weapons had been securely holstered and—luckily for him—totally unreachable during the fight.

He looked up to see Nell peeking out from underneath the bed.

"Are you all right?" she asked, her eyes wide. "Oh, God, you're bleeding."

His cheek had been cut by the fancy ring the gunman wore on his pinky finger. Crash used the back of his hand to blot it. "I'm fine," he said. A little scrape like that didn't matter. Nor was the bruise he was going to get along his ribs even worth mentioning.

He'd hurt when he laughed for the next few days.

But since he couldn't remember the last time he'd laughed, he didn't think that would be much of a problem.

Crash pulled the man's wallet from the back pocket of his pants. There was a driver's license inside, along with several suspiciously new-looking credit cards. There were no papers, no receipts, no photos of child or wife, no little scraps of life.

"Who is he?"

"He's currently going by the name Sheldon Sarkowski," he told her. "But that's not his real name."

"It's not?" She began inching out from her hiding place, gingerly pushing Sheldon's handgun in front of her.

"Nope. He's a pro. He probably doesn't even remember his real name anymore." Crash took the weapon, pulled out the clip and stored both pieces in his vest, along with the other weapons he'd taken from the gunman.

"What are we going to do with him?"

"We're going to tie him up and take him with us. I have a question or two to ask him when he wakes up."

Nell had climbed to her feet, but then backed up so that she was sitting on the edge of the bed. She was so pale, she looked almost gray.

"Are *you* all right?" he asked. "We've got to get out of here right now before this guy's backup comes to see what's taking him so long. Are you going to be able to walk?"

"Yeah, I'm just…getting used to the idea that someone named Sheldon came in here to kill me."

Crash stood up. "I'm not going to let anyone hurt you, Nell. I swear, I'll keep you safe if it's the last thing I do."

Nell gazed up at him. "I believe you," she told him.

Chapter 12

"What exactly are we going to do with the guy in the trunk?" Nell laughed in disbelief as she turned slightly in her seat to face Crash. "I can't believe I just said that. I can't believe we've actually *got* a guy in the trunk. Isn't that very uncomfortable for him?"

Crash glanced at her. "That's his tough luck. He should've thought of that before he broke into your hotel room to kill you."

"Good point." Nell was silent for a moment, staring out the windshield at the stars. She looked over at Crash again. "So where *are* we going?"

"To California."

"By *car?*"

He glanced at her again. "They'll be looking for me at all the airports."

"Of course. I'm sorry. I…" Nell shook her head. "How long is it going to take us to get there?"

"Depends on how many times we stop to sleep. We've got to stop at least once so that I can question Sarkowski."

At *least* once. He wasn't kidding. They were going to drive all the way from the District of Columbia to California and they were quite possibly going to stop to sleep only once.

The car was luxurious. It was compact, but the seats were covered with soft leather that would be comfortable for sleeping.

The back seat was big enough for her to curl up on. Currently, it was covered by several gym bags, a suitcase and what looked to be a laptop computer case.

"Where did you get all this stuff?" she asked. "This car?"

"The car belongs to a Navy officer who's doing a six month tour on an aircraft carrier. I liberated it from storage. Same with the gear."

Liberated was just a fancy word for stole.

"I have every intention of returning everything," he told her, as if he knew what she was thinking. "Except maybe the bullets and some of the explosives."

Explosives? Bullets? Nell changed the subject.

"So what's in California?" she asked. "And where in California are we going? It's a pretty big state."

He gave her another glance before turning his attention back to the road. He turned on the radio to a classic rock station, adjusting the controls so that the signal only went to the speakers in the back. "In case Sarkowski wakes up," he explained. "I don't want him to bored."

What he *really* didn't want was for the man who was tied up in the trunk to regain consciousness and overhear their conversation.

Nell waited for him to answer her question, but one mile rolled by and then two, and he still didn't speak.

"Oh, please," she said, exasperated. "We're not going

to play this game again, are we? I ask you a question and you don't answer it. Can't you do something different for a change? Like tell me the truth about what's going on?''

It was starting to rain, and Crash put on the windshield wipers. He glanced at her again, but he didn't say a word.

"Because if we're going to play that old, dull game," Nell continued, "you'd better get off at the next exit. In fact, if you don't tell me everything, and I mean *everything,* starting from what happened at Jake's house, you can just pull over and let me out right now."

"I'm sorry," Crash said quietly. "I wasn't purposely not answering you. I was just thinking that..." He hesitated.

"Your apology will go a whole lot further if you actually finish that sentence."

"I was thinking that as a SEAL, I can't talk about any of this." He glanced at her again. His eyes looked almost silver in the darkness, his face shadowed and mysterious. "But I'm not a SEAL anymore."

Crash had been stripped of his commission, his pride, his very soul. There was a very strong chance that he was going to lose his life as well, finding and taking down the mysterious commander.

The truth was, he was prepared to die, if necessary. Most of what he'd already lost was more valuable to him than his life.

But if he *was* going to die, he wanted someone to know the whole story. He wanted someone to know what had *really* happened.

And he knew he could trust Nell.

"You already know that I do—did—special assignments for Jake," he said.

"Yeah." Nell nodded. "But I'm not really sure what that entailed."

"Jake would send me a coded file, usually electronically.

These files were specially programmed so they couldn't be copied, and they were designed to self-delete after a very short time, so there'd be no information trail.''

Crash could feel her watching him. She was all but holding her breath, waiting for him to continue. With the exception of that one time he'd told her the story of how Daisy had pulled him out of summer camp, he knew she'd never heard him string together so many sentences.

''The file would contain information about a situation that needed checking into, or correcting or…some other type of…revision, shall we say,'' he continued. ''It would include a mission objective as well as recommended courses of action. Sometimes the objective was simply to gather more information. Sometimes it was more… complicated. But when I was out in the real world, working the op, my team and I—and Jake usually only assigned two or three other SEALs to work with me—we were on our own.

''Anyway, Jake sent me an encoded file on the morning he was shot. I had just flown in to D.C. from California that same day. I was coming home after spending nearly six straight months out of the country. Usually the first thing I do when I get stateside is take a few days of leave— get a haircut and go out to the farm to see Jake and Daisy.'' He caught himself and shook his head. ''Just Jake, now. But when I arrived at the base, Captain Lovett called me into his office and told me that he was organizing a special team. He said he'd received orders to go out to the farm and provide additional security. He said the admiral had been receiving death threats. And he asked if I wanted to be part of this special security team.''

''Of course you said yes.''

Crash nodded. ''I tried calling the farm as soon as I left Lovett's office, but I couldn't get through. And then I didn't have time to do much more than organize my gear before I had to meet Lovett and the other members of the team.''

It had been lightly raining that night, too.

He glanced at Nell and cleared his throat. "When I got to the chopper—our means of transport out to the farm—there were three men there I'd never seen before. I was tired. I hadn't slept in a full forty-eight hours, so I passed my suspicions off as fatigue-induced paranoia. Lovett knew these men, and he seemed to know them well. I figured everything was kosher.'' He paused. "I figured wrong.''

"When we got to the farm, Jake seemed really surprised to see us, like no one had told him a SEAL Team would be coming out,'' Crash continued. "That should have clinched it for me. I should have known then that something was off.'' He clenched his teeth. "But I didn't, and Jake died. But before he died, he told me about the file he'd sent.'' He turned to glance at Nell. "He believed that he was shot in an attempt to cover up the information he'd sent me in that file—that to keep his investigation from going any further, someone had set up this hit.''

Nell nodded slowly. "And you think he was right, don't you?''

"Yeah.'' The rain was turning slushy and thick against the windshield. The night was getting cold, but it was nice and warm inside the car.

Too warm.

He glanced at Nell again. The way she was sitting, turned slightly toward him, her knee was only an inch and a half away from his thigh. Because of the car's compact design, she was sitting close enough to touch. She was close enough so that even if he'd wanted to, he couldn't have avoided breathing in her sweet perfume. He looked at the odometer. They'd only traveled forty-seven miles. Two thousand six hundred and fifty-three to go.

Crash stared at the road, trying to clear his mind, to desensitize himself to the scent of her perfume and the sound of her voice. He tried to focus on the feel of the leather-covered steering wheel beneath his hands, but all he could think about was the soft down that grew at the nape of her neck, and the silky smoothness of her bare back. Her skin was impossibly soft, like a baby's.

He'd let himself touch her, that night she'd spent in his room. After she'd fallen asleep, he'd allowed himself the luxury of running his fingers across her shoulders, down her back and along her arm until he, too, had fallen into a deep sleep.

He forced the image away. This was *not* the time to be thinking of Nell that way—at the beginning of a 2700-mile journey, at the start of a mission that in all likelihood was not going to end well.

"Can you tell me what was in the file Jake sent you?" she asked softly.

Crash kept his eyes on the road. "No, but I'm going to tell you anyway."

"You…are." Nell couldn't believe what she was hearing. He was going to tell her top-secret, classified information.

"The mission objective was investigation. Jake believed there was a cover-up going on—that someone had screwed up bad during a SEAL training operation that took place six months ago.

"See, there's a small island nation in Southeast Asia," Crash told her, "that for the past forty years has been one of the major ports for illegal drug trafficking. When the United States began actively trying to cut off drug dealers closer to their source, we worked to establish an alliance with this island's government.

"Right up until recently," he continued, "we'd managed

to build a foundation for a relationship that would be good for both countries.''

Nell leaned back against the headrest, watching Crash as he drove. He was a good driver, always checking the mirrors, holding the wheel with both hands. She felt safe sitting next to him, despite the fact that he was number one on FInCOM's most-wanted, armed-and-dangerous list.

''But then, about six months ago, I was part of a team that intended to use this island as a training site. I'd hooked up with some SEALs from Team Ten's elite Alpha Squad, and we took four FInCOM agents to this island on a training mission to show them how we can kick ass in a potential terrorists-with-hostage situation. We were going to execute a rescue op, going up against some Jarheads on the island, who were going to play the part of the tangos.''

''Whoa,'' Nell said. ''Back up a sec. You lost me. *Jarheads* and *tangos?*''

''I'm sorry. Jarheads are marines—the nickname comes from their haircut. And tango's radio talk for the letter *T*, which is short for terrorists.''

''Got it. Go on,'' she ordered him.

''When we inserted onto the island, we found ourselves jammed in the middle of one of the biggest training op snafus I've ever dealt with. See, as we approached the site where the simulated rescue mission was to take place, we found two KIAs.'' He interpreted before she could even ask. ''We found the bodies of two of our marine friends—killed in action.''

''My God.'' Nell sat up, transfixed by his story. ''What happened?''

He glanced at her. ''Apparently a firefight had broken out between the two major drug lords on the island between the time we left our ship and the time we hit the training site.''

"Firefight. You mean, a gun battle between the two gangs, right?"

"Yeah," Crash told her, "but I wouldn't call them *gangs*. Both the drug lords had private armies with state-of-the-art technology. We're talking thousands of men and name-brand firepower. These armies were more powerful than the government's own armed forces. What started that day was more like a full-scale civil war." He glanced at her. "The average yearly income of the men who owned these armies was higher than the entire GNP of this country. One of 'em was an American expatriate named John Sherman—a former Green Beret, which really pissed off the Jarheads. The other was a local man named Kim, nicknamed 'the Korean,' because his father was from there.

"Sherman and Kim had been careful not to go into each other's territory for years, and more than once, they'd helped each other out. But on that day, whatever agreement Sherman and Kim had between them disintegrated. And when they clashed, lots of innocent people were caught in the crossfire."

He took a deep breath. "It wasn't easy, but we finally got all of Alpha Squad and the surviving marines off the island. But the fighting went on for days after that. When the smoke cleared, the body count was in the tens of thousands, and property damage was in the millions. The only good thing that came of it was that both Sherman and Kim were killed, too."

He was silent for a minute, and the sound of the windshield wipers beat a rhythm that wasn't in sync with the Christmas pop song playing on the radio. "Rocking Around the Christmas Tree."

"I don't get it," Nell finally said. "You said there was some kind of cover-up. What was there to cover up?"

"The file Jake sent me contained a copy of a secret deposition taken from Kim's widow," Crash told her. "She claimed to have overheard a conversation in which an American Naval commander supposedly approached Kim and told him that the Americans would look the other way when he did business, on the condition that Kim use his army to destroy John Sherman and his troops. There's no single officer in the entire U.S. Navy—admirals included—who has authority to make this kind of bogus deal, but apparently Kim didn't know that. The deal was done and the Korean began planning a surprise attack on Sherman's stronghold.

"But news of the so-called agreement and the impending attack was leaked—for all we know, Kim's wife sold him out—and Sherman struck first. It was during this initial attack that our marines were targeted, too, and two of them were killed."

Crash glanced at Nell. Her face was only dimly illuminated by the greenish dashboard light, but he could see that she was hanging onto his every word, her eyes wide.

It was clear that she trusted him. She believed every word that fell from his lips. Even now, after the way he'd abused her friendship—all those letters he never answered, all those times he'd kept himself from calling—she had total faith in him. Something inside him tightened and twisted, and he knew with a sickening certainty that he'd let far more than he'd ever dreamed possible walk out of his room when Nell had left that morning, nearly an entire year ago.

And now it was too late.

He held the steering wheel tightly, telling himself that he'd been right to let her go. He'd been home all of five weeks in the past twelve months. Of course, he'd volunteered for every overseas assignment he could get his hands on. If he'd wanted to, he could have spent most of that time in the States.

But still, what he felt, what he wanted, shouldn't really matter.

The truth was exactly the same now as it had been a year ago. Nell deserved better than he could give her. Of course, in Crash's opinion, she deserved better than Dexter Lancaster, too, but even the lawyer won points simply for being available.

"Hey," Nell said. "Are you going to tell me the rest of this story, or do I have to figure out where to drop the quarter in to get you talking again?"

Crash glanced at her. "Sorry. I was—"

"Thinking," she finished for him. "I know. Trying to figure out how to track down this commander, right?"

"Something like that."

"Are you sure it's not just a rumor? You know, things go bad, and everybody tries to figure out who's to blame."

"In the aftermath, there were tons of rumors," he admitted. "There were people who believed that the U.S. *did* make a deal with Kim. There were people who believed that rumors of the agreement between Kim and the United States were falsely planted *by* the U.S. to cause Kim and Sherman to wipe each other out. But none of that was true. I'm very familiar with the policies used in dealing with this island, and I know we stood to gain far more by playing by the rules.

"If this commander really *did* make a deal with Kim, and I believe he did, he's responsible for starting a war. Thousands of innocent civilians were killed. Not to mention the fact that our alliance with this country has totally crumbled—all of their trust in us is gone. All the work we'd done to maintain goodwill and cooperation in stopping the drug traffic closer to its source was for nothing. The entire program's been set back a good twenty years."

"But if you don't know who the commander is," Nell said. "How are you going to find him? There must be *thousands* of commanders in the U.S. Navy. Kim's wife didn't know his name? Not even his first name? A nickname?"

Crash shook his head. "No."

"Can she describe him?" Nell asked. "Maybe make some kind of police composite sketch?"

He glanced at her again. "She's disappeared."

"And Jake really seemed to think she was telling the truth, huh?" Nell asked.

"He told me," Crash said. He had to stop and clear his throat. "After he was shot, he was still conscious for a while, and he told me that whoever this commander was, he had to be behind the shooting. I believe that, too. This son of a bitch killed Jake and framed me. And now he's trying to kill you, too."

Nell was silent, her eyes narrowed slightly as she stared out at the mixture of sleet and snow falling on the windshield. "What was his motive?" she finally asked. "This commander. What did he stand to gain by starting this civil war between Kim and what's-his-name?"

"John Sherman," Crash supplied the name. "I've been running that same question through my mind ever since I read the file. It's entirely possible that things went as wrong for the commander as they went for the rest of us. And in that case, his intent probably *wasn't* to start a civil war." He glanced at her. "I have a theory."

"Spill."

He looked at her again. Yes, that was kind of what it felt like. After so many years of silence, everything inside of him was in danger of spilling out.

"My theory is that the commander's motive was exactly what he'd told Kim. He wanted John Sherman dead. My theory is that this commander didn't give a damn about the drugs or the armies. My theory is that it was personal."

"Personal?"

"A man like Sherman's got to have lots of enemies. Over in Vietnam, his unit specialized in liberating large shipments of drugs and confiscating stashes of weapons. He spent quite a few years taking half of everything he liberated for himself—and turning around and selling it back to the highest bidder. It didn't matter that he was selling it to the enemy. Word got out that he was doing this, but before he was arrested he went AWOL."

"And you think, what? This commander was getting back at him for having gotten away?"

"I think it's possible that our commander served with Sherman in 'Nam. In fact, I've gained Internet access to some Navy personnel files, and I've hit on a list of three names—two commanders and one recently promoted rear admiral. They all served in Vietnam at the same time as Sherman. And they're all still on the active-duty list. I sent them vaguely threatening E-mail messages—you know, 'I know who you are. I know what you did.' But so far none of them have responded. I didn't really expect them to—it was kind of a long shot." He shook his head.

"Think about all the people we called last year, about Daisy and Jake's wedding," Nell said. "It seemed like every other man was Colonel This or Captain That. The guy you're looking for could have been retired for years and still be addressed as 'Commander.'"

"I know. And the list of *retired* Navy commanders who served in 'Nam when Sherman did is probably ten pages long." He looked over at Nell and smiled grimly. "If I want to find this bastard—and I do—my best bet is to try to shake some information loose from our friend who's napping in the trunk. But first I'm going to get you to a safe place.''

"Excuse me?'' She was giving him her best are-you-kidding? look, brows elevated and eyes opened wide. ''I thought we'd decided that help was a two-way street—that I'd let you help me, on the condition that you let me help *you*.''

"There's nothing you can do to help me.''

"Want to bet? I have an idea how I can help you get that information you need from our dear friend Sheldon. Without me, it'll be much harder. I may not be enough of an actress to win an Oscar, but I'm good enough to pull *this* off. We just need to stop at a convenience store and—''

"Nell, I don't want your help.'' Despite everything that Crash had told her, there was still so much that he hadn't said—so much that hadn't spilled out. He hadn't told her how sitting so close to her in this car was slowly driving him crazy from wanting to touch her. He hadn't told her about the sheer terror he'd felt when he picked up that newspaper and saw the picture of Nell's house engulfed in flames. He wasn't going to tell her about the way he'd stood in that hotel room and watched her as she'd slept, feeling a possessiveness he knew he had no right to feel, feeling an ache of longing and desire and need that he recognized as being something he had to push far, far away.

Separate, distance, disengage.

No, he didn't want any help from Nell.

"Maybe you don't want my help,'' she said quietly. "Maybe you don't even need it. But this guy in the trunk came to kill *me*. I'm involved in this, Billy, as much as you are. At least hear me out.''

Chapter 13

Nell was too nervous to eat. She tossed her half-eaten slice of pizza back into the box and watched as Crash unzipped one of the gym bags he'd brought in from the car.

"Here's what we're going to do," he said in his deceptively soft voice, as he reached inside and pulled out a cylindrical tube that he screwed onto the barrel of his *Dirty Harry*-sized handgun. "I'm going to ask you some questions, you're going to answer them and no one's going to get hurt."

Sheldon Sarkowski's left eye was swollen shut and his lip was puffy and still bleeding slightly. He'd still been out cold when Crash had stopped along a deserted stretch of road and pulled him from the trunk and into the back seat. Sheldon's hands had been cuffed and his feet tied, but Crash had covered both rope and handcuffs with a blanket as he'd then carried the smaller man into the cheap motel room they'd rented for the night.

There were only two or three other cars in the entire

parking lot—none of them within shouting distance of their drafty room.

And that was good—in case there was going to be shouting. And Nell suspected that there *was* going to be some shouting. Not that Crash would be doing it. She'd never heard him raise his voice to anything louder than mezzo piano.

Crash had managed to rouse Sheldon once inside the room. An ice bucket full of cold water in the face had done the trick. The man now sat, sputtering and belligerent, tied very securely to a chair.

The gunman clearly wasn't in a position of power, yet he still managed to laugh derisively at both Crash and the gun. "I'll tell you right now, I'm not saying anything. So what are you going to do, kill me?"

Crash sat down on the bed, directly across from him, his gun held loosely on his lap. "Damn, Sheldon," he said. "Looks like you called my bluff."

Nell spun to face him, turning away from the window where she'd been furtively peeking out at the parking lot. "Don't tell him that!"

"But he's right," Crash said mildly. "Killing him doesn't do anyone any good."

Nell took a deep breath, aware that her first line had been terribly overacted, and that she was in danger of breaking into giddy laughter. She went back to peeking out the window, praying that this would work.

"I don't have a lot of options here," Crash was saying. He sounded kind of like Clint Eastwood—his voice was soft, almost whispery but with an underlying intensity that screamed of danger. "I guess I could shoot you in the knee, but that's so messy. And it's unnecessary. Because all I really want is to be put on the commander's payroll."

Nell turned around again. "Hey—"

Crash held up one hand, and she obediently fell silent.

"Here's my deal, Sheldon," he said. "I've been set up. I didn't kill Admiral Robinson, but somehow those ballistic reports were fixed to say that I did. I haven't figured out yet how the commander managed that, but I will. And I haven't quite figured out the commander's connection to John Sherman, but I'll figure that out, too. Sooner or later, I'm going to know the whole nasty story—all the sordid little details."

He paused and then said, still in that same quiet voice, "What I'm thinking right now is that my silence is worth *some*thing. See, I think both you and the commander know as well as I do that even if I were to prove myself innocent, even if I were acquitted for the charges that have been brought up against me, I'm never going to shake the damage that's been done to my name and my career. In fact, I know for a fact that my career with the SEALs is over. No one's going to want me on their team.

"And since I'm no longer gainfully employed by my Uncle Sam," Crash continued, "I'm finding myself in a situation where I need a new source of income. I figure if the commander wants all the dirt I've already uncovered, and all the dirt I'm *going* to uncover about him to stay neatly under the rug, then he's going to have to pay. Two hundred and fifty thousand in small, unmarked bills."

Crash stopped talking. Nell gave him several beats of silence just to make sure he really was done. Then she spoke. "I can't believe what I'm hearing."

She really *was* a lousy actor. First she'd sounded too outraged, too over-the-top, and now she sounded too matter-of-fact. She wanted this guy to believe that she was intensely angry with Crash, not that she was bipolar.

Anger, anger. How did people look and act when they were angry?

More specifically, how did they look and act when they were angry with *Crash?*

Nell had quite a bit of personal experience to draw on in *that* department.

Over the past year, she'd spent a good amount of time angry as hell at herself, and angry at him, as well.

Why hadn't he at least scribbled a two-line postcard, acknowledging her existence? "Dear Nell, got your letters, no longer interested in being your friend. Crash. P.S. Thanks for the sex. It was nice."

Nice. He'd actually used that horribly insipid word to describe what they'd done that incredible, amazing, one-hundred-million-times-better-than-nice night.

Nell had been too emotionally overwhelmed to react at the time. But she'd had plenty of time to smolder in outrage since then.

She invoked those feelings now, and shot a lethal look in Crash's direction. "I *can not* believe what you just said." Her voice had just the slightest hint of an angry quiver. Nice. Nice. He thought making love to her had been *nice.* "You're actually planning to sell out to these scumbags?"

"I don't see too many choices here." Crash made himself sound wound tight with tension. "So just shut the hell up and keep watch."

Shut the hell up? The words were so un-Crash-like, Nell took a step backwards in surprise before she caught herself.

"No, I won't shut up," she shot back at him. "Maybe you don't have a choice, but—"

He stood up. "Don't push me." The expression on his face was positively menacing. His eyes looked washed out and nearly white—and flatly, soullessly empty.

Nell faltered, unable to remember what she was supposed to say next, frozen by the coldness of his gaze. It was as if nothing was there, as if nothing was inside him. She'd seen him look this way before—at Daisy's wake and funeral. She remembered thinking then that he may have been able to walk and talk, but his heart was barely beating.

Had it been an act back then, too, or was he really able to shut down so completely upon command?

He turned back to Sheldon. "You give up the commander's name, and seventy-five thousand of that money is—"

"What about Jake Robinson?" That was what she was supposed to say.

"Excuse us for a minute, Sheldon." Crash took her arm, and pulled her roughly toward the bathroom.

He didn't turn on the bathroom light because there was a fan attached, and he didn't want it to drown out their whispered words. Part of the plan was for Sheldon to be able to hear what they were saying.

"I thought you wanted to stay alive," he hissed through clenched teeth.

The tiny bathroom was barely large enough for both of them. Even though she had pulled her arm free from his grasp, they were still forced to stand uncomfortably close. She rubbed the place where his fingers had dug into her arm.

"I'm sorry about that," Crash said almost soundlessly. "I had to make it look real. Did I hurt you?" Concern warmed his eyes, bringing him back to life.

He cared. Something surged in her chest, in her stomach, and just like that, her anger faded. Because just like that, she understood why he hadn't returned her letters.

As much as she professed to want only to be friends, deep inside she wanted more.

She'd given *that* truth away on the morning she'd begged him to give their relationship a try.

He'd known that, and he'd also known that if he'd written to her, or if he'd called, his letters and phone calls would have kept alive the tiny seed of hope buried deep inside of her—the seed of hope that still fluttered to life at something so trivial as a flare of concern in his eyes.

God, she was pathetic.

She was pathetic, and he smelled so good, so familiar. She wanted to wrap her arms around him and bury her face in his shirt. It wouldn't have taken much—just a step forward an inch or two.

Instead, she jammed her hands in the front pockets of her jeans and shook her head, no. "I thought you wanted to get back at the bastard who killed Jake Robinson!" she whispered loudly enough for the man in the other room to overhear.

"Yeah, well, I changed my mind," he told her. "I decided I'd rather take the money and run. Disappear in Hong Kong."

"Hong Kong? Who said anything about going to *Hong Kong?*" Nell lowered her voice. "Do you think he's buying this?"

Crash shook his head. He didn't know. All he knew for certain was that it had been too damn long since he'd kissed this woman. She was really getting into this game they were playing. Her cheeks were flushed and her eyes were bright, making her impossibly attractive. He tried to put more space between them, but his back was already against the wall—there was nowhere else to go.

"No *way* am I letting you drag me to Hong Kong!" she continued. "You *promised* me—"

He cut her off. "I promised you nothing. What—do you think just because we got it on that suddenly you own me?"

Nell took a step back and bumped into the side of the tub. Crash caught her even as she reached for him, and for one brief moment, she was in his arms again. But he forced himself to release her, forced himself to step back.

What was wrong with him? True, bringing up the issue of sex would make their arguing more realistic, but it was definitely dangerous ground. And the words he'd spoken couldn't have been farther from the truth. They'd got it on, indeed, but then she'd let him go. Even the letters she'd written to him had been carefully worded. There was no question—she didn't have any expectations or demands.

Some of the sparkle had left her eyes as she looked up at him. "Oh, was *that* what you'd call what we did?" she said in a rough stage whisper loud enough for Sheldon to hear. "Getting it on? I think it's got to last longer than two-and-a-half minutes to be called anything other than 'getting off.' As in *you* getting off and me faking it so that you won't feel bad."

She was making it up. Crash knew that everything she was saying was based on some fictional joining. But still, he couldn't help but wonder.

The night they'd spent together *had* been over pretty quickly. He hadn't even managed to carry her all the way to the bed. But the way she had seemed to shatter in his arms—that couldn't have been faked, could it?

Something, some of his doubt, must have flickered in his eyes because Nell reached out to touch the side of his face. "How could you forget how incredibly perfect it was?" she asked almost inaudibly.

She lightly touched his lips with one finger, her eyes filled with heat from her memories of that night. But then her gaze met his and she pulled her hand away as if she had been burned. "Sorry. I know I shouldn't have…sorry."

"Just do what I say and keep your mouth shut," Crash harshly ordered her for Sheldon's benefit. "Don't make me wish I'd let Sarkowski shoot you."

He abruptly turned and went out of the room, afraid if he didn't leave he'd end up doing something incredibly stupid, like kiss her. Or admit that he *hadn't* forgotten. He'd tried to forget, God knows he had. But his memories of the night they'd spent together were ones he knew he'd take to his grave.

She stayed in the bathroom as he sat down again across from Sheldon.

"Women are always trouble," the gunman told him.

"It's nothing I can't handle," Crash replied tersely.

Nell slunk out of the bathroom then, her body language much like a dog with its tail between its legs. Despite everything she'd said to the contrary, she *was* good at acting. Unless her kicked-puppy look was the result of him rejecting her again. It was on a much smaller scale this time, but his lack of response to her nearly silent words *was* a rejection of sorts.

Nell reached the other side of the room and, just as they'd planned, she bolted for the door, throwing it open and running out into the darkness of the night.

Sheldon snorted. "Yeah, right, man, you can really handle her."

Crash checked to see that the gunman was still securely tied to the chair and then he went after Nell, slamming the door behind him. He didn't have far to go—she was waiting for him right outside the door.

"You should gag me," she whispered quietly. "Because if this was real, you better believe that I would scream. And if you just covered my mouth with your hand, I'd have to bite you."

"I don't have anything to gag you with." Of course, if this was real, if he were desperate, he'd use one of his socks. He didn't think she'd go for that, though.

Nell pulled the tail of her shirt out from her jeans. "Tear off a piece of this."

Crash took out his knife to cut through the seam. And then, as the fabric tore with a rending sound, Nell met his eyes.

He knew she was thinking the exact same thing that he was—that this was actually kind of kinky. With the undercurrent of sexual tension that seemed to follow them around, the idea of him tearing her shirt to gag her, with the intention of dragging her back into the motel room and tying her up...

She gave him a smile that was half embarrassed and half filled with excited energy as he put his knife away. Damned if she wasn't getting into this.

"You got the juice?" he asked. She'd poured some of it into a plastic baggie back in the car.

"I put it under the bed that's farthest from the door. Remember, when you knock me onto the ground, let me crawl under the bed to get it. Give me a minute to stick it under my shirt."

"How?" Crash asked. "I'm going to tie your hands behind your back. I thought you were going to have it on you now."

"Are you kidding? And have it open too early?" His news slowed her down, but it didn't stop her. "Well, *you're* just going to have to do it. When you grab me to pull me out from under the bed, stick it up under my shirt."

"I can't believe we're doing this. If this actually works, I'm going to be amazed."

Nell smiled at him. "Prepare to be amazed," she said. "Come on. Let's make this look real." She took off, running out into the parking lot.

Crash sighed, and went after her. He caught her in less than four steps and grabbed her around the waist, swinging her up and into his arms. She was harder to hold on to than he'd thought, though—she was fighting him.

"Nell, take it easy! I don't want to hurt you," he hissed.

She took a deep breath and opened her mouth, and he knew without a single doubt that she was going to scream. Talk about taking role-playing a *little* too seriously. He wadded up the fabric from her shirt and put it in her mouth, trying really hard to be careful. She bit his fingers and he swore.

He all but kicked the motel room door open and *did* kick it closed behind them, swearing again as one of her legs came dangerously close to making him sing soprano for a week. He flung her onto the bed, flipping her onto her stomach, and holding her hands behind her back.

He had to sit on her as he tied her wrists together, resting nearly his full weight upon her after she tried to kick him again. Dammit, she was actually *trying* to kick him in the balls.

He cursed as he tied her, choosing words he couldn't remember using in years, and she was trying to get free, kicking and wriggling beneath him like a wild woman.

Her torn-off shirt rode up, exposing the pale smoothness of her back and making him feel like a total degenerate. How could this possibly turn him on?

But this was just a game. He wasn't trying to hurt her— in fact, he was trying to do the opposite. He was tying her up using knots that she'd be able to slip out of. He was taking care that the roughness of the rope didn't abrade the soft skin of her wrists.

It was the sight and feel of Nell beneath him on a bed, his body pressed against hers, that was making him heat up. It wasn't the ropes or the struggle—that wasn't real. But Nell was real. Dear God, she was incredibly real.

He grabbed another rope from his bag and tied her feet,

also with slipknots, aware that Sheldon Sarkowski was watching, disgust in his eyes.

He lifted Nell up, depositing her on the floor as gently as he could while making it look to Sarkowski as if he'd damn near thrown her there.

As she said she would, she immediately began wriggling, rolling all the way under the bed. She was smart—she didn't leave a leg or a foot sticking out for him to grab. He had to lift up the dust ruffle and crawl halfway under himself just to pull her out.

There, just where she said it was, was a thin plastic baggie, closed with a twist-tie like a little balloon, filled both with air and tomato juice, ready to be popped. Of all the absurd ideas he'd ever tried, this one had to take the cake.

Nell had rolled onto her back, and he grabbed the baggie, careful not to pop it, and thrust it up, underneath her shirt. He hooked part of the loose plastic around the front clasp of her bra, trying to ignore the sensation of his fingers brushing against her smooth, warm skin. God, why was he doing this?

Because there was a .001 percent chance that it would work. As ridiculous as it was, it could work. People often saw what they expected to see, and as long as Sarkowski didn't have *too* acute a sense of smell, he wouldn't see tomato juice spilling out onto Nell's shirt, he'd see blood.

Crash hauled Nell out from under the bed, making it look as if he'd hit her hard enough across the face to make her lie still, dazed from the blow.

He stood up then, straightening his combat vest and quickly running his fingers through his hair, putting himself back into order. He drew his weapon from his holster, and sat down across from Sarkowski as if none of that had happened.

"I want the commander's name," Crash said, "and I want it now. My patience is gone."

"Sorry, pal." Sarkowski shook his head. "The best I can do for you is to pass along your message about the two hundred and fifty thousand. But you're not dealing from a position of strength here. Unless you can guarantee the girl's silence as well as your own, my employer isn't going to consider paying that price."

"I can guarantee the girl's silence."

The gunman laughed derisively. "Yeah, right."

Crash didn't blink. He didn't move a muscle in his face. He simply turned and discharged his weapon, aiming directly at Nell's chest.

She rolled back, as if from the force of the bullet, and then fell forward. She struggled briefly against the ropes that held her and then was still.

Crash took a deep breath, but all he could smell was the pizza—its box left open on the top of the TV set.

He watched Sarkowski's face as a red stain slowly appeared from beneath Nell's body. The gunman had lifted his heavy eyelids higher than usual, and when he turned to look at Crash, there was wariness in his eyes.

Crash set his weapon in his lap, the barrel pointed casually in the other man's direction. "I want to know the commander's name," he said again. "Now."

Sarkowski was searching his eyes for any sign of remorse, any hint of emotion, and Crash purposely kept his face devoid of expression, his eyes flat and cold and filled with absolutely nothing. From the gunman's perspective, he had no heart, no soul—and absolutely no problem with doubling the current body count.

"Kill me and you've got nothing," Sarkowski blustered. "You'll never know who I work for then.

But he spoke a little too quickly, his anxiety giving a little too much of an edge to his voice.

"That would only be a temporary problem," Crash pointed out. "I'd just have to wait for the commander to send someone else after me. Chances are *that* guy will talk. And if not him, then maybe the next. It doesn't matter to me. Time's one thing I've got plenty of." He lifted his weapon with the same kind of blasé casualness that he'd pointed it at Nell and aimed directly at Sarkowski's forehead.

"Wait," Sarkowski said. "I think we can make some kind of a deal."

Jackpot.

Nell didn't move. Crash couldn't even tell that she was breathing, but he knew that she was smiling.

Chapter 14

The motel window was dark as Crash pulled back into the parking lot.

A string of blinking Christmas lights had slipped from the edge of the roof, drooping pathetically across the front of the motel. The artificial tree visible through the lobby window listed to the left, its branches sagging under the weight of garish decorations.

Christmas was a grim undertaking here at this fleabag motel in the middle of nowhere. The festive trappings had all been brought out, but there was nothing merry about them. There was no hope, just resignation. Another season of bills that couldn't be paid and dreams that couldn't come true.

Somehow it all seemed appropriate.

Crash was exhausted. It had taken him longer than he'd hoped to find another motel in which to deposit Sheldon Sarkowski.

He'd planned to take Sarkowski out to the state park and

leave him locked in the men's room, but the two men had made a deal of sorts. Sheldon had been bought by the promise of a cut of the blackmail money and the hope that if he gave up his employer's name, Crash wouldn't kill him.

The deal was bogus, of course. Crash had no intention of taking any money from the commander who had engineered Jake Robinson's death. His goal was still—and had always been—justice.

But Sheldon thought they were a team now. And team members didn't lock other team members in a freezing-cold men's room. Instead, Crash had taken the highway, going nearly twenty miles back in the direction they'd come before finding another appropriately ancient motel. And once inside, he'd handcuffed Sheldon to the radiator in the bathroom. He'd even apologized before tapping him on the side of the head with the butt of his handgun.

His apology was accepted. Sheldon would have done the very same thing to him. They were supposed to be teammates now, but unlike members of a SEAL Team, they didn't fully trust each other.

And Sheldon Sarkowski—or whoever he *really* was—was the last person Crash ever would have trusted. The man liked his work way too much. Just from the short conversations they'd had, Crash knew Sheldon enjoyed pulling the trigger and delivering death. He'd volunteered to get rid of Nell's body and Crash got the sense that the offer was made not so much to help Crash, but for the pleasure doing so would give Sheldon.

The thought of Sheldon touching Nell was enough to make Crash's skin crawl.

He fought a wave of fatigue as he unlocked the door to the first motel room. He didn't have time to be tired. It was probably true that Sarkowski wouldn't be found by the maid until morning, but he wasn't about to take any chances. He'd wake up Nell and they were going to get back on the road.

She would be shocked to find out that she'd danced with the man responsible for this entire fiasco at Jake and Daisy's wedding. Senator—and retired U.S. Navy Commander—Mark Garvin was the man they were after.

There were no lights on at all in the room. Nell had no doubt showered and climbed into bed by now. God help him, he was going to have to stare down temptation and pull her out of bed rather than climb in with her, the way he so desperately wanted to and—

Nell hadn't moved. In the darkness, Crash could see her, still lying on the floor where he'd left her.

Dear Lord, the bullet he'd fired at her *had* been a blank, hadn't it? He'd double-checked and triple-checked it. But God knew he was exhausted. And when men were exhausted, they made mistakes.

He slapped the light switch on the wall and the dim light only verified what he already knew. Nell was lying on the floor, hands still tied behind her back, eyes closed, almost exactly the way he'd left her.

Crash's chest was tight with fear, and his throat was clogged with the closest thing to panic he'd ever felt in his life as he crossed toward her.

''Nell!'' She still didn't move.

He knelt next to her and pulled her into his arms, tearing at her clothes, praying that the sticky redness was indeed the result of the tomato juice they'd picked up at the convenience store, praying that he wasn't going to find some awful, mortal wound beneath the stained fabric.

Buttons flew everywhere as he ripped her shirt open. He swept his hands across the smoothness of her skin and looked down in her eyes, which were now opened very, very wide.

She was all right. The blood wasn't blood after all, the bullet he'd fired *had* been a blank. Relief made him so dizzy he nearly lost his balance.

But he wasn't too dizzy to realize that his hand was still on her chest, his fingers against her delicate collarbone, his wrist between her lace-covered breasts.

She was in his arms, her face inches from his, her shirt torn and stained, her hands and feet still tied.

Nell cleared her throat. ''Well, this is quite the little fantasy come true.''

Crash moved his hand, but then didn't quite know where to put it. ''Are you all right? When I saw you still lying here, I thought...''

''I couldn't get free.''

''I purposely used slipknots to tie you.''

''I tried,'' she admitted, ''but they just seemed to get tighter.''

''You're not supposed to pull at them.'' He helped her up into a sitting position and swiftly used his knife to cut her hands free. ''You're suppose to finesse them. Pulling just tightens them.''

''So much for my lifelong dream of becoming an escape artist.''

Crash's ribs hurt as he cut her feet free, and he realized that she had made him laugh. He wanted to pull her back into his arms, but she had turned away from him, as if suddenly self-conscious that her torn shirt was hanging open, all its buttons neatly removed.

She rubbed her wrists. ''Damn—that tomato juice stings!''

''It's acidic. Come here.''

Nell let him help her up and lead her to the set of double sinks right outside the bathroom door. He turned on the water and she held her wrists under the flow as he turned on the light.

"I'm sorry about this." His hands were so gentle as he lifted her hands to look at her rope burns.

She looked up at him. "It worked, didn't it?"

"Yeah."

"Then it's worth it."

His gaze flickered down to the open front of her shirt. "You better take a shower. I'll find you something clean to wear."

He was still touching her, still holding her hands. Nell knew that it was now or never—and she couldn't bear for it to be never. Not without trying one more time.

She reached out and touched the edge of the front pocket of his pants. In his haste to make sure she was all right, he'd knelt in the puddle of tomato juice. "You look like you could use a shower yourself," she said softly. "And I could use a little company."

Crash didn't move. For a minute, she wasn't even sure if he was still breathing. But the sudden rush of heat in his eyes left her little doubt. The sexual tension she'd felt building over the past few days was *not* a figment of her imagination. He felt it, too. He *suffered* from it, too. Thank God.

"That was your big cue," she prompted him. "That was where you were supposed to kiss me and pull me with you into the shower."

"Why are you here?" he asked hoarsely. "What do you want? Why did you even come to the jail?"

Nell knew she should break the spell by saying something funny, something flip. But in a flash of clarity, she realized that she used humor to maintain a distance—much in the same way that Crash separated from his emotions. So she didn't make a joke. She told him the truth.

"I want to help you prove your innocence. You once told me that I didn't really know you, but you were wrong." She held his gaze, daring him to look away, to step away, to pull away from her. "I *do* know you, Billy. My heart knows you. Even though your heart doesn't seem to want to recognize me."

He touched the side of her face, and she closed her eyes, pressing her cheek into his palm, daring to hope that he felt even a fraction of what she did.

"So that's why you're here," he whispered. "To try to save me."

"I'm here because you need me." Nell opened her eyes and let slip another dangerous truth. "And because I need you."

He was looking at her, and she could see everything he was feeling mirrored in his eyes. For once, he wasn't trying to hide from her. Or from himself.

"I want you," she told him softly. "All these months, and I still haven't stopped wanting you. I dream about your kisses." She smiled crookedly. "I've been sleeping a lot lately."

Crash kissed her then.

It was so different from that night after Daisy's funeral, where one minute he was looking at her and the next he was inhaling her. It was different, because this was a kiss that she actually saw coming.

She saw it in his eyes first, in the way his gaze dropped to her mouth for just a fraction of a second. And she saw it in the way his pupils seemed to expand, just a little. Then he leaned toward her, slowly, as his hand tilted her chin up. And then his mouth met hers, softly, sweetly.

He tasted like tomato juice.

He deepened the kiss, pulling her gently toward him, and Nell felt herself melt, felt her pulse kick into double time, felt her heart damn near burst out of her chest. This was what she'd been waiting for. This was why she had never invited Dex Lancaster inside after a dinner date.

She'd tried to deny it so many different times. It wasn't pure attraction and simple sex. It wasn't friendship, either. It wasn't anything she'd ever felt before.

She loved this man. Completely. Absolutely. Forever.

"Nell." He was breathing hard as he pulled back slightly to look at her. "I want you, too, but…" He took a breath and let it out quickly. "We shouldn't do this. Bottom line— nothing's changed between us." He laughed. "Truth is, it's gotten even more impossible. I can't give you—"

She stopped his words with a kiss. "Honesty's all I need. I know exactly what you can't give me and I'm not asking for that. All I want is another night with you." She knew he didn't love her, but she told herself that she didn't need him to love her. And she didn't need false promises of forever, either. She just wanted this moment. She kissed him again. "I can't think of anything I want more than to spend tonight in your arms."

She watched his eyes, holding her breath, praying he wouldn't turn away, knowing that she was risking so much by telling him this.

He touched her face again, the edges of his mouth twisting up into what could almost be called a smile. "You're looking at me like you don't have a clue what I'm going to do next," he said perceptively. He softly traced her lower lip with his thumb. "You don't *really* think I'm strong enough to hear you say all that, then walk away, do you?"

Nell's breath caught in her throat. "I think you're the most remarkable man I've ever met, and you're right. I *never* have a clue what you're going to do next."

"Tonight I'm going to be selfish," he said quietly.

He kissed her slowly, completely. It was a kiss that

promised her all of the passion of their first joining and even more. She clung to him, breathless and dizzy and giddy with desire, barely aware as he pulled her with him into the tiny bathroom.

They'd stood right here just hours ago.

Nothing had changed, Crash had said. But everything had changed. Two hours ago she'd had her hands in her pockets to keep from touching him. Now those same hands were unfastening the buckle of his belt, even as his hands helped her out of her own clothes.

She was covered with tomato juice and he stepped into the tub, pulling her with him, and turned on the water, rinsing her clean.

He washed her so slowly, so carefully, stopping to give her deliciously long, exquisitely sweet kisses that made her weak-kneed with desire. She could feel his arousal, hot and hard against her, and she opened herself to him, winding one leg around him in an attempt to pull him even closer.

He'd taken a foil-wrapped condom from his vest and tossed it into the soap-holder as they'd stepped into the shower. He opened it now, covering himself.

She kissed him again and he groaned, pulling her up, lifting her, pressing her back against the cool tile wall as he filled her.

It was heaven. The water raining down from the shower seemed to caress her sensitized body as he kissed her, touched her, claimed her so completely.

She was moments from release when he pulled back, breaking their kiss to gaze down at her. His gaze was hot, his breathing ragged. "I want to make love to you in a bed," he told her. "I want to look at you and touch you and taste every inch of you. I want to take my time and be absolutely certain that you're satisfied."

She pushed herself more deeply on top of him. "I'm

satisfied," she told him. She was already more satisfied than she'd thought she'd be ever again. "Although the bed thing sounds really nice. Maybe we can do that later."

"We don't have time. We have to leave," he told her.

Nell opened her eyes. *"Now?"*

"Soon." He kissed her. "I'm sorry. I should have told you right when I came in."

She tightened and released her legs around him, setting a rhythm that he soon obligingly matched. "You were too busy tearing off my shirt."

"I was." He held her gaze as he drove himself deeply inside of her again and again and again.

His beautiful eyes were half-closed and he was smiling very, very slightly—for him it was the equivalent of an all-out grin. He knew damn well what he was doing to her. He knew damn well that she was seconds away from total sensual meltdown.

But she could feel his heart pounding and she could read the heat in his eyes. She knew that when she exploded, she would take him with her. He was that close, too.

"Can we pretend tonight doesn't end when the sun comes up?" he asked softly. "I want to drive as far from here as possible before we stop again and…Nell, I need to make love to you in a bed."

He *needed* her. Dear God, he was actually admitting that he needed her.

"I would like that, too." She laughed. "Understatement of the year."

Hope filled her. The tiny seed that she'd tried to crush for so long burst to life inside her. He needed her. He didn't want tonight to end. She never dreamed he'd ever confess to either of those things.

At that moment, anything was possible. At that moment, she didn't need wings to fly.

She left the ground in an explosion of sensation and emotion that was deliriously intense. She felt herself cry out, heard an echo of her voice shouting his name. She felt him kiss her, possessing her mouth as completely as he possessed her body, felt him shake from his own cataclysmic release.

It was wonderful.

And it was even more wonderful knowing this time that she was going to get a chance—soon—to make love to him like this again.

Nell slept in the front seat of the car, her head resting in Crash's lap.

She'd folded up her jacket to use as padding over the lump from the parking brake. She was wearing one of his shirts and a pair of his pants, the cuffs rolled up about six times and the waistband cinched with a belt.

Her golden hair gleamed in the dim light of dawn. He ran his fingers through its baby-fine softness, loving the sensation.

She slept so ferociously, her eyes tightly shut and her fists clenched.

What on earth had he done?

Crash felt sick to his stomach. It could have been from fatigue, but he suspected it was, instead, a result of that look he'd seen in Nell's eyes while they were making love.

He'd made a mistake and admitted that he wanted more—more than quick, emotionless sex in the shower.

He'd opened his mouth, and now she was no doubt dreaming of their wedding.

He glanced down at her again and had to smile. She looked so fragile and tiny, nearly lost in his too-large clothes. And yet even in sleep she looked like she was ready at any given moment to hold her own in a boxing match.

No, she wasn't dreaming of their wedding. She was probably dreaming about getting her hands on Senator Mark Garvin and tearing him limb from limb.

He was the one who was dreaming about their wedding. God help him, he was in love with this woman.

Crash wasn't sure exactly when he'd realized it. Maybe it was when he walked into that motel room and thought for one god-awful moment that he'd actually shot and killed her. Or maybe it didn't sink in until she looked him in the eye and bared her soul, telling him that she needed him, that she wanted him, that she ached for him. Or maybe it was when they made love in the shower, and she held his gaze while he moved inside her. Maybe it was the realization that mere sex had never felt remotely like what he was feeling at that moment.

Or maybe it was when he hadn't been able to keep his fool mouth shut. Maybe it was when he'd told her that he wanted more, and she just lit up from within, her eyes shining with hope. His initial reaction hadn't been instant regret. No, he was double the pathetic fool. He'd actually been glad. That light in her eyes had made him feel happy.

That was when he knew he loved her. When he'd found himself happy at the thought that maybe she loved him, too.

The really stupid thing was that he'd been in love with her for years. *Years.* Probably since the very first time they'd met. Certainly during the previous year, while they'd lived together in Jake and Daisy's house, their beds separated only by one thin wall.

He'd loved her, but he'd refused to acknowledge it, refused to believe that she would want the kind of life she'd have with him.

She was the real reason he'd spent most of last year out of the country.

Somehow he knew that if he'd seen her again, if he'd so much as run into her on the street, he wouldn't have been able to keep away from her. Somehow he knew that he had no control at all when it came to Nell.

The sky lightened behind him as he drove relentlessly west.

The morning sky was pewter-gray and dull, promising rain or maybe even more sleet or snow.

His future was just as bleak. As hard as he tried, Crash couldn't see any kind of happy ending for him and Nell.

What he *could* see was heartbreakingly tragic.

Unless he was able to hunt down and destroy Commander Garvin, USN Retired, the woman he loved was a target. Unless Crash could win, Nell would die.

But Crash *would* win.

His career might be over. His name and his reputation were definitely ruined. He was wanted by every law-enforcement agency in the country, and probably some that were outside of the country as well. He had no kind of life left and what he did have, he didn't deserve—not after the way he'd let Jake die.

First Daisy, then Jake. There was no way in *hell* he was going to let Nell die, too.

He was willing to give up everything he had left to save her—and all he had left was his life.

Nell awoke to find herself alone in the bed.

They'd stopped shortly after crossing the border into New Mexico, and she had fallen asleep with Crash's arms around her.

But first, they'd made the most incredible love.

Crash had delivered everything he'd promised and then

some. He'd made love to her so thoroughly, so sweetly, Nell had almost let herself believe that he loved her.

Almost.

Now he was sitting, half-naked, in front of a powerful-looking laptop computer that he'd hooked up to the room's phone system. His hair stood up, as if he'd frequently run his fingers through it, and the screen lit his bare chest with a golden glow.

He pushed his chair back with a sigh and stood up, stretching his long legs and twisting a kink from his back. He turned, as if he felt her watching, and froze. "I'm sorry, did I wake you?"

Nell shook her head, suddenly uncertain, suddenly wondering if their night together had officially come to an end. "Have you slept at all?"

"Not yet." He looked exhausted. His eyes were rimmed with red and he reached up to rub the back of his neck with one hand. "I've been trying to find the connection between Garvin and Sherman. But I need to sleep. I'm starting to go in circles."

He sat down on the second of the two double beds in the room, and Nell thought for a second that he was sending her a message. Their night *was* over. He was going to sleep alone. But when he looked at her, she realized that he was feeling as uncertain as she was.

"You look like you could use a back rub," she said softly.

He met her eyes. "What I really want is to make love to you again."

Nell's mouth was suddenly dry. She tried to moisten her lips, tried to smile. "The odds of that actually happening will increase enormously if you sit on this bed instead of over there on that one."

He smiled tiredly at that. "Yeah. I just didn't want to…"

He shook his head, running his hand down his face. "I don't want to take advantage of you."

"Come here. Please?"

He stood up, crossing the short distance between the two beds. Nell sat forward, pulling him down so that he was sitting, facing slightly away from her. The covers fell away from her as she knelt behind him, gently massaging the tight muscles in his shoulders and neck.

He closed his eyes. "God, that's good."

"Did you find anything about Garvin at all?"

"He was definitely in 'Nam in '71 and '72—the same time as John Sherman served with the Green Berets."

Nell gently pushed him down, so that he was lying on the bed, on his stomach, arms up underneath his head. She straddled his back to get real leverage as she tried to loosen the muscles in his shoulders.

"I hacked my way into Garvin's tax records. He inherited a substantial sum of money in 1972—money his first wife used to buy a house while he was still in Vietnam. I searched the tax records of the elderly relative he claims the inheritance came from, but there's no record of income from the interest for a sum of money that large. Unless the old guy kept a quarter of a million dollars under his mattress."

"So what are we going to do?"

"I sent him a coded message that should be easy enough for him to break. I told him I had proof that his so-called inheritance was really the money he'd made dealing in the black market with John Sherman."

"But you don't have proof."

"He doesn't know that. I need to talk to him, face-to-face, record the conversation, and hope that he slips and says something that incriminates him."

Nell paused. "Face-to-face? This is a man who wants to kill you."

"That makes two of us."

"Billy—"

"I could just go after him. Take him out. An eye for an eye. A commander for an admiral. It wouldn't be the first time I've played the part of the avenging angel."

Nell took a deep breath. "But—"

"But if I do it that way, no one will know what he did. He killed Jake, he killed all those people in that war he started, and I want the world to know it. God, you're beautiful."

Nell turned her head, following his gaze, and realized that he was watching her in the wall mirror opposite the bed. The only light in the room was from his computer screen, but it was enough to give her breasts and her stomach and the curve of her rear end an exotic cast.

She looked like some wild, hedonistic version of herself. A naked love slave ministering to the needs of her master. All he had to do was turn over, and he could watch as she kept caressing him, kissing her way down his chest, down to his stomach, down…

She met the fire of his gaze in the mirror, feeling her cheeks heat with a blush. It wasn't the first time she'd believed him capable of reading her mind.

He didn't look tired any longer.

He turned, rolling beneath her so that he could look up at her, so that the hardness of his arousal pressed against her.

"This is the closest I figure I'll ever actually get to heaven," he said softly.

Nell leaned forward to kiss him and he held her close, telling her again, although not in so many words, just how much that he needed her.

She kissed his neck, his throat, his chest, trailing her mouth across his incredible body as she reached between them to unfasten his pants.

She turned to look, and, just as she'd imagined, found him watching her in the mirror. She smiled at him.

And then she took him to heaven.

Chapter 15

"I'm *not* going."

"Nell—"

"But you don't even have a plan to..." Nell broke off, gazing at him wide-eyed from the other side of the car. "Oh, my God," she said softly. "You *do* have a plan to get the evidence you need against Garvin, don't you? And you weren't even going to tell me."

It would have been easier if she'd shouted at him.

He tried to explain. "There are some things that are better if you don't know."

She turned to look out the window. "The things I don't know—particularly about you—could fill a book."

"I'm sorry."

She looked back at him. "You say that a lot."

"I mean it a lot."

"So this is it," she said. "You're just going to drop me off here in Coronado, at the house of somebody named

Cowboy. And I'm just supposed to hide until you either come back or you don't.''

The southern-California streets were filled with lengthening shadows and heavy traffic as the sun began to set. Crash had never been to the house that his swim buddy Cowboy shared with his young wife and infant son. But he had the address and he'd checked the map back when they'd last stopped for gas. He knew exactly where he was going.

"Silence," she said quietly. "With you, silence tends to imply an affirmative." She turned toward him then, reaching for him. "Billy, please don't shut me out now."

He let her take his hand, lacing their fingers together. "I know you want to help me, but the best way you can help me right now is to let me make sure that you're someplace safe." He braked to a stop at a traffic light and turned to look at her. "I need to know that you're okay, so that I can do what I have to do without being distracted—without worrying whether or not you're in danger."

"Please." Nell's husky voice broke very slightly. "Please tell me what it is that you're going to do."

Crash lost himself for a moment in the perfect blue of Nell's eyes. The car behind him honked—the light had turned green and he hadn't even noticed. He looked back at the road as he drove, wishing he had an eternity to fall into the blue ocean of her eyes and knowing that he only had hours left. Minutes. "A guy I know, a SEAL instructor, has a cabin in the mountains, not far from here. I know he's not going to be using it—the latest class of candidates are going through Hell Week. This guy's disabled and he does almost all of his teaching in a classroom, but he's still going to be busy this week."

"So you're going to use his cabin to wait for Garvin to contact you?"

He glanced at her again. "Actually, I got a response from Garvin this morning. Via E-mail. He's accepted my deal."

"My God. Isn't that the proof that you need? I mean, if he's letting himself be blackmailed…"

Crash smiled. "Unfortunately he didn't send me back a message that said. 'Yes, I'll pay you a quarter of a million dollars to make sure that you keep silent about the fact that I not only killed Jake Robinson but also started a war in Southeast Asia.' No, I've got to go face-to-face with Garvin, try to get something he says down on tape. I need something concrete."

"Face to…? But he's going to try to kill you! There's no way he's going to *pay* you all that money to be quiet when killing you guarantees your silence."

Crash signaled to make a left turn onto the street where Cowboy lived. "I'll be ready for him. I have enough C-4 in my bag to take out the entire mountain if I have to."

"C-4?"

"Explosives."

"Oh, God."

There was a break in the oncoming traffic and Crash made the left turn into the residential neighborhood. He swore sharply as he saw the cars idling further down the street. "Nell, kiss me, then laugh, make it big, like we're on our way to a party. No worries."

She didn't hesitate. She slipped her arms around his neck, turning his head, forcing him to watch the road with only one eye as she kissed him full on the mouth. She tasted like coffee with sugar, like slow, delicious early-morning lovemaking, like paradise on earth. When she finally pulled back, she threw back her head and laughed—just as he'd asked. "Who's watching us?" she asked, nuzzling his neck again.

He had to clear his throat before he could speak. That

was such a good performance, she'd nearly fooled *him*. "I'm not sure exactly, but there's at least one car that's got to be FInCOM, one I *know* is NIS, and one other a little further down the road, a little harder to pick out, that I'd bet my life savings belongs to whoever's working for Garvin."

She kissed him again, even longer this time. "Where did they come from? Are they following us?"

"No." He glanced in the rearview mirror. None of the cars had moved. "They're all doing surveillance outside of Cowboy's house—waiting for me to show up." He swore again. "They found the one man I know I can still trust. I should've known they'd figure that out."

"Is there some other way you can contact your friend? By phone or at work?"

Crash shook his head. "If they're watching Cowboy's house this closely, they've surely put a tap on his phone. And they'll follow him to work. Besides, my goal was to bring you into his house, not just talk to him. But there's no way that's going to happen now."

"So what happens now?"

"We go to Plan B."

"Funny, I didn't know about Plan A until minutes ago, and now we're already onto Plan B. What's Plan B?"

He checked the rearview mirror again before he glanced at her. "I'll let you know when I figure it out."

As Nell got an apple from the car and went back across the clearing toward the cabin, she could feel Crash's eyes on her.

She knew what he was thinking. He was wondering what on earth he was going to do with her.

It didn't matter how many times she protested. It didn't matter how brilliantly she argued with him. He was convinced that he needed to find some kind of haven for her, while he went one-on-one with a man they both *knew* had killed before to keep his secrets safe.

She sat down next to him on the cabin's front steps. "What's that?" He'd taken several blocks of gray, putty-colored modeling clay and several spools of wire from one of his gym bags. The clay was soft, so he was easily able to tear it into smaller chunks.

He looked up at her. "It's C-4."

She nearly choked on her apple. "*That's* an explosive? Don't you need to be really careful with it?"

He gave her one of his rare smiles. "No. It's stable. I could hit it with a hammer if I wanted to. It's no big deal."

She tossed what was left of her apple into the woods. "I remember watching western movies where the bank robbers all sweated bullets when they got out the nitroglycerine."

"We've progressed a long way since those days."

"That depends on your definition of progress." Nell looked around. "It's nice here. So peaceful and quiet. So naturally, you've decided to blow it up."

Crash put down the chunk of C-4 he was working with and kissed her. Of all the things she'd expected him to say or do, a kiss wasn't one of them. It wasn't just a quick kiss, either. It was a very well-planned kiss, as if he'd been thinking about doing it for a good long while.

It was more than just an I-want-your-body kiss. It was filled with a flood of emotions, most too complicated to name, and the rest too risky to acknowledge. He couldn't quite meet her eyes when he pulled away. Instead, he held her close for several long moments, lightly running his fingers through her hair.

"I've been thinking," he finally said.

Nell held her breath, praying that he'd finally come to the realization that what tied them together was uncontrollable and inevitable. He loved her. She *knew* he loved her. He wouldn't have been able to kiss her that way if he didn't.

"At sundown we're heading back into town. There's a SEAL I know, the executive officer of Alpha Squad. His name's McCoy. He was at the hearing, and he signaled me, you know, with hand signals—asked if I was all right. He wasn't like the guys from Team Twelve, ready to help strap me in for the lethal injection without even hearing my side of the story." Crash took a deep breath. "So I'm going to tell Blue McCoy my side of the story and ask him to take care of you. I know that he might feel obligated to turn me in, but I won't give him that opportunity. And I also know if I ask him, he'll make damn sure that you stay safe."

Nell fought her disappointment, keeping her face pressed against his shoulder, breathing in his warm, familiar scent. Those weren't the words she'd wanted to hear. In fact, they were words she *hadn't* wanted to hear. "Can't we stay here until the morning? Spend one more night together?"

His arms tightened around her. "God, I wish we could." He spoke so quietly, she almost didn't hear him. "But I've already sent Garvin an encoded message, giving him these coordinates. He's up at his home in Carmel right now. By the time he breaks the code—and I know he won't be able to do that in less than six hours—by the time he gets down here, even if he takes a private plane, it'll be dawn."

She straightened up. "Don't you think he's going to take those coordinates and send an army of Sheldon Sarkowskis here to kill you?"

"My message was very clear. If he doesn't make an in-person appearance, I'll evade whoever he *does* send. I'll disappear—until I conjure myself up some night in one of the dark corners of his bedroom. And then—I told him—I'll show him how a covert-assassination op is done right.

No one will ever know it was me—except for him. I'll make sure *he* knows.''

Nell shivered. ''But you're only bluffing, right? I mean, you wouldn't really just kill him...would you?''

He released her and went back to his work with the C-4 explosives. Silence. A silent affirmative. Dear God, what was he planning to do?

''I know you believe Garvin killed Jake, but Billy, God! What if you're wrong? You'd be killing an innocent man!''

''I'm not wrong. Garvin's credit-card records show him paying for a plane ticket to Hong Kong three days before the fighting started between Sherman and Kim. There's no record of him leaving Hong Kong during that time, but there wouldn't be. He would've paid cash and made sure that any side trips he took wouldn't show up on his passport.''

''That's all circumstantial evidence.''

He gave her a long look. ''Maybe. But when you put them together with a few more facts I dug up, such as that the Hong Kong trip was a week before his wedding to Senator McBride's daughter... He didn't try to claim the trip as a business expense on his tax return, and I find it hard to believe he took a three-day vacation in the middle of the week, five days before his wedding to the daughter of the man who would secure him the Vice Presidential nomination in two years' time.''

''Yeah, okay, that looks bad, but it's not *proof*—''

''I've also found out that Dexter Lancaster has been Mark Garvin's tennis partner for fifteen years.''

Nell sat back. ''What?''

Crash nodded. ''I figure Garvin was being blackmailed by John Sherman for a while—probably since he won the senate seat last November. Certainly by the time he attended Jake and Daisy's wedding. My bet is that six months later, after everything hit the fan, Garvin remembered that his pal Dex couldn't take his eyes off you and—''

"Wait a minute. Are you telling me that you think *Dexter* is somehow involved in Jake's murder?'' Nell felt dizzy.

"No.'' He shook his head. "Actually, I don't. Not knowingly, anyway. But I think if you ask Lancaster, he'll admit that Garvin was the one who urged him to call you. You'll probably also find out that it was Garvin's idea to steer you in the direction of working for Amie and the theater. You'll also find that the theater recently received a private donation to help defray the cost of a personal assistant for its director—Amie. If you want, I'll get my laptop and show you the records that state the name of the donor. Guess who? Mark Garvin.''

"But...why?'' She didn't understand.

"My thinking is that Garvin was well-connected enough to know that an investigation had been started. He probably knew about the deposition Kim's wife gave, found out Jake would be handling the file. The fact that he was responsible for starting a war wouldn't have gone over real well when the time came to run for Vice President. And that's not even taking into consideration whatever despicable thing he did back in 1972—whatever Sherman was blackmailing him about. He had a lot to lose.''

"Garvin was probably covering his bases by keeping track of you,'' he continued. "He probably suspected that you and I had something going and figured that keeping track of you could possibly be the only way he'd even remotely keep track of me.''

"He must've been disappointed.''

"He figured—correctly—that I would be his biggest threat if he had to take Jake out. One thing I'm still not sure of, though, is if he knew that I worked for Jake as part of the Gray Group. And if he *did* know, how did he find out?"

"I haven't said anything to *anyone,* Billy. I swear it. I wouldn't do that."

"I know you wouldn't."

He was quiet for a moment, but then he looked up at her again. "So all that—along with his message agreeing to meet me—makes Garvin look extremely guilty. I still haven't figured out what leverage he used to make Captain Lovett and the Possum sell out. But that's something I may never know."

"You'll definitely never know if you kill Garvin," Nell said hotly. "You'll never get his confession, either. And you may never find the proof you need to clear your name."

He glanced up at her. "Even if I'm cleared of all charges, my good name's gone. It'll always be connected to betrayal, no matter what I do. There's always going to be this cloud of doubt hovering over me. How much did Hawken really know? Why did he let those killers into the admiral's house?" He laughed, but there was no humor in it. "Truth is, I am at least partly responsible for Jake's death."

Nell couldn't believe what she was hearing.

"But this is all moot," he continued. "Garvin *is* going to show up here at dawn. He's not going to risk having me hunt him down—particularly since I led him to believe I'd enjoy it. And on top of that," he added, "he knows that I don't have a whole hell of a lot to lose."

He was serious. He honestly didn't believe that despite everything he'd been through, he had more to lose than most men even started with.

"If I agree to go to this SEAL's house," she said slowly, "What's-his-name's house—McCoy's—then you've got to promise me that you'll be careful."

"I'll be careful," he told her. "But..."

She looked at him in disbelief. "How can you dangle a 'but' off a promise to be careful?"

He wasn't even remotely amused. In fact, when he looked up at her again, his eyes seemed distant, his expression detached. "Whatever happens with Garvin—whoever's left standing when the smoke clears—it will mean only one thing to you. If he's the one who's still standing, then you've got to run and hide because you'll be next on his list. But I'm telling you right now that I'm going to do everything humanly possible to make sure that's not going to happen. By this time tomorrow, you're not going to have to worry about Garvin anymore."

Nell stood up, wiping the seat of her pants with her hands. "Good. Then let's make a date to have dinner tomorrow night when you come back from—"

"I won't be coming back," he said quietly.

She stared at him. "But you said—"

"There's no tomorrow night, Nell. Whatever happens with Garvin," he said again, "it won't change the fact that we have no future. *I* have no future. Even if I live, I won't come back."

Nell was aghast. Won't, he'd said, not *can't*. Even if he lived, he *wouldn't* come back. He didn't want to come back for her. "Oh," she said, suddenly feeling very small.

He cursed. "You only wanted one more night, remember? It was sex, Nell. It was *great* sex, but it wasn't anything more than that. Don't you dare turn it into something that it's not."

She couldn't breathe. "I'm sorry," she somehow managed to say even though there wasn't any air left in her lungs. "I just..." She shook her head.

"I thought I'd made my feelings clear," he said tightly.

"You did," she whispered. He had. He'd been up-front

and direct about the impossibility of a relationship right from the very beginning. "I guess I just let my imagination run away with me for a while."

He didn't look up from the work he was doing, building bombs that would allegedly protect him from a man who would go to great lengths to see him dead.

"You still have to promise that you'll be careful," she told him before she turned away.

The colorful lights of a Christmas tree shimmered through the side window of Blue McCoy's house. It was a nice house, quietly unassuming, rather like the man himself.

Crash had driven around the block four times but had seen no sign of surveillance vehicles. He'd finally parked on a different side street, cutting through a neighbor's yard to approach Blue's house from the back.

Blue was at home—he could see him passing back and forth in front of the kitchen window. Cooking dinner. Crash hadn't known that Blue could cook.

There was a lot he didn't know about Blue McCoy, he realized, crouched there between a pickup truck and a little subcompact car that were parked in the drive alongside the man's house.

He felt Nell shift beside him. "What are we waiting for?"

Good question.

He motioned for her to hang back as he approached the back door. He could tell from one quick glance that the door didn't open into the kitchen, but rather into a smaller area—a mud room.

The door was locked, but he had the tools to get through it in about fifteen seconds. It opened and he nodded to Nell, gesturing with his head for her to follow him.

He drew his sidearm and slipped inside the house.

Crash could smell the fragrant aroma of onions sautéing. Blue was standing at the counter, with his back to him, chopping green peppers on a cutting board.

He didn't turn around, didn't even stop chopping as he said in his deep Southern drawl, "We missed y'all at Harvard's wedding."

Crash held his weapon on the other man as he spoke from the shadows. "I sent my regrets. I was out of the country."

Blue set down his knife and turned around. His quiet gaze took Crash in from the top of his too-long hair to the tomato-juice stains on the knees of his black BDUs. He focused for about a millisecond on the barrel of Crash's sidearm, but then dismissed it. He knew as well as Crash did that the weapon was a formality. Crash was no more prepared to use it on Blue than he was likely to use it on himself or Nell.

"Ma'am." Blue nodded a greeting at Nell before he turned back to Crash. "Before I invite you in, Hawken, I've got to ask you just one question. Did you kill, or conspire to kill, Admiral Robinson?"

"No."

"Okay." The blond-haired SEAL nodded, turning back to stir the onions that were sizzling in a saucepan on the stove. "I was wondering when you were going to show up. Why don't you sit at the table? Stay low, the window's got no shade."

Crash didn't move.

"I'm guessing you're here because everyone and their dim-witted second cousin is watching Cowboy's place," Blue continued. He laughed as he added the chopped peppers to the pot and stirred the vegetables together. "Every time that boy goes anywhere, there's about four cars behind him. At first he thought it was funny, but now it's kind of getting on his nerves.'' He turned back to Crash. ''So what can I do to help?''

''Wait a sec,'' Crash said. ''Rewind. You ask me *one question,* and that's it? I say no, I didn't kill Jake, and you're satisfied?''

Blue considered that for a moment, then nodded. ''That's right. I just wanted to hear you say what I already knew. Everyone in the Spec War business with half a brain can see as clear as day that you've been set up.'' He laughed in disgust. ''Unfortunately it looks as if Alpha Squad is the only team with more than half a brain these days.''

''You understand that by helping me, you'll be an accomplice.''

''But you didn't do anything wrong. To believe that—and I do—and do nothing to help you…now, *that* would be a real crime.'' Blue lifted one shoulder in a shrug. ''Besides, I figure you wouldn't be here if you weren't close to catching whoever did kill the admiral. Am I right?''

Crash still didn't move. He didn't lower his weapon, he didn't do much more than breathe as Blue added several cans of whole tomatoes and some spices to the saucepan.

Blue glanced at him again. ''I can understand how you might be a little paranoid right about now, so I won't take that weapon you're holding on me personally. But I have to tell you that—''

''You may not hold it personally, but I sure as hell do.'' There, in the door to the dining room, stood a pretty, dark-haired woman wearing a well-tailored pantsuit and holding an automatic pistol in her hand, aimed directly at Crash.

''Lucy will,'' Blue finished.

Crash hadn't heard her come in. He'd heard no cars approaching or pulling into the driveway. He hadn't heard the front door open or shut.

But of course, she'd been home all along. There'd been

two cars in the drive when he'd approached. He'd made the mistake of assuming that simply because Blue was cooking dinner, his wife wasn't home.

That would teach him to make assumptions based on gender-role stereotypes in the future. Except he didn't *have* a future.

Crash lifted his sidearm higher, holding it on Blue. "Please put down your weapon, Mrs. McCoy."

The brunette's mouth tightened. "I'm going to count to three, and if *you* don't—"

Blue moved, crossing the kitchen in two very long steps, stepping directly in front of his wife's deadly-looking pistol.

"Everything's fine," he said to her, gently pushing the barrel down toward the floor. "You can put that away. Hawken's a friend of mine."

"Everything's *not* fine! There's a man in our kitchen holding a gun on you!"

"He'll put it away."

"I can't do that," Crash said tightly.

"It looks like he can't put his weapon away right now," Blue told his wife. "I'm not sure I'd be able to do it myself if I were in his shoes." He turned back to Crash. "Can you do me a favor and at least lower it?"

Crash nodded, his eyes never leaving Lucy's handgun.

As Lucy reholstered her weapon, he lowered his.

"Good." Blue kissed his wife gently on the lips before he went back to the stove. "Lucy, meet Crash Hawken. You've heard me talk of him plenty of times."

Lucy's brown eyes widened as she turned to look at Crash again. "*You're* Lieutenant Hawken?"

"Crash, this is Lucy, my wife," Blue continued. "She's a detective with the Coronado police."

Crash swore softly.

"And you must be Nell Burns," Blue greeted Nell with a smile. "On the news, they're saying you were abducted. But it looks to me like you're here of your own free will."

Nell nodded. "Billy and I both thought that I'd be safer with him—after the second attempt was made on my life."

Blue lifted his eyebrows as he looked at Crash. "*Billy,* huh?"

"Look, we're just going to turn around and walk out of here," Crash said. Blue McCoy's wife was a police detective. His current streak of dismal luck was absolutely unending.

Blue turned to his wife. "Yankee, you better plug your ears, because I'm about to ask a suspected felon to join us for dinner."

"Actually, I'm long overdue for a soak in the tub," Lucy said. "And your friend looks like he's got someplace he needs to be in a hurry." She nodded to Nell and Crash. "Nice meeting you, Lieutenant. Or was it Captain? I'm sorry, I've never been very good with names. I've already forgotten yours."

As Crash watched, she disappeared into the darkness of the other room. He could hear the sound of her footsteps going up a flight of stairs.

He could sense Nell standing right beside him, her anxiety nearly palpable. He ached to reach out and slip his arm around her shoulder, to pull her in close for an embrace. But doing that would undermine everything he'd worked so hard to do this afternoon—telling her how he wouldn't come back, making it sound as if he had a choice when the real truth was he honestly didn't think he'd live to see another sunset.

And touching her would also undermine all that he'd done today to separate from the tornado of emotions that threatened to throw him into uncharted territory.

"Tell me what you need me to do," Blue said simply.

Crash glanced in the direction in which Lucy had disappeared.

"She's not calling the SWAT Team, I promise. She knows we're friends."

"Are we?"

Blue turned back to stir his tomato sauce. "I thought so."

Crash looked at Nell, and forced himself to detach even more completely than he had earlier that afternoon, after he'd allowed himself one more kiss. One *last* kiss. This was one of the most difficult decisions of his life, but he knew it had to be done. "I need a place for Nell to stay that's safe," he said, as ready as he'd ever be to put the one person he cared more about than anyone on the planet into another man's hands.

The blond-haired SEAL nodded as he turned back to meet his gaze. "I'll see to that."

Nell's throat felt tight. Just like that, Crash was handing her over. Just like that, he was going to walk out of the house, into the darkness. And just like that, she was never going to see him again.

"Are you set for supplies?" Blue asked. "Ammunition?"

"I could use an extra brick of C-4, if you've got any lying around."

Blue didn't blink. "You know we're not allowed to bring that stuff home."

"I know the rules. I also know that when a team is called out on an op in the middle of the night, there's not always time to go back to the base to pick up supplies."

Blue nodded. "I can spare half a block. But unless you're intending to take out more than a single house, that ought to be enough."

Nell couldn't believe what she had just heard. A half a block of C-4 could "take out" an entire house? Crash had already used at least three entire blocks, strategically planting the bombs he had made around the edges of the clearing surrounding the cabin. If a half a block could destroy all that, then surely he'd *already* used enough to blow up the entire mountainside.

She'd realized with icy-cold shock that she'd figured out Plan B.

Crash was prepared to blow himself up if necessary, in order to take down Commander Mark Garvin.

Chapter 16

The warm golden light of the kitchen seemed suddenly washed-out and much too bright. And Nell's ears were roaring so loudly, she almost couldn't hear as Blue said, "It's locked in the basement. I'll get it and be right back."

He vanished through the same door his wife had disappeared through earlier.

Nell fumbled for one of the kitchen chairs, nearly knocking it over in her haste to sit down. She actually had to put her head between her legs and close her eyes tightly to keep from falling over.

"Are you all right?"

Crash had crouched next to her. She could sense him, smell his familiar scent, hear the concern in his voice, but he didn't touch her. She didn't expect him to.

She shook her head no. "I'm in love with you." She opened her eyes and lifted her head slightly to find herself gazing directly into his eyes. Her words had shocked him.

Her blunt non sequitur had penetrated the emotional force field he'd set up around himself. "I've been in love with you ever since that night you made me go sledding. You remember that night, don't you?"

He stood up, moving away from her. "I'm sorry, I don't."

She sat up, indignation replacing dizziness. "How could someone who's such a bad liar specialize in covert ops?"

He shook his head. "Nell—"

"Let me refresh your memory," she told him. "That was the night you told me about Daisy coming to get you from that summer camp. Remember? That was the night you told me how it had felt to know, to *really* know that Daisy and Jake both wanted you around. You told me how strange it had felt to know that you were loved. Totally. Unconditionally."

He moved closer to the door, and she stood up, following him, angry and upset enough not to care any more that she was making him uncomfortable. This could well be the last time she ever spoke to him. If he had his way, it would be. Because—oh God!—he believed that in order to bring down Garvin, he was going to have to die.

"Well, guess what?" she said, stepping in front of him so that he was forced to look at her. "Jake and Daisy are gone, but I'm here to carry on. I love you unconditionally. And I want you to come back to me after this is over."

To her total shock, she saw that there were tears in his eyes. Tears, and absolute misery. "I didn't want this to happen. This is *exactly* what I was trying to avoid." He ran his hands down his face, trying hard to get back into control. "If you love me, then I'm going to hurt you. And God help me, Nell, I don't want to hurt you."

Back in control was the last place Nell wanted him to

be. She couldn't believe she'd managed to break through his detachment as much as she already had. She pushed, trying to see more, to get more from him. "So don't hurt me. How are you going to hurt me?"

He lowered his voice. "The odds of my surviving this altercation are low. I've known that from the start. If you love me—and please, Nell, don't love me—then I'm going to hurt you the same way Daisy hurt Jake." He met her gaze and she knew at last that she had uncovered the truth. He was doing unto others the way he wished they would do unto him. He was so terrified of losing someone he loved, he tried to keep himself from loving, he tried to shut all his feelings down. And he'd tried to keep her from loving him, to prevent *her* from being hurt as well.

Nell reached for him, touching his arms, his shoulders. "Oh, my God, is that really what you think? That Daisy hurt Jake by dying?"

His voice was ragged. "I know she did. If Jake had lived, he still wouldn't be over her, he still would be in pain, missing her every day for the rest of his life."

"Yes, Daisy made Jake hurt. Yes, he missed her right up to the moment he drew his last breath, but think of all she gave him along with that pain. Think of all those years, all the laughter they shared. I've never known two people who were as happy as they were. Do you really, *honestly* believe that Jake would've traded all that joy simply to avoid the pain he felt at the end?"

Nell touched the unrelenting lines of his face. "I can tell you absolutely that he would not have traded even one single moment, because I wouldn't trade, either. If I could, I wouldn't choose to go back and keep myself from falling in love with you. I don't care, even if you *are* hell-bent on killing yourself."

She stood on tiptoe, pulling his head down to kiss the grim line of his mouth. "There's one more kiss I'll always remember," she told him. She kissed him again, longer this time, lingering. "One more moment I'll cherish forever."

She kissed him a third time, and with a groan, he pulled her close, kissing her with all the passion and longing and sweet, sweet emotion he'd tried so hard to keep buried deep inside.

"Please," Nell whispered as he held her so tightly she could barely breathe. "Come back to me." She was begging again. This man had the power to force her to abandon her pride, force her to her knees. "Is avenging Jake's death really worth losing your own life?"

"Is that what you think I'm doing?" He pulled back to look at her, searching her eyes. "Don't you know I'm doing this for *you?*"

She shook her head, not understanding.

"Unless Garvin is in custody with absolute proof connecting him to his crimes, or unless he's dead, I'd never know for certain that you were safe."

She gripped his arms. "I'd be safe if you were with me."

An avalanche of emotions crossed his face. "I can't ask you to do that—to come away with me, to run and hide, to spend the rest of your life hiding."

"Try asking!"

"That's no way to live!"

She wanted to shake him. "Getting yourself killed isn't living either, in case you haven't noticed!"

He shook his head. "This way I'll know you're safe."

"So you're doing this for me?" She couldn't keep her eyes from brimming with tears. "You're telling me that you're willing to die. For *me*."

"Yes."

"Why?"

He kissed her and she knew that he was telling her why. He loved her. He couldn't say the words, but she knew it to be true.

"If you're willing to die for me," she asked him, her heart in her throat, "then why won't you *live* for me?"

He just looked at her for several long seconds as Nell prayed her words would make him stop the chain of events he'd already set in motion.

But then he shook his head, turning away. Following his gaze, Nell saw that Blue had come back into the kitchen.

As Crash stepped back, away from her, Nell knew with a sudden wrenching pain that she'd lost. He wasn't going to stay. And he wasn't going to come back.

She pushed her pain away, refusing to stand there weeping as the man she loved walked away from her for the last time. She forced everything she was feeling, all that terrible emptiness and loss, far, far back, deep inside of her. She'd have plenty of time later on to mourn.

She'd have all the rest of her life.

She watched as Crash took the C-4 Blue had wrapped up for him and slipped it into one of his pockets. She watched as the two men shook hands. Did Blue know it was the last time he was going to see his friend? She watched, feeling oddly detached and remarkably in control as Crash paused in front of her.

Was this how he did it? Was this how he stayed so cool and reserved and distanced? It almost didn't hurt.

He kissed her again, his mouth sweet and warm, and she almost didn't cling to him for just another few seconds longer.

And when he walked out the door and vanished into the night, she almost didn't cry.

* * *

Crash left his car out by the main highway and traveled the last ten miles to the cabin on foot.

He sat in the darkness outside the cabin as one hour slipped into two, watching and waiting—making sure that no one had approached the area while he had been gone.

He went into the cabin cautiously, then searched it to be doubly certain he was alone up here.

He *was* alone.

In fact, he couldn't remember the last time he'd been so totally alone.

Normally, he didn't mind sitting quietly with his thoughts. But tonight, his thoughts wouldn't behave.

He couldn't stop thinking about Nell, about what she had said.

If you're willing to die for me, then why won't you live for me?

I love you, unconditionally.

Unconditionally.

When he closed his eyes, he saw her, her face alight, laughing at something Daisy or Jake had said. He saw her, her eyes filled with tears at the thought that she'd ruined one of Daisy's last sunsets. He saw her, blazing with passion as she leaned forward to kiss him. He saw her, that first time he'd seen her again in close to a year, sitting in the visitors' room at the jail, hands folded neatly on the table in front of her, her expression guarded, but her eyes giving away everything she was feeling, everything she hadn't dared to admit aloud until just hours ago.

She loved him. Unconditionally.

And he knew it was true. If she could sit there, loving him even as she visited him in jail, an accused murderer, then she truly did love him unconditionally.

As Crash got out his roll of wire and laid out his tools

to rig the last of the explosives that would guarantee Garvin's death—and his own death as well—he stopped for a moment.

Because when he closed his eyes, if he concentrated really hard, he could see a glimmer—just a tiny flicker—of his future.

If he didn't die here this dawn, he *could* have a future. It might not have been the future he'd always imagined, working for the Gray Group as a SEAL until he hit his peak, then moving into more standard career as a SEAL instructor until he was too old to do the job right.

He'd always figured he'd be with the Teams, or he'd be dead.

But now when he closed his eyes, he could see a shadowy picture of himself, a few years from now, with Nell standing at his side.

Loving him unconditionally, whether he was a SEAL or working nights at the counter of a Seven-Eleven. What he did didn't matter to her. And Crash realized that it wouldn't matter to him, either. Not as long as she was there when he came home.

He looked down at the C-4, at his own private cup of hemlock, and he knew in that instant, without a single doubt, that he did *not* want to die today.

He had been wrong. He *wasn't* expendable, after all.

He should have asked Blue McCoy and the rest of Alpha Squad for help.

It would've have been a whole lot easier.

Crash stood up. It was too late to contact Blue, but it wasn't too late to do a little rewiring.

He smiled for the first time in hours.

Maybe his luck was finally about to change.

* * *

Nell couldn't stand it another second.

She put down her fork, done pushing the pasta around her plate, done pretending that she had any kind of appetite at all. "He's going to die if we don't do something."

Blue McCoy glanced across the table at his wife before putting his own fork down. He knew Nell was talking about Crash. "I'm not sure exactly what it is we *can* do at this point."

In a low voice, Nell told the SEAL about all the C-4 that Crash had rigged, about the cabin, about the message to Senator Garvin, about *everything*. She didn't need to speak of the low odds of Crash's survival. Blue had already figured that out.

"There's got to be a way for Billy to beat Garvin," she said. "To implicate him in Jake's death, and to stay alive as well. But he's going to need help. Lots of help."

As she watched, Blue glanced again at his wife.

"This sounds more like your department than mine, Superman," Lucy said softly.

"You told Billy how your squad—Alpha Squad—all thought he was being set up," Nell persisted. "Who do I have to call to ask them to help?"

Blue lifted one hand. "Whoa. Do we even know where Crash is?"

Nell's heart was pounding. Was he actually considering her outrageous request? "Yes. I could find my way back there, I'm sure of it. I could lead you there."

Blue was silent for a moment. "It's one thing for *me* to offer to help a man I personally trust," he finally said. "It's a whole other story to bring Alpha Squad in. If this goes wrong…"

"Billy spoke so highly of the Alpha Squad," Nell said. Her heart was beating so hard she could hardly speak.

Please, God, let them agree to help. "If the men of Alpha Squad have even one-tenth the respect for him that he has for them, how can they refuse to help?"

"You're asking a lot." Lucy leaned forward, her brown eyes sober. "They'd be putting their careers—not to mention their lives—on the line."

Blue pushed back his chair and stood up. "I'll call Joe Cat—Captain Catalanotto," he told Nell. "I can't promise anything, but…"

He reached for the phone.

Nell held onto the edge of the table, allowing herself to dare to hope.

Garvin appeared, right on schedule.

Dawn was breaking, but the west side of the mountain was still in heavy shadow. As Crash watched, Garvin drove right up to the cabin, the headlights of his car still on, still necessary.

He'd brought a half a dozen shooters with him, but they'd come in a different vehicle and parked down the road—as if they didn't think Crash would notice them, creeping through the woods, not quite as noisy as a pack of Boy Scouts on a camping trip, but pretty ridiculously close.

Garvin was a tall, handsome man with a full head of dark hair. He didn't look capable of starting a war or conspiring to kill a U.S. Navy admiral, but Crash knew that looks could often be deceiving. As he watched, Garvin climbed out of his car, hands held out to show that they were empty, that he was unarmed.

Crash, too, had left his weapon inside the cabin. But he was far from unarmed. "Call your shooters off."

Garvin pretended not to understand. "I came alone, just as you said."

Crash stepped forward, opening his jacket, letting Senator Garvin, a former commander in the U.S. Navy, get a good look at all of the C-4 plastic explosive he'd rewired and attached directly to his combat vest. He also showed the man the trigger mechanism that he'd rigged. He'd turned himself into a walking bomb.

"Call your shooters off," he said again. "If one of them makes a mistake and shoots me, my thumb will come off this button, and this entire hillside will be one big fireball."

Garvin raised his voice. "He's got a bomb. Don't shoot. Don't anyone shoot. Do you understand?"

"There now," Crash said. "Isn't the truth so much more refreshing?"

"You are one crazy son of a bitch."

"Hey, I'm not the one who wants to be Vice President."

Garvin was backing away, slowly but surely, inch by inch.

Crash laughed at him. "Are you trying to sneak away from me? Turn around and look down the trail," he ordered the older man. "See that tree with the white marker tied around it? I tied it there, just for you. Can you see the one I'm talking about, *way* over there?"

Garvin nodded jerkily.

"That's the edge of my kill zone," Crash told him. "Start there and draw a circle with me in the middle. Anyone and anything inside that circle is going straight to hell when I lift my thumb from this trigger."

Garvin's face was chalky as he realized that edging away wasn't going to do him much good. "You'd never do it."

Crash lowered his voice, leaning forward until he was mere inches from Garvin's face. "Is that a dare?" He raised the trigger so the man could see his thumb, started to move his thumb—

"No!"

Crash nodded, backing down. "Well, then. It seems like I've got something you want—your life. And since you've got something *I* want—the truth—I think we can probably—"

"I *do* have something you want," Garvin interrupted. Sweat was rolling down his face. "I have something you want bad. I have that girl. Nell Burns."

Crash didn't move, but something, *something* must have flickered in his eyes. Some uncertainty. Some doubt.

"Am I bluffing? That's what you're thinking right now, isn't it?" Garvin somehow managed to smile. "That's a very good question."

"You don't have her."

"Don't I? Maybe you're right. Maybe I didn't send Mr. Sarkowski into your SEAL friend's house. Maybe he didn't put a bullet into your friend's brain. Maybe he doesn't have the girl with him right now. And maybe he's not waiting for 7:00 a.m. to come—knowing that if I don't show up by then, he'll get to do whatever he wants with your girlfriend. Poor thing."

Crash didn't move. Garvin was bluffing. He *had* to be bluffing. There was no way Sarkowski could have gotten past Blue. No *way*.

"The real beauty of it is that the ballistics reports will show that the bullet that killed her came from *your* gun," Garvin continued. "So unless you disarm that bomb you're wearing—"

"No." Crash turned to look at him. "You don't know it, but by telling me you've got Nell you lost the game. I just won. Check and mate, scumbag." He kept his voice low, his face expressionless, his eyes empty, soulless. "Because if you have Nell, I truly have nothing left to lose. If you have Nell, I'd just as soon die as long as it means that I'd kill you, too."

Everything he was saying had been true. Just hours ago, it *had* been true. He could say it with a chilling believability because he knew exactly what it felt like to be ready to die.

"Here's what I'm thinking," he told Garvin. "If I disarm this bomb, you'll kill me, and then you'll kill Nell, too, anyway. Hell, if Sarkowski really *does* have her, she's probably already dead. So you see, Senator, you've just severed the last of my ties to this world. I have no reason at all not to start my search for inner peace in the afterlife right now." He smiled tightly. "And I know I'll go to heaven, because my last act on this earth will be ridding the world of *you.*"

Garvin bought it. He swallowed it whole. Every last word. "All right. Jesus. I *was* bluffing. I *don't* have the girl. Christ, you're a crazy bastard."

Crash shook his head. "I don't believe you," he said in the same quiet voice. "In fact, I think you already told Sarkowski to kill her." He moved his thumb on the trigger.

"I didn't—I swear!" Garvin was nearly wetting himself with panic.

Crash reached into his jacket and took out his cell phone. "If you want to live, here's what you've got to do." With his spare thumb he dialed Admiral Stonegate's direct number. It would be after 9:00 a.m. in D.C. right now. The admiral would be in.

"Stonegate," the admiral rasped.

"Sir, this is Lt. William Hawken. Please record this conversation." Crash held the phone out to Garvin. "Tell him everything. Start with the money you got illegally in 'Nam, and the house you bought with it. Tell him about your meeting with Kim and how you killed Jake Robinson to keep it covered up. Tell him *everything*, or I'll be more than happy to escort you straight to hell.''

Garvin took the phone and began to talk, his voice so low that Crash had to step closer to hear him.

He'd made over one hundred thousand dollars selling confiscated weapons back to the Viet Cong. It was a one-time thing, a temporary, momentary lapse in judgment. John Sherman had orchestrated the deal. He'd merely had to look the other way to earn more money than he'd ever dreamed of having.

But then just last year, after he'd won the senate seat, he'd been contacted by John Sherman and blackmailed. Over the next few months, he'd paid nearly five times the money he'd made illegally, with no end in sight. He'd finally gone to Hong Kong in an attempt to rid himself of Sherman once and for all. He'd worn his old naval uniform when he'd met with Kim and led the man to believe he was acting on behalf of the United States. He'd had no idea that the battle between the two rival gangs would get so out of control. He'd only wanted Sherman dead. He'd had no idea thousands of innocent people would die as well.

He knew when word came down that Jake Robinson was looking into the matter that he had to stop the investigation at the source. He was in over his head, but it was too late to stop. He set Crash Hawken up for the fall, had the ballistics report falsified—and it would have worked, too, if Hawken hadn't been so damned hard to kill.

On and on he talked, giving details—times, dates, names. The three men who'd been part of the alleged SEAL Team assigned to protect Jake had been compatriots of Sheldon Sarkowski's. Captain Lovett and the Possum hadn't been part of the conspiracy to kill the admiral. They'd been told that Admiral Robinson had been acting oddly since the death of his wife. They were told they were being sent in to make certain he didn't harm himself or become a threat to national security. They'd been told that the three strangers on the team were psyche experts—men in white coats—who were going to restrain the admiral and bring him to a special hospital. Lovett had been ordered not to tell Crash the "real" reason they were going out to the farm. The entire affair had been a serpent's nest of lies.

Finally, Garvin handed the phone back to Crash. "The admiral wants to speak with you," he said. But then he dropped the phone, and the batteries came out. By the time he got them back in, the line had been disconnected.

It didn't matter. Crash pocketed the phone. "Tell your shooters to come forward and surrender their weapons."

Garvin turned toward the woods and repeated Crash's order.

Nothing moved.

The silence was eerie and the hair on the back of Crash's neck suddenly stood on end. There *had* been at least six men out there, he *knew* there had been. But now they were all gone. The rising sun was starting to thin out the shadows, but the early morning was misty, making it even harder to see.

The strangest thing was, Crash hadn't heard anyone leave. Yet he'd heard them all approach. It didn't seem possible, or likely, that they'd been able to leave without his being aware of it.

"Tell them again," Crash ordered.

"Come forward and surrender your weapons!"

Still no movement.

But then a man stood up, stepping from the cover of the

bushes. It was as if he'd been conjured out of thin air. One moment he wasn't there, and the next he was.

It was Blue McCoy, his face streaked with black-and-green greasepaint. "We've taken care of the opposition and already confiscated their weapons," he told Crash.

We?

Crash turned, and not one or two but *five* men appeared silently from the woods. SEALs. He recognized them first as SEALs by the way they moved. But then he realized they were the men of Alpha Squad. He recognized Harvard beneath his camouflage paint. And the captain—Joe Cat. Lucky, Bobby and Wes—they were all there. All except Cowboy, who no doubt was still being trailed by FInCOM and NIS.

They moved to stand behind him in a silent show of force. And with the streaks of black and green and brown on their faces, they put on one hell of a show.

And then, damned if Nell didn't step out of the bushes, too. She was actually carrying an M-16 that was nearly as big as she was. She had greasepaint on her face as well, but as she moved closer, he saw that her eyes were filled with tears.

"Don't be mad at me." Nell wanted to touch him. She wanted to throw herself into his arms, but she was holding this huge piece of hardware, and he was still covered in C-4. "Please, will you disarm that bomb now?"

Crash looked at Garvin. "Looks like you *were* bluffing about Nell." He held up the trigger and released his thumb. Nothing exploded. Nothing happened at all. "I was bluffing, too."

He looked at Nell. "I was only bluffing," he repeated, as if he wanted to make absolutely certain that she knew that.

He took off his jacket, and peeled off his combat vest and the heavy weight of all that C-4.

Garvin stared at Crash. And then he started to laugh. "You son of a bitch."

Captain Catalanotto stepped forward, motioning to Garvin. "Let's get this piece of garbage into custody."

But Garvin stepped back, away from him. "You still don't win," he told Crash. "I disconnected that call to Stonegate before I started to talk. It's your word against mine. You have no proof of *any* wrongdoing on my part." He looked at the captain and the rest of Alpha Squad. "You'll go to jail—all of you. *He's* the one you should be arresting. He's the one wanted for murder and treason."

Crash reached down into one of the pockets of his combat vest and pulled out a hand-sized tape recorder—one of those little things people used to record letters and take dictation. "Sorry to disappoint you, Senator, but I've got every word you said on tape. This game *is* over. You lose."

The game *was* over. And Nell had won. She knew she'd won from the look in Crash's eyes as he turned to smile at her.

But then, as if in slow motion, Garvin drew a gun from the pocket of his jacket.

And, in slow motion, Nell saw the early-morning sun glinting off the metal barrel as he aimed the weapon directly at Crash.

She heard herself shout as, in the space of one single heartbeat, Garvin fired the gun.

The force of the bullet hit Crash square in the chest and he was flung back, his head flopping like a rag doll's as he was pushed down and back, into the dirt.

Crash was dead. He had to be dead. Even if he *was* still alive, there was no way they could get him to a hospital in time. The nearest medical center was miles away. It would take them hours to get there and he'd surely bleed to death on the way.

She ran toward him and was the first at his side as the SEALs disarmed Garvin and wrestled him to the ground.

Crash was struggling to breathe, fighting to suck in air, but she didn't find the massive outpouring of blood that she'd expected. She took his hand, holding it tightly. "Please don't die," she told him. "Please, Billy, don't you die...."

Harvard—the big African-American SEAL—knelt in the dirt, on the other side of Crash's body. He tore open Crash's shirt and she closed her eyes, afraid of what she would see.

"Status?" another man asked. It was the squad's captain.

"He got the wind knocked out of him," Harvard's rich voice said. "Could be he's got a broken rib, but other than that, as soon as he catches his breath, he should be fine."

He should be...?

Nell opened her eyes. "Fine? He's got a bullet in his chest!"

"What he's got is a bullet in his body armor—his bulletproof vest." Harvard smiled at her. "Just be careful not to hug little Billy too hard, all right?"

Crash was wearing a bulletproof vest. She could see the bullet embedded in it, flattened. He *had* been bluffing with the C-4. She hadn't quite believed it—until now. He'd had no real intention of blowing himself up along with Garvin. If he had, he wouldn't have bothered wearing a bulletproof vest.

He was alive—and he wanted to be.

Nell couldn't stop herself. She burst into tears.

Crash struggled to sit up. "Hey." His voice was whispery and weak. He reached for her, and she slipped into his arms. "Aren't you always telling me that you never cry—that you're not the type to always cry?"

She lifted her head to look at him. "This must be just another fluke."

He laughed, then winced. "Ouch."

"Will it hurt if I kiss you?"

"Yeah," Crash said quietly, aware that Alpha Squad had taken Garvin away, that he and Nell were alone in the clearing. He touched her cheek, marveling at the picture she made with that war paint on her face. Nell, his unadventurous Nell, who'd rather stay home and sit by the fire with a book than risk getting her feet cold, was cammied up and ready for battle. She'd done that for him, he realized. "It's always going to hurt a little bit when you kiss me. I'm always going to be scared to death of losing you."

"You can't lose me," she said fiercely. "So don't even try. I've got you, and I'm not going to let go."

Crash kissed her. "And if I ever leave you, it won't be because I want to."

Her eyes filled with fresh tears as she kissed him again.

"I don't know where I'm going from here," he pulled back to tell her bluntly. "Even if the Navy wants me back, I'm not sure the SEAL Teams will want anything to do with me. I *know* the Gray Group won't touch me after this. Too many people know my face now. And I also know I can't handle some backroom Navy desk job, so…"

"You don't have to decide any of that right now," she told him, smoothing his hair back from his face. "Give yourself some time. You haven't even let yourself properly mourn Jake."

"I feel like I…" He stopped himself, amazed at what he'd almost revealed, without even thinking. But now that he *was* thinking, he knew he had to say it. He *wanted* to say it. "I feel like I can't ask you to marry me without making sure you realize that right now my entire life is kind of in upheaval."

"*Kind of* in upheaval? That's *kind of* an understatement, don't you..."

Crash knew the moment when she realized exactly what he had said.

Ask you to marry me...

She started to cry again.

"Oh, my God," she said softly. "I know about the upheaval. So you can. Ask me. I mean, if you want."

"You're crying again," he pointed out.

"This doesn't count," she told him. "Tears of happiness don't count."

Crash laughed. "Ouch!"

"Oh, God, I've got to stop making you laugh."

He caught her chin, holding her so that she had to look into his eyes. "No," he said. "Don't. Not ever, okay?"

"So...you love me because I make you laugh..."

Crash lost himself in the beautiful blue of her eyes. "No." He whispered the words he knew she wanted to hear, the words he could finally say aloud. "I love you...*and* you make me laugh." He kissed her, losing himself in the softness of her lips. "You know I'd die for you."

She fingered the edge of his bulletproof vest. "I know you'd live for me, too. That's much harder to do."

"So, do you want to..." his lips were dry and he moistened them "...marry me?" He realized how offhanded that sounded and quickly reworded it. "Please, will you marry me?"

Nell made a noise that sounded very much like an affirmative as she reached for him. He held her tightly, aware that she was crying. Again.

He tasted salt as he kissed her. "Was that a yes?"

"Yes." This time she was absolutely clear.

Crash kissed her again as the shadows finally shifted, as the sun finally cleared the mountain, bathing them in warmth.

And he knew that the next leg of his journey—and he hoped it was going to be a long, long stretch—was going to be made in the light.

Chapter 17

"Where are we?" Crash asked.

The driver didn't answer. He simply opened the door and stood back so that Crash could climb out.

He snapped to attention, and Crash realized that there was an admiral standing by the front door of the building. An admiral. They'd sent an *admiral* to escort him to his debriefing...?

Crash was glad Nell had made him wear his dress uniform. The row of medals across his chest nearly rivaled those the admiral was wearing.

The admiral stepped forward, holding out his hand to shake. "Glad to finally meet you, Lieutenant Hawken. I'm Mac Forrest. I don't know why we haven't met before this."

Crash shook the older man's hand. Admiral Forrest was lean and wiry, with a thick shock of salt-and-pepper hair and blue eyes that looked far too young for a face with as many wrinkles as his had.

"Is this where the debriefing is being held?" Crash looked up at the elegant architecture of the stately old building as the admiral led him inside. He took off his hat as he looked around. The lobby was large and pristine, with a white-marble-tiled floor. "I don't think I've ever been here before."

Forrest led the way down a hall. "Actually, Lieutenant, not many people *have* been here before. This is a FInCOM safe house."

"I don't understand."

Mac Forrest stopped in front of a closed door. "Hold on to your hat, son. I've got an early Christmas present for you." He nodded at the door. "Go on in," he said as he turned and started down the hall. "I'll be back in a bit."

Crash watched him walk away, then looked at the door. It was a plain, oak door with an old-fashioned glass doorknob, like a giant glittering diamond. He reached out and turned it, and the door swung open.

He wasn't sure what he'd expected to see on the other side of that door, but he sure hadn't expected to see a bedroom.

It was decorated warmly, with rich, dark-colored curtains surrounding big windows that made the most of the weak December sunshine.

In the center of the room was a hospital bed, surrounded by monitors and medical equipment.

And in the center of the bed was Jake Robinson.

He looked pale and fragile, and he was still hooked up to quite a few of those monitors, with an IV drip in his arm, but he was very, very, *very* much alive.

Crash couldn't speak. Tears welled in his eyes. Jake was *alive!*

"Let me start by saying that I wanted to tell you," Jake

said. "But it was a week before I was out of intensive care, and nearly another week before I was even aware that you didn't know I was still alive. And then you were gone and there was no way to let you know."

Crash closed the door behind him, fighting the emotion that threatened to choke him, to make him break down and cry like a baby. Detach. Separate. Distance...

What the hell was he doing?

This was *joy* he was feeling. This was incredible relief, heart-stopping happiness. Yes, he wanted to cry, but they would be good tears.

"I'm sorry you had to go through all that thinking that I was dead," Jake said quietly. "Mac Forrest made the decision to release the news that I'd died. He thought I'd be safer that way."

Crash laughed, but it sounded kind of crazy, more like a sob than real laughter. "This is so unbelievably great." His voice broke. As he crossed to Jake, he pulled a chair over to the bed and clasped the older man's hand in both of his. "Are you really all right? You look like hell, like you've been hit by a truck."

If Jake noticed the tears that were brimming in his eyes, he didn't comment. "I'm going to be fine. It's going to take a little while, but the doctor says I'll be up and walking in no time. No permanent damage—a few more scars."

Crash shook his head. "I should have known. It was so easy to escape after the hearing. I should have realized I was being let go."

"They gave you a little bit of help, but not much. There were only a few people who were allowed to know I was alive." He squeezed Crash's hand. "Good job with Garvin. That was one hell of a tape you made."

"I'm lucky I had Alpha Squad there to back me up."

"Speaking of Alpha Squad—you met Mac Forrest on your way in?"

Crash nodded.

"Alpha Squad's under his command. He asked me to let you know that there's been a special request made for your reassignment. Captain Joe Catalanotto's asking for you to be placed on his team. He sent a personal note to Mac along with all the paperwork. These guys really want you to work with them."

Crash couldn't speak again. "I'm honored they want me," he finally said.

"I'm glad to see you finally got a haircut. The pictures they kept flashing of you on the news were pretty scary-looking."

Crash ran his hand back through his freshly cut hair. "Yeah, Nell likes it better this way, too."

"Nell." Jake said. "Nell. Would that be the same Nell who used to work for Daisy? Pretty girl? Great smile? Head-over-heels in love with you?"

"Don't be a jackass."

Jake grinned. "That's Admiral Jackass to you, Lieutenant."

"Jake, I can't tell you how glad I am that you're not dead."

"Back at you with that, kid. I'm also glad you finally opened your damn eyes and saw what you had right there in front of you, ready to fall into your lap." He paused. "You *did* manage to get yourself straightened out about Nell?"

"Actually, I haven't," Crash admitted. "I'm totally tied in knots when it comes to her." He smiled ruefully. "But I'm loving every minute of it. She's crazy enough to want me, and I'm sane enough to know that I'd be an idiot to let her get away. You know, she's marrying me on Christmas. Will you stand up for me, Jake—be my best man?''

Now there were tears in Jake's eyes, but still he tried to joke. "I'm not sure if I'm going to be standing by then."

"Can we have the wedding here? There's no law that says the best man literally has to stand."

Jake held his hand more tightly. "I'd love that. It would be an honor."

It had only been a year since Crash had done Jake that very same honor.

"Daisy always knew that Nell was perfect for me," Crash said quietly.

"Daisy was…extraordinarily good at seeing the truth, even when it was hidden from the rest of the world's view." Jake looked away, but not before Crash saw the flash of pain in his eyes. "God, I still miss her so much."

"I'm sorry, I shouldn't have…"

Jake looked up at him. "Shouldn't have what? Said her name? Remembered how much we both loved her? Are you kidding?"

"I don't know. I just thought—"

"Twenty years," Jake said. "I had her for over twenty years. I would've loved forty or sixty, even. But twenty wasn't bad. Twenty was a gift." He looked up, pinning Crash with the intensity of his gaze. "Make every minute count, kid. Pay attention and really make sure you experience every step of the dance. You never know how many times you'll get to go around the floor."

Crash nodded. "I'm glad you didn't die."

"Me too, Billy. Me too, kid."

It was supposed to be a private wedding.

But when Nell's father opened the door to Jake Robinson's hospital room in the FInCOM safe house, there were so many people there, he and Nell almost couldn't fit inside.

Lucy and Blue McCoy were there. Harvard and his wife, P.J., were there, too. Even Captain Catalanotto and his family had come. Bobby and Wes and Lucky were present, as was Crash's swim buddy Cowboy and his new wife. Cowboy was holding a baby who was his exact spitting image— and he was holding the little boy comfortably, as if the kid were an extension of his arm. It was a pretty amazing sight to see.

But it wasn't half as amazing as the sight of Nell, walking into that room on her father's arm. She was wearing a beautiful antique gown she'd found downtown in a secondhand shop. Although it was a traditional-style wedding dress, with long sleeves and a high collar, it looked incredible on her. Even Daisy would have approved.

"I thought this was supposed to be a wedding," she said, still looking around at all the extra guests with a smile, "not a surprise party."

"I called Blue to see if anyone was going to be in town, because we needed another witness," Crash told her. "Turns out everyone was in town."

Nell looked around, and Crash knew she realized that each and every one of his friends had come here purposely to support him. Like her parents, they'd changed all of their Christmas plans to be here today.

Her father raised her veil and kissed her before giving her to Crash.

"I'm so glad all your friends could come," she whispered to him as she squeezed his hand.

The ceremony passed in a blur. Crash tried to slow it down, tried to pay complete attention to the promises he was making, but the truth was, he would have promised this woman anything. And he would fight with his last breath to keep those promises.

The pastor finally told him that he could kiss his bride, and as he kissed his new wife's sweet lips, he tasted salt.

She was crying again.

He looked at her questioningly, touching her cheek, and she shook her head.

"Tears of joy don't count," she whispered.

He laughed and kissed her again, holding her close and knowing that no matter how long they had together—one year or one hundred—he would cherish every moment.

* * * * *

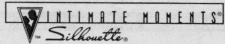
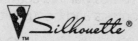

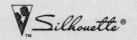

Catch more great

◆ HARLEQUIN™ Movies

featured on **the movie channel** tmc

Premiering December 12th
Recipe for Revenge
Based on the novel *Bullets Over Boise*
by bestselling author Kristen Gabriel

Don't miss next month's movie!
Premiering January 9th
At the Midnight Hour
Starring Patsy Kensit and
Simon McCorkindale
Based on the novel by bestselling
author Alicia Scott

If you are not currently a subscriber to
The Movie Channel, simply call your
local cable or satellite provider for more
details. Call today, and don't miss out
on the romance!

the movie channel tmc   ◆ HARLEQUIN®
Makes any time special ™

100% pure movies.
100% pure fun.

COMING NEXT MONTH

#901 MURPHY'S LAW—Marilyn Pappano
Men in Blue
Detective Jack Murphy and psychic Evie DesJardien had been in love—
until the night Jack was told she'd betrayed him. They were passionately drawn
back into each other's lives when Jack enlisted Evie's help to catch a killer. Could
the two learn to trust in their love again…before it was too late?

#902 CODE NAME: COWBOY—Carla Cassidy
Mustang, Montana
When Alicia Randall and her six-year-old daughter answered Cameron Gallagher's
ad for a housekeeper, she knew that she could never let him discover the truth
about her. Then she found herself immediately attracted to this sexy stranger. Was
this the happiness she had been searching for, or would her past catch up with her
and ruin her future?

#903 DANGEROUS TO LOVE—Sally Tyler Hayes
Sexy spy Jamie Douglass knew she was falling for her strong and irresistible
instructor Dan Reese. He was a difficult man to get close to, but Jamie was
determined to break down his barriers. Then a routine mission turned deadly,
and Jamie was forced to admit just how much she felt for this tough, sensual
man. She trusted him with her life…but did she trust him with her heart?

#904 COWBOY WITH A BADGE—Margaret Watson
Cameron, Utah
When Carly Fitzpatrick's determination to find her brother's killer brought her
back to the McAllister ranch, she met Devlin McAllister, the son of the man
accused of the murder. Torn between her growing feelings for Devlin and her
desire to discover the truth, Carly found herself falling in love with this strong,
sexy sheriff—but what would he do when he found out why she'd really come to
town?

#905 LONG-LOST MOM—Jill Shalvis
Stone Cameron thought life was moving along nicely for himself and his
daughter—until Cindy Beatty came to town. Deeply distrustful of women after
his long-ago love abandoned him, Stone tried to resist her sensuous appeal. But
there was something oddly familiar about this beautiful stranger that made her
impossible to resist…and he knew that it was only a matter of time before he gave
in to the attraction.…

#906 THE PASSION OF PATRICK MacNEILL—Virginia Kantra
Families Are Forever
Single father Patrick MacNeill's time had been consumed with caring for his son,
leaving him no room for a social life—until he met Dr. Kate Sinclair. Suddenly he
began to remember what it was like to feel…and to fall in love. So when Kate
tried to deny the attraction between them, he planned on showing the lovely doctor
his own bedside manner!